Elizabeth Harris was born in Cambridge, and now lives with her husband and two sons on the borders of Kent and Sussex. She graduated from Keele University with a degree in English and Psychology, and has recently gained a Certificate in Archaeology from the University of Kent, at Canterbury.

She spends much of her time travelling and researching, and lives for part of the year in an ancient stone cottage on the edge of a forest in Brittany.

*Singing in the Wilderness* is the sequel to a *A Good Man's Love*.

# SINGING IN THE WILDERNESS

After the tragic death of her first husband,
Jo Dillon has finally built a new life around
Hal, her one-year-old son Edmund, and
new baby, Sammie. But Hal's increasing
preoccupation with work leaves Jo isolated
and resentful. Sensing a growing rift
between them, Hal travels alone to Crete.
There, he finds solace in the company of
Angela Swayne: charismatic, free-spirited,
and everything Jo used to be . . . Jo knows
she must act. She remembers the small
house in Kent which came to her rescue
once before. Inside its peaceful walls, she
at last understands what she must do to
save her marriage — and her true self.

*Books by Elizabeth Harris*
*Published by The House of Ulverscroft:*

THE EGYPTIAN YEARS
A GOOD MAN'S LOVE

ELIZABETH HARRIS

◆

# SINGING IN THE WILDERNESS

*Complete and Unabridged*

# ULVERSCROFT
*Leicester*

First published in Great Britain in 1997 by
Severn House Publishers Limited
Surrey

First Large Print Edition
published 1999
by arrangement with
Severn House Publishers Limited
Surrey

British Library CIP Data

Harris, Elizabeth
Singing in the wilderness.—Large print ed.—
Ulverscroft large print series: romance
1. Domestic fiction
2. Large type books
I. Title
823.9'14 [F]

ISBN 0–7089–4108–7

Published by
F. A. Thorpe (Publishing) Ltd.
Anstey, Leicestershire
Set by Words & Graphics Ltd.
Anstey, Leicestershire
Printed and bound in Great Britain by
T. J. International Ltd., Padstow, Cornwall

This book is printed on acid-free paper

'*A Flask of Wine, a Book of Verse — and
Thou*
*Beside me singing in the Wilderness —*
*And the Wilderness is Paradise enow.*'

*Edward Fitzgerald,*
*The Rubaiyat of Omar Khayyam*

# Part One

## May – December 1984

# 1

It was late May, and San Francisco was sullen with fog.

'When's it going to clear?' Jo asked Hal dispiritedly, gazing out of the window at drops of condensed mist falling off the trees. 'I want some sunshine.'

Hal looked up from the breakfast table, smiling slightly. 'Maybe never,' he said. 'You ought to be used to it, after two years.'

'Not quite two years. And it's never once managed to be like it was that first time I came, in the summer of 1981.' Hal felt she was taking an unreasonably pessimistic view of the Californian climate, and was aware of his detached clinical thought, don't take everything out on the weather.

He said, 'You were just lucky, then. In any case, you came later. It was June, wasn't it?'

'July.' She managed, in the short syllables, to sound reproving, as if he ought to have remembered the month without her telling him. It was when they'd first met.

He wanted to go back to the file he'd been reading before her remark and her

3

discontent had interrupted him. He was due to lecture in a couple of hours, and he needed to cocoon his mind in Ancient Greece. He heard her sigh, and glanced up. Her face was dejected as she stood staring at the mess the children had left on the table.

'Look at me,' she said, very quietly, as if she knew he didn't want to listen. 'I'm turning into a bored, boring housewife.' She stacked cereal bowls, picking up crusts of chewed toast and dropping them into the milky remains with an expression of infinite disgust. 'And I don't think I like myself much.'

'I like you,' Hal remarked.

'That's only because you're very tolerant.' She turned her back on him, heading for the sink. 'I don't think I'm at all likeable any more.'

Hal wiped a splash of milk from his glasses: she'd dropped one of the toast crusts with some force. You're not happy, are you, kid? he thought. And I can't say I'm surprised. She'd had all these months in another country, perpetually coping with the different needs of the baby and his adventurous half-brother — five years between them, a gap that was impossible to bridge, at the ages of seven and not-quite two, with any common interests other than hollering at each other.

Hal could see Jo's frustration, and although he was sympathetic — he couldn't have lived her existence for more than a couple of days without losing his marbles — the traitorous thought occasionally surfaced: other women manage it.

But she wasn't other women. He'd known that well enough when he married her, and it came às no surprise to find she had no wish to slip unprotesting into American middle-class suburbia. She didn't want coffee mornings and tupperware parties, nor intense conversations about disposable diapers and the best way to deal with sibling rivalry. She didn't particularly want long evenings entertaining Hal's colleagues to dinner, with or without their wives, because no matter how intellectually capable she was of joining in the conversation, inevitably her contribution would be interrupted by a child's need, or by her own failure to have given sufficient thought to the meal for it to progress without more attention. Often considerably more — on one occasion he'd gone out to the kitchen to investigate a delay that was becoming embarrassing, to find her frantically opening cans to make a fruit salad because she'd forgotten about the chocolate soufflé and it had exploded all over the inside of the oven. Hal saw it all, and ached for her.

She wanted the freedom to live in her own head, at least for some of the time, and her problem was that nobody would let her.

Before they'd met she'd written children's stories. Good enough to be published, and one of them — about a boy whose dead father returned to be his guardian angel — was under offer to a TV company who were considering making it into an animated film. She didn't write stories any more. Poor kid, he thought with compassion, she hasn't written a word in two years except for those outpourings she confides to her diary at night. He never asked her what she wrote, but he knew it wasn't often very joyful because the expression on her face, as she quickly scribbled it all down before the next interruption, was usually anxious and miserable.

He took off his glasses to watch her at the sink, shoulders hunched with tension. She was muttering something, but he couldn't make it out over the combined noise of the washing machine starting on its fastest spin and the impossible racket Jo was making with the crockery. Above everything came the sudden enraged wail of Sammie: 'Teddy pinch my bum!'

'*Shit!*' Jo tore off her rubber gloves and raced out of the kitchen.

Hal dropped his face in his hands and shut it all out for a moment. My wife is unhappy and frustrated. I love my wife. Therefore I have to help her. What the hell do I do? It's no more my fault than hers that we have two kids and she has to be the one who stays home. We have two kids. It was automatic to think that way, since Edmund was as much Hal and Jo's son as Sammie was. Hal had a sudden vivid picture of Ben, Edmund's father and Jo's first husband. Hal and Ben had been close friends; he could still remember how he'd felt the day he was told Ben was dead, killed in a diving accident that left Jo a widow with a baby only just over a year old.

What would you make of your son, Ben? Hal wondered. Would you reckon I'm making a good job of bringing him up? A picture flashed into his head of the haphazard ward in an English hospital where he had sat by Edmund, caring for the child while Jo slept off her exhaustion. He had asked himself that long day whether he was prepared to bring up Edmund as his own son, because he'd known it'd be required of him if he married Jo. Required not only by her, but by his own sense of what was owed to Ben. I reckon Ben would agree Teddy's OK, Hal thought. He smiled faintly. If he could be persuaded to stop pinching his brother's butt.

Maybe I should try harder to make Jo OK.

★ ★ ★

Jo returned to the washing-up, her right hand smarting from the smack she'd just swiped across her elder son's leg. He's seven, she thought angrily, he's too big to tease his little brother so persistently. Anyway, he's certainly too big for me to smack much longer. She smiled despite herself — she'd only gone for the leg as a sort of first reserve, having been unable to manoeuvre the struggling child onto his front in order to smack his bottom.

'I'll finish this. You go have a quiet cup of tea.' Hal was by her side, taking the saucepan out of her hands.

'Oh! No, it's all right, you'll have to go in a minute.'

'Not for half an hour. Go on.' He grinned at her, and she felt guilty for being so objectionable. She opened her mouth to say something, but he bent down and kissed her before she could form the words.

It's not like you think it's going to be, she thought dismally as she settled with her tea in the living-room. I wonder if anyone ever truly realises how much having children messes things up? Not that I'd be without them, she added swiftly, in superstitious dread that some malicious intelligence might be listening which would pounce on her for her disgruntled complaint and wipe out her children like an avenging Fury. But all the same . . .

It had been easy, with Edmund. The first one was always relatively easy, although nobody ever thought so at the time. And Edmund's babyhood had been different because his father had died: Jo had been plunged into single parenthood like a lobster thrown screaming into boiling water, losing the mate who'd smoothed the frustrations just as he'd augmented the joys. And Ben would have gone on being a great father as Teddy grew up, too — people as easy-going as him made wonderful parents, provided they didn't slide into lazy selfishness. But Ben hadn't been like that. His only act of selfishness had been to get himself killed while Jo still loved him to distraction.

She sighed. Teddy had gone upstairs to get ready for school, grumbling over his slapped leg. She could see Sammie through the half-open door, sitting in the hall with a stack of plastic bricks that he was determined to make into a wall. A small wall; you couldn't emulate Hadrian with twelve bricks. Sammie was born too soon, Jo thought. Not that he was premature in the biological sense, but he'd probably been premature in her marriage to Hal, making his entrance a mere eleven months after the wedding. Jo had sworn, when her pregnancy had been confirmed, that she'd never put her trust in an IUD again. Poor little Sammie — she smiled as the child's careful wall fell over again and, with a quaintly adult sigh, he began once more to rebuild it — your Dad's a bit too intellectual for someone as small and limited as you. But he's improving, slowly. He's doing his best. And you won't be small for ever.

★ ★ ★

The day ran its course, Jo's hours frittered away, crammed with a hundred small tasks. Whatever interest can I hold for Hal? she thought despairingly as she peeled vegetables. We'll sit over supper and he'll tell me some fascinating fact about the Greek City States, and he'll wonder what happened to the bright girl who used to ask lots of intelligent questions. If he's lucky and I'm not totally overcome with yawning, I'll say, 'that's nice, Sammie crapped his pants four times, I must stop giving him so much stewed fruit, and Edmund got a B+ for his essay on redwoods — more painstaking than his father, isn't he?'

She made a special effort with dinner, fighting the sourness of her thoughts. The table was prettily laid, she put wine on ice and worked out an appetising menu. After she'd put Sammie to bed and settled Teddy watching TV upstairs, she showered and put on a velvet dress that had hung in her wardrobe for far too long. I'm getting thin, she thought, zipping it up. That's something — most miserable young mothers seem to stuff themselves till they grow gross, which no doubt adds to their misery.

'Did you have a good day?' she asked Hal when they were sitting down to the homemade asparagus soup. He kept smiling, and she thought he was probably thinking about something else.

'I had a great day,' he replied, with unexpected enthusiasm.

'Oh! That good?' She wondered what had happened.

'Wonderful soup, did you make it?'

'Yes.'

He grinned across the table at her, his face bright in the candlelight. 'And you've made something for the main course that

11

smells terrific, and had time to dress up smart, too.'

She laughed shortly. 'I wouldn't bank on the main course. It's a new recipe, I'm not at all sure how it'll turn out.'

Hal shrugged. 'The takeaway's still open.' Then, with hardly a pause, 'How d'you fancy going sailing?'

'Oh!'

He was watching her intently, as if waiting for her to say more, but she wasn't going to risk getting excited until she was sure she had good reason.

'We'll go spend the weekend with Dad,' he said. 'I don't have to go into college tomorrow, Teddy can miss out school for one day, so we'll set off early and come back Sunday night. What d'you reckon?'

Three whole days away, with Hal to share the kids, and the pleasure of seeing Sam thrown in. It sounded marvellous. She reached across the table and he grasped her hand, squeezing it. She felt absurdly near to tears as she muttered, 'I'd love it.'

★ ★ ★

They were on the road by seven-thirty the next day. Jo's excitement had galvanised her into action, and she'd rushed the

12

children through the morning routine with the slickness of a military exercise.

'OK,' she panted, leaning against the kitchen door. 'They're strapped in the car.'

Hal finished his coffee and rinsed the cup. 'I'm only half awake,' he said. 'Will you drive?'

'You bet.' Her impatience to get away was better suited to driving than sitting passively in the passenger seat. 'But it means you'll be in charge of the sick bags.' The idea of Hal having to cope with bulging bags of sick gave her a malicious pleasure, which wasn't at all fair when he'd organised this break for her.

Hal put his arms round her. 'Ain't nothing I can't handle.' He turned her face up to kiss her. 'Happy weekend.'

She kissed him back, suddenly confident. 'It will be.'

★ ★ ★

'Hal says you need a rest,' Sam remarked, bringing a couple of cold beers out to where Jo was sitting on his verandah with her feet up, watching the sunset. 'Reckon I could do with one too, so it looks like Hal'll be doing most of the work.'

Jo took her beer. She loved being with Sam; he had a marvellous calm, supportive quality.

13

'It'll do him good,' she said. 'Academics ought to get their hands dirty regularly. We can watch him changing nappies and doing all the cooking with impunity.'

'Hope he remembers to wash between times.'

Jo laughed. 'Sammie only wears one at night now. I could cope with that, at a pinch.'

'Not allowed,' Sam said. 'You have to sit out here with me listening to sweet music. When Hal has put the boys to bed, maybe I'll let you go stroll along the shore with him.'

'If I've been good?' She looked at him affectionately.

'Right.'

★ ★ ★

I am perfectly content, Jo thought the next morning. She had been brought breakfast in bed by Sam, reminding her poignantly of how he'd done the same thing the day she and Hal got married. Sam had come to stay at Jo's house in Kent; she'd been aware even at their first meeting that she and Sam would get along. Now Hal had disappeared with both the boys. Laden with life-jackets, food, flasks of hot drinks, warm sweaters and changes of clothes, he was going to take them out in Sam's boat. Seeing Jo's expression as they left, he'd turned back.

'Tears you in half, doesn't it?' he said. 'You want to watch over them yourself, but when someone else'll take them off your hands, you have to say yes.'

She felt a shiver of emotion: he understood so well. She answered flippantly, 'You bet. It doesn't happen often enough.' It would have been unnecessary, ungrateful and insulting to say, 'take good care of them'.

Sam went off to shop, and in his absence Jo sat, thinking and reading, for an uninterrupted two hours. I could live out here on Sam's verandah, she thought. The low white house stood on a grassy slope, overlooking the small-boat harbour and the strange volcanic rock that stood out in the middle of Morro Bay. Long before Jo had ever come here, Hal had described it to her: 'It gives the illusion there's a dip in the ocean floor just there and a monstrous camel is walking in it with only its hump showing.' He'd been right.

Sam had enclosed his verandah with sliding glass screens, which could be closed if the wind got up. The furniture was well-worn and supremely comfortable; big, saggy armchairs, cushions and a footstool, tables for all that a person would need for his day sitting in the sun: binoculars, bird book, pencils, notebook, and, taking up most of the space, a cassette player and a box of tapes. When you eventually become tired of sitting, Jo thought, getting up and stretching, you can stroll down by the water. She crossed the quiet road that ran in front of the house, stepping carefully onto a wooden pontoon. It was tightly packed with small boats, most covered with tarpaulins. A few people were pottering about, and there were faint sounds of quiet conversation. A gap to Jo's right indicated where Sam's yacht was usually moored; she wondered how Hal and the children were getting on, whether they'd taken enough food with them. The thought made her realise she was ravenous. She saw that Sam was back, unloading bags of groceries from his car. She hurried to help him. 'I hope you haven't forgotten we're only staying till tomorrow,' she said.

Sam grinned. 'Nope. Round about this time of the month, I always stock up. And I reckoned I'd get some extras, with you here.'

Jo peered into the bag nearest to her. 'Six-packs of beers, a bottle of bourbon and a carton of popsicles,' she said. 'How well you know us.'

'I'm hungry,' Sam announced. 'Too hungry

16

to wait to cook, so I got us pizza.'

'Great! I'll get plates and a beer each, and we'll eat as soon as we've put this lot in the kitchen.'

★ ★ ★

'I guess,' Sam reflected as they ate the pizza, 'we oughta drink red wine with this.' He looked at Jo questioningly.

'Oh, no,' she said quickly, 'beer's much more thirstquenching.'

Sam smiled. 'It's no surprise your kids have such nice manners. Reckon they take after their mom.'

She was pleased on the children's account, even more on her own. 'They like being with you,' she said. 'So do I.'

They sat listening to a Brahms piano concerto while they had coffee. When it was over, Jo delved into the box of tapes to make another choice.

'There's twice as many again in the house,' Sam said. He led the way into the house, across the hall into his room, which looked like an indoor version of the verandah except that there was a bed, covered with a patchwork bedspread. The room was orderly; there was a slight smell of polish, and fresh flowers stood in front of a group of photographs. She went over to have a better look.

The right-hand picture was Hal and herself, on their wedding day. She smiled; the memory of the day she married Hal always made her happy. The left-hand picture had to be Hal. He must have been about eighteen, with long hair and a slightly truculent expression.

The middle photo was of a dark-haired woman, perhaps in her twenties. She looked out with an expression that at first appeared to be wide-eyed innocence, until, Jo discovered, you went closer and saw the amusement and intelligence in the face. For a moment she thought it must be Magdalena. Hal had loved Magdalena. Why wouldn't Sam have her photo in his room?

Then suddenly she knew. It was Hal's mother. 'She's beautiful,' Jo said. 'I've always wanted to know what she looked like. Sam, she's really lovely.'

Sam came to stand beside her. He put out his hand and stroked a gentle finger across the woman's cheek. 'Yes, she's beautiful,' he said softly. 'I guess Ruth was the loveliest woman I ever saw.'

Jo thought of what she knew about Hal's mother, which wasn't much. She had died when Hal was five, in the middle of a bleak post-war Chicago winter; without much of a struggle, she'd succumbed to pneumonia. Hal had said she'd never been strong. Jo stared at the photograph. Yes, she thought, Ruth looks delicate — that dark, heavy hair round the heart-shaped face makes her seem all eyes and cheekbones. But she's strong, too. Self-confident, in a quiet sort of way. It's hard to imagine her letting go of life unless she had to.

'She died of pneumonia, didn't she?' she asked tentatively. She was reluctant to probe, but remembered that when she lost Ben, thinking people didn't want to know hurt even more than talking about him.

'Yes.'

'Hal said she was frail. But she has strength in her face.'

'Oh, she was strong.' Abruptly he opened a cupboard, reaching for a cardboard box on a top shelf. Going quickly through the contents, he picked out a sealed envelope and, opening it, passed the enclosed photo to Jo. Ruth again, this time laughing, her face rounder as she turned to look into the camera. Her body, in profile, was full with advanced pregnancy.

'That's the very last picture of her,' Sam said.

Jo knew without him saying. Yes, that

would weaken even the strongest woman, physically and emotionally. Even an Amazon might have succumbed to pneumonia if she'd just lost a baby. 'Why didn't you ever tell Hal?'

Sam shook his head. 'I have no idea. At first, he was so sad and lost without her, it just would have hurt too much. Then, I guess I got used to him not knowing. Maybe I even thought I'd forget, if he didn't know.'

'I don't think you'd ever have done that.'

'No. Probably not.' He took the photo back from Jo, staring at the happy face, touching the curve of the belly. 'She was a little girl. We both would have loved a daughter.' He sighed, then put the photograph back in its envelope, resealing it with a strip of sellotape.

Jo realised that she had become a conspirator. She turned away, struggling between sorrow for Sam's long pain, pleasure that he'd confided in her, and worry that she now shared a secret that apparently she wasn't to tell Hal. Her eyes went back to the photograph of Ruth in the frame. Can't I tell him? she asked silently. And the answer came back, no. He'll know, one day.

'Here's the music,' Sam said behind her, deliberately cheerful. He pulled out a box, and as they rummaged through it together,

Sam took her hand. His expression was apologetic. 'Jo, I'm sorry. I didn't think you'd mind, but I guess maybe you do.'

She found it hard to speak. 'It's OK, Sam.' She couldn't manage any more.

Sam patted her hand. 'We have to find something real bright, huh?'

'Yes. What about Mendelssohn's Italian Symphony?' She looked up and he met her eyes. She said quietly, 'We shouldn't be sad, listening to that.' She wasn't sure if it was an opinion or an order.

★ ★ ★

By the time Hal and the children came home, Jo and Sam had played all the cheerful works they could find. They had also broached the bottle of bourbon; it was almost half-empty. The children were sandy, salty and exhausted; Edmund sagged under the weight of the life-jackets and the food bag, Sammie was asleep in Hal's arms. Hal stood looking down at his wife and his father with an ironic expression, which made Jo giggle.

'Sam bought it specially,' she said, nodding towards the bourbon. 'It would have been rude not to drink it with him.'

'Sure,' Hal said. Then, as Sam got up unsteadily to help Teddy carry his burden into the house, he leaned towards her and said quietly, 'You'd better sober up by tonight. Sea air makes me horny as hell.'

Her eyes flew open. Then, watching Hal's retreating back as he took Sammie inside to bed, she started to smile.

# 2

Jo's happiness during the Morro Bay weekend proved a temporary reprieve. Hal hadn't expected it to be more, but still he was sad to see the look of anxiety return to her face as the weeks went by. She didn't complain, but in a way that would have been easier to bear. He didn't think it was the work that got her down; she'd never shown disinclination for hard work. He knew what upset her so much — it was, as she'd confessed when he'd woken in the night once to find her crying silently, 'never having the time to finish a thought'.

Hal wondered what that'd be like. How would I feel if my endless hours spent in pursuit of a theory, the answer to one small question, even, were doomed to be interrupted by other people's needs? It'd be unbearable. Jeez, it'd be awful! He tried to give her more time to herself, suggesting to the boys that he take them out, just the three of them, guys together. But Sammie, too young to be either subtle or anything other than egocentric, would look at Jo out of enormous eyes and say in a small voice, 'Mummy coming?' And Hal, irritated, would watch with an ache in his heart as she reluctantly said, 'All right'.

As the summer term passed, he became increasingly aware of the extra load he was about to dump on her. He would never have imagined they could descend to a state where he kept his plans secret, but the situation had crept up apparently under its own momentum. She had withdrawn into unhappiness, and what he had to tell her was going to push her further in. He had sheered away from delivering the blow; now he had no idea how to make it easier on her. On both of them.

He came in late one evening, delayed by a student hotly disputing the assessment Hal had given him for an essay. Hal, his mind on the forthcoming scene at home and in no mood for diplomacy, had justified his marking in a few sharp sentences, adding fuel to the growing campus opinion that Dr Dillon was a mean son of a bitch. Jo had already put the children to bed, and Hal found her sitting on the sofa, staring in front of her with blank eyes. She started as he came into the room. 'Sorry!' She sounded guilty. 'I'll get supper.' Before he could greet her, hug her, talk to her, she'd gone, hurrying off into the kitchen to fetch a meal for which neither of them had any appetite.

'Jo,' he said as they sat making an effort to eat, 'Jo, I may have to go away.' I've never been subtle enough, goddam it, he thought, watching as her face fell into distress. He was about to say more, but she forestalled him.

With an effort, she managed a smile. 'Oh yes? Where to?'

Her eyes are too bright, Hal thought. Shit, how did I get into this? 'Cairo.'

She nodded sagely. 'Yes, of course. Your Minoan thing.'

'Right. My Minoan thing.' How important was it anyway? he thought bitterly, angry with the part of himself that drove him on so that he had to bring her this sorrow. 'I can't get on till I've been to Cairo, I have to look at the evidence for cultural cross-influences between Egypt and Knossos,' he went on, more sharply than he'd intended; he was justifying his actions to himself as much as to her. 'Then I'll need to go to Crete, although that can wait a while.'

She sat watching him. 'I can't come with you, you know,' she said flatly.

'I know.' He reached out and took her hand. 'I wish you could.' He saw her expression lighten briefly. He'd seen her look at him that way so many times. It endured, apparently, her feeling for him, even through the thickets of problems and the weariness of bringing up children.

'I couldn't take Sammie and Teddy to Cairo in summer, could I?' She sounded wistful. 'Big, dusty, dirty city, full of traffic, and hundred degree heat?'

'No. No way. They'd hate it. So would you, if they did.'

'You couldn't go another time, when we could all go together?'

'No. It'd have to wait till the Christmas vacation. And I have to write this thing now.'

'OK.' He didn't have to tell her. She knew well enough how he operated: from inspiration to paper, as quickly as he could. And this work had been stewing on the back burner since Sammie's increasing size in Jo's belly had taken them home to England in 1982. Their itinerary, that carefree year, had been Rhodes, Crete and Cairo. Only Jo had got pregnant in Rhodes.

'I'm sorry, kid.' He was, deeply sorry. But there wasn't an alternative. Lecturing he did because he had to. Writing he did because he loved it, and with any luck it'd eventually be all that he needed to do. And the next thing he had to write was his long-postponed 'Minoan Thing'.

She looked up at him desolately. He knew

this summer was going to be hard on her, whereas he, once he was enmeshed in the tantalising lines of enquiry that were pulling him to Cairo . . . Her expression changed suddenly, almost as if she was reading his mind. She got up from the table with their half-full, abandoned plates. Her green eyes regarded him coolly. She said distantly, 'No doubt I'll manage.'

★ ★ ★

Jo was in the shower one morning, her mind busy on matters connected with Hal's imminent departure for North Africa, when she thought: why don't I go away, too? The voice of reason instantly answered: with two little children? Come off it!

'Why the hell not?' she said aloud. 'All right, so I can't take a child and a toddler to Cairo, but there are plenty of other places in the world.' Her heart lurched with a sudden homesickness for Europe — Greece, Italy, France . . . England! She sat on the edge of the bath towelling her hair. Why not? Why can't I go away as well? God knows, my need's as great as Hal's, for different reasons. Without thinking beyond the desire for a break, she dug out a large suitcase and stood it firmly beside Hal's, half-packed in

27

the middle of the bedroom floor. There! she thought. That'll show him!

She looked at the clock on the bedside table. Half past eight. Yes, she could ring England now — it'd be early evening. She picked up the phone, throwing herself across the bed and beginning to dial her mother's number. She wondered fleetingly if she ought to talk to Hal first, but then she thought, no. *He's* going away, he won't be around to mind if I'm here or not. With sudden vehemence she thought, *sod* Hal. In her distress she forgot where she was, and had to start the dialling all over again.

Her mother greeted her with the usual warmth, which never failed to make Jo feel better even before Elowen had said anything beyond, 'Hello, darling, how lovely!'

'Can I come to stay, Mum? With the boys?'

'Oh, Jo! No, you can't, because Dad and I are off to Cannes in three days.'

'Oh.' Jo hadn't stopped to think that her plans would have to fit in with any arrangements her parents might have. Selfish cow, she berated herself.

'Why don't you come too?' Elowen said.

'What did you say?'

'Come to Cannes. Dad and I are renting an apartment, but there'd be room for you, if you don't mind going in with the boys or sleeping on a couch.'

'No, no, I wouldn't mind.' I don't mind *anything*.

'What about Hal?'

'He's going to Cairo.' Amazing how I don't mind so much, all of a sudden, Jo thought. 'It's much too hot and stinky for us, though.'

'Yes, I'm sure it is,' Elowen said. 'Your father was there in the war, he says his abiding memory of Cairo is of dust and the smell of donkey pee.'

'Not the Pyramids?'

Elowen laughed. 'He only saw them from a distance. You'd better not tell Hal, but he got as far as the terrace of the Mena House Hotel, where the appeal of several cold glasses of lager outweighed the thought of tramping across more miles of dust to look at a group of little triangles on the horizon.'

'No, I won't tell Hal.' Jo was smiling at the thought of Hal's reaction to anyone calling the Pyramids a group of little triangles. She added charitably, 'I expect Dad was battle-weary.'

'Shall we meet you at Nice, then, darling?'

'Yes. You'd better tell me your address and phone number in Cannes, then I can let you know when we're coming.' She wrote to

Elowen's dictation. 'Avenue Floriana. Sounds nice. Is it right on the front?' She recalled childhood visits to Cannes, picturing its well-kept sophistication, the air of wealth of its inhabitants.

'No, it's right at the back — it's a long walk to the beach and you'll have to help us cart the shopping up from Monoprix.' Clearly, Elowen wasn't having her coming out under false pretences.

'Oh. Well, I'd better bring Sammie's pushchair. And a shopping trolley.'

'You *do* sound keen,' her mother commented.

'Oh, I am, I am! It doesn't sound much like Dad, though, walking and shopping?'

'You haven't heard anything yet. But I'll tell you when I see you — or rather, you'll see for yourself.'

'I can't wait!'

They said their goodbyes, and Jo put the phone down. I feel better, she thought. Not absolutely all right, but better. She stared down at her suitcase, standing expectantly on the floor. Much better!

* * *

Elowen and Paul Daniel had reached the decision some time ago that they preferred

30

driving to flying; time was an increasingly less important factor in their lives. Elowen would never have been so foolhardy as to suggest that Paul had retired; as long as he breathed, she knew he'd keep a watchful eye on the business which he had spent his working life building up.

She refrained from questioning him; it would be pointless, anyway, since he'd only humph and pretend to have misunderstood. But she suspected she already knew the truth: that he was actually beginning to find as much pleasure in other things — holidays, for example, or simply being at home with her in the gracious old house in Cornwall — as he'd once derived from the fiercely competitive world of high finance. Now their two sons looked after the day-to-day running of their father's company, and Elowen tried with careful diplomacy to stop him making spur-of-the-moment phone-calls to Zurich. The boys were making a good enough job of filling in the vacuum left by their father, and reverse-charge calls from all over Europe whenever something surprising happened in the stock market did not, in Elowen's opinion, help matters.

Long knowledge of his ways told her she now had as much of him as he was likely to give her, which was considerably more than she had expected. They had grown apart over the years; with retaliatory determination, Elowen had entrenched herself as securely in her life in the old house in Cornwall — the Family Stronghold, they called it — as Paul and, later, their two sons had in the challenging environment of Zurich. She had given up all hope of any other way of life when, unexpectedly, Paul had agreed to her half-hearted suggestion that they take a holiday together. She'd been making that suggestion routinely once in a while for years, and she still had no idea what it was that made him suddenly agree.

It didn't matter. Nothing mattered, Elowen thought, except that the holiday had been wonderful. They had gone to Italy, to stroll in the Renaissance beauty of Siena and Florence, brilliant in the springtime light and a world away from what either of them had become used to. Then, with a peace and contentment re-established between them that Elowen would have thought impossible, they had lost themselves in the mountains of Tuscany.

Paul had returned to Zurich afterwards, and Elowen to Cornwall. She hadn't minded; she had known it wouldn't be for long. Sure enough, he had come back to her, arriving unannounced one evening with a stack of travel brochures and asking her where she fancied going next.

The only clue she ever found to explain Paul's change of heart came on a day of dazzling sunshine in Capri. They had left the triteness of the tourist town behind them, taking a taxi up to a little place in the hills where they had lunch on a vine-covered terrace overlooking the sea, dizzyingly far below. They were discussing Maugham's *Lotus Eater*, and Elowen remarked that twenty-five years on Capri still seemed a pretty fair exchange for a lifetime as a Hendon bank manager.

Paul laughed shortly. 'Work and play. So few of us get the balance right.' Elowen waited in silence; he had more to say, she was sure. 'Mark Anderson's dead,' he went on abruptly. 'Died last November. Heart attack, sitting at his desk. Killed him instantly — he was dead before his forehead hit the page of figures he'd been studying.'

'I didn't know,' Elowen said softly. She remembered Mark Anderson. He had been a lifelong friend of Paul's, successful in both his business and his private life. He had driven himself on relentlessly, partly because he was going to retire to Spain and wanted enough money to do it in style, but more so because of sheer love of his work. 'What about the villa in Marbella?' she asked.

'Valerie sold it. Said she couldn't bear to go there without Mark, and anyway she didn't like the heat. Poor old bugger. All that effort, and his widow says she didn't like the heat. She'd have been there on her own most of the time, anyway — I don't seriously think he'd ever have torn himself away from the business.' He stared out over the tumbled, scrubby hillside to the vivid blue of the distant sea. He sighed deeply, then turned to look directly at Elowen. Taking her hand in an uncharacteristic gesture, he said quietly, 'He forgot there was anything else.'

Vindication, Elowen thought, for my having persuaded him into this new way of life. She knew he would never say more; he didn't need to. His staccato comment had made her very happy.

★ ★ ★

Now Cannes was a leisurely drive ahead of them. Perhaps not leisurely exactly, Elowen thought, glancing at Paul, supremely content as he drove the Rolls down the Autoroute at a smooth and uninterrupted 90 mph, but it felt that way. He was humming fairly tunelessly to a tape of Beethoven's Pastoral Symphony which Jo had given him.

It amused Elowen to see her daughter try to introduce Paul to new, more challenging works, but he steadfastly stuck to Beethoven since he liked something with a *tune*.

'But so do I!' Jo had exclaimed in despair. 'Don't you think Brahms liked a tune? And Mozart? Ravel? Bach? Berlioz?'

'Dah-dah-dah-DUM,' Paul replied, in a way that allowed no room for argument. '*Now that's* a tune! You can get me that, if you like.'

'Beethoven's Fifth,' Jo grumbled. Elowen had been amazed she'd recognised it. 'All right, if you must.'

So Elowen's travels with Paul had perforce to be travels with Beethoven as well. She thought she must have heard the Fifth Symphony over a hundred times in the last two years, and she was considering making enquiries about earphones.

'Why hasn't she gone with Hal?' Paul asked suddenly.

Elowen sighed. She had been working very hard on not thinking about that. Jo's reason for coming to Cannes with the boys was quite plausible, and Elowen was unwilling to let any sinister thoughts intrude on her happy holiday mood. Especially when they had such a tenuous basis. 'Cairo's not exactly where one would choose to have a summer holiday, especially with two small boys.'

'Isn't it?' Paul sounded surprised. 'Interesting, I'd have thought. Arabs, souks, donkeys, that sort of thing.'

Elowen thought his impressions of Cairo seemed to have stagnated in 1945. 'Well, Hal will be working, researching in the museums and so on,' she said tactfully, 'and I suppose Jo thought she might as well take the children somewhere more suitable.'

'She could be a great help to him.' Paul's mind had leapt on. 'Sometimes I wonder if he appreciates how bright she is.'

'Oh, I think he does.' Elowen thought of suggesting that Jo, given the time, would want to pursue her own interests rather than help Hal with his. But she dismissed the idea: given Paul's tendency to get right to the bottom of things, they'd still be on the subject in Avignon. 'There isn't much about her that he doesn't appreciate. He's a very clever man.'

'She's a very clever girl.'

Elowen agreed. 'She's — developed, since she met him,' she went on, after a pause.

'How do you mean?'

'Mentally. She was at a lower level, with Ben. His level.' Elowen felt she was betraying Ben, whom she had loved more dearly than either of her own sons. 'I'm not saying Ben wasn't bright,' she went on hastily, 'but his was a more practical, common-sense sort of intelligence. He and Jo didn't do anything intellectual together. I think she would have been content to stay at that level.'

'I don't.' Paul spoke vehemently. 'Mind you, I always thought she was too clever for Ben.'

'You didn't say so at the time.'

'No, but I thought it.'

'So what are you saying?'

Paul looked taken aback. 'I don't think I'm saying anything, other than what is implied by the superficial meaning of my words.' Elowen smiled; he often had a touch of the Gladstone, but it was understandable. He had, after all, had decades of addressing public meetings. 'But I don't think she's too clever for Hal,' Paul went on. 'I imagine not many people are. Who are the Minoans, anyway?'

'They lived on Crete, years ago.'

'Oh.' Elowen could feel the next question cantering towards her for quite a while before Paul asked it. 'Then why is he going to Cairo?'

'You'll have to ask Jo,' she said, when she had finished laughing. She was incapable of telling Paul what was so funny.

They arrived in Cannes in the late afternoon, plunged into a heaving mass of undisciplined homeward-going traffic. Paul, anxious for the Rolls' immaculate coachwork, switched off the air-conditioning and wound down his window to address remarks liberally. 'Lunatic drivers,' he said loudly to Cannes in general, when nobody would break the stream to let him in after he'd wrong-laned himself. 'No road sense whatsoever. Shouldn't be allowed anything more lethal than a horse and cart.'

'Left here, then follow the main road till the next major intersection, where we go left again.' Elowen was calmly reading from the street plan on her lap.

'This is a pedestrian crossing,' Paul enunciated clearly through his window to a large Frenchman in a Peugeot trying to overtake on the nearside, '*un passage pour piétons*. We stop for pedestrians!' A volley of horns from behind suggested that the lights had changed.

'Green light, darling,' Elowen said serenely.

Soon they were in quieter residential streets, and after some wrong turnings, they emerged into the correct avenue and found their apartment block, hidden away behind a sheltering fringe of trees and flower beds.

'Tomorrow, after we've collected Jo, we'll put the car down there,' Paul said, nodding towards the entrance to the block's underground car-park, 'and that's where it will stay.' He had made a careful inspection all the way round the car, but had found nothing worse than half a million dead flies spread evenly all over the forward-facing surfaces. 'Do you think those boys of Jo's would wash it for me?'

'I don't think you can expect much of Sammie, since he's only two. But Edmund might. You'll have to pay him, he is on holiday, after all.'

'Hmm. We'll see.'

They unloaded the car, carrying into the apartment in addition to the cases several boxes of groceries. Elowen glanced at the contents: muesli, wheatgerm, dried fruits, soya protein. She had been unable to convince Paul that taking food to the South of France was superfluous. Another effect of Mark Anderson's death had been Paul's preoccupation with his health, and he was now extremely fussy about what he ate. A routine check-up with his doctor had elicited the comment that his blood-pressure was a bit up but otherwise his constitution was AOK, and despite the general cheery tone of this, Paul had been panicked into a fitness routine. His enthusiasm for it came and went; we must be in a waxing phase at the moment, Elowen thought. She wished she could develop a taste for wheatgerm.

They settled into the apartment, and Elowen unpacked their clothes and toiletries while Paul arranged his vitamin supplements. 'I don't want to live on bran and orange juice,' she remarked, coming into the kitchen. 'Let's go shopping. We haven't got any wine,' she added craftily.

'Ah. No.' She could see conflicting desires in Paul's face. Then he smiled, putting his arm round her affectionately. 'Of course, there is one school of thought that says a certain amount of wine is essential to break down fatty deposits in the arteries.'

'I for one am one big fatty deposit,' Elowen said, returning his hug, 'so for my sake, let's get a bottle of red, a bottle of white and some vermouth as an *apéritif*.'

They took the car down to Monoprix, and Paul waited outside while Elowen hurried in to buy food and drink. She came out in record time, conscious that Paul would hate having to park in so vulnerable a spot. There didn't in fact seem to be any place to park in the streets of Cannes that wasn't a vulnerable spot. She sat clutching the brown paper bags, trying to keep them upright as Paul weaved through the traffic, amusing herself at the incongruity of bringing the groceries home in a Rolls.

Later they went for an evening promenade, arriving on the Croisette in time to buy a copy of that day's *Times* from the *presse* before it closed. Then they crossed the road to a bar for cold beers. 'Would you like to read the news?' Paul asked, folding the financial section to the stock exchange prices.

'Yes, thank you.' Elowen didn't particularly care what was going on in England and the rest of the world, but she knew Paul would feel uneasy about shutting himself off inside the business section if she was sitting there apparently waiting for him to talk to her. She heard him go 'hmph!' as he settled into his reading; she left him to it.

The extraordinary cast of his mind continued to amaze her. As she watched him, his face taut, muttering under his breath and occasionally making rapid jottings in a leather-bound notebook, she reflected that she had still never met anyone quite like him. It was as if the beam of his mind's power were focused more narrowly than most people's. The complex intricacies of the financial world

41

were to him like well-lit, straight pathways, and he was totally at home with anything to do with money. But, really, that was about it: he was rather like a toned-down version of an *idiot savant*, outstanding in the one area, fairly useless outside it. Elowen smiled at her thoughts — I shouldn't be too critical, my husband's one great talent has made him an extremely wealthy man. And one outstanding talent is more than most people have.

But oh, he makes me laugh. She thought back to their conversation about Jo and Hal. She wondered what Paul really thought of his second son-in-law. What, indeed, Hal thought of him. The two of them had found plenty to talk about on the few occasions when they'd had the chance, but Elowen realised that this said more about the flexibility of Hal's mind than any ability of Paul's. Hal, she thought, can apparently manage anything cerebral; she didn't imagine it had been his choice to talk for an hour and a half about the benefits of denationalisation.

Elowen hadn't intended to think about Hal. I'm on holiday, she said to herself, and Jo's coming tomorrow. I shall see my grandchildren, who no doubt will wear me out and annoy me as often as they make me overflow with happiness. But I shall still be very pleased to see them.

Paul closed the newspaper, returning it to a neat, folded shape. 'Stock market's up,' he said cheerfully. 'I'll buy you another beer.'

# 3

Nice Airport had changed in eleven years; it looked sufficiently like any other international airport for Jo not to be overcome by memories of racing across the concourse in the summer of 1973 to fall into Ben's arms. Before the vapour trails of memory could clarify, she caught sight of her parents, looking fit and tanned. Ben's benign ghost retreated; this is *now*, she told herself firmly, I've got quite enough on my plate without keening for the past.

With the perversity of childhood, Sammie, who had bawled most of the way from San Francisco, was instantly all smiles and enchantment for his grandparents. Jo watched her father setting off for the car park, a happy grandson holding on to each hand, and collapsed against Elowen.

'Bad journey, darling?' her mother asked sympathetically.

'Awful. Teddy was OK — there was a Bond film, and he loves James Bond. But Sammie's been a little sod.'

'Never mind.' Elowen patted her cheek.

'You're here now, two more pairs of hands to help.'

'Oh, Mum, don't be nice to me!' Jo felt stupidly like crying. I'm tired, damn it, she told herself. 'You look great,' she went on quickly, 'I love you in yellow.'

'Not too bright, for a woman of my mature years?'

'Definitely not. Especially against your tan.' Jo was aware of looking pale, by comparison. 'It's been dreadful in San Francisco. So much fog! And I've longed to see the sun.' Why couldn't she get away from subjects that made her feel sorry for herself?

Elowen started to push the luggage trolley towards the exit. 'Your father seems to have left this to us,' she said, 'but then he's got the boys.' She shot a comradely glance at Jo. 'I know which I'd rather have.'

'Me too,' Jo agreed fervently. 'Suitcases don't winge.'

★ ★ ★

Jo wondered later whether her sudden lift in spirits was merely a result of the large amount she seemed to have drunk. Elowen and Paul had suggested they spend a lazy day, as befitted people who had just flown the Atlantic and the width of North America into

45

the bargain, so they spent the afternoon by the apartment's swimming pool. As Elowen firmly told Edmund, the beach would still be there tomorrow. The children were yawning by seven o'clock, and Jo put them to bed before they could change their minds and decide to be lively again.

She strolled out on to the terrace, a glass of pastis in her hand, to join her father. He was on the top right-hand corner of the *Times* crossword. 'Poseidon was god of the sea, wasn't he?' he asked as she sat down.

'Yes.'

'Damn. Too many letters.'

'What about Neptune? That was his Roman name.'

'Hmph. No, that won't do. I think I'll leave that one to you.'

'Mum says supper's in half an hour,' Jo said, smiling. 'If you move over, I'll lay the table.'

She was hit with a lovely holiday somnolence. Paul got up to refill their glasses, and her torpor increased. Quiet sounds floated on the still air: the murmur of voices, talking quietly on other balconies; distant laughter from the pool; the cooing of a pair of collared doves from a roof-top, and, closer, a rattle of plates as her mother worked tranquilly in the kitchen and her father's obbligato of muttered comment as he struggled with the crossword.

The terrace was at ground floor level, and gave on to a garden. There was a wide space of bright green lawn, and the flower beds surrounding it were full of well-established shrubs. Lavender, rosemary and marjoram exuded their competing scents into the evening warmth, the soft colours of their foliage contrasting with hibiscus and oleanders. The blooms of hibiscus always made Jo think of people putting their tongues out and going *bleah*.

'Paul, will you open the wine?' Elowen's voice brought her back from half-sleep. Her father disappeared inside the apartment. There was a pop, and he returned carrying a tray of glasses.

'Champagne,' he said unnecessarily, 'to celebrate your arrival.' Jo looked at his smiling face, and at Elowen, bringing out a plate of snacks. It was such a luxury to be looked after, so heavenly to be brought food and drink that she hadn't had to think about, buy or prepare. Again she felt dangerously emotional, although she refused to let herself cry; it would hardly have been the response her father expected to his champagne. Mum would understand, she thought. But I'm not going to give in.

The three of them chattered ceaselessly over supper, with the enthusiasm of family members who hadn't had a long conversation, just between themselves, for years. Jo tried to analyse what was different about the mood between them, and came to the conclusion that the answer lay with her father. She studied him as he sat relaxed, relating how he and Elowen had made friends with a retired doctor in Levadia, who had taken them to a cherry festival in a village up in the mountains. I didn't know they'd been to Greece, Jo thought, I must ask them later what they thought of it.

'Our doctor seemed to be something of a local celebrity,' Paul was saying, 'and your mother and I were therefore accorded double honours, both as his guests and as the strangers at the feast.'

'Entertaining angels unawares,' Jo commented. 'The Greeks are good at that, aren't they? And you might have been gods descended, after all.'

Paul went on to describe how the doctor had kept dancing with Elowen, and as he spoke he reached out and took her hand. That's what it is, Jo realised. He's not wishing he was somewhere else any more. He wants to be here, with Mum. She thought back over the years of childhood. She pictured her father arriving for flying visits, spoiling them all rotten with treats and expensive presents, which he bestowed with one eye on the clock and his mind still on his work. She had realised — early enough for it not to disturb — that her father preferred life in his other existence, the one that didn't include wife and family. It had always been so, and it didn't hurt. Perhaps, she thought, it had hurt her mother.

Elowen looked happy now. But she still kept her air of seeming to observe events rather than participate. Too strong a habit to break? Jo wondered. Elowen had a quality of imperturbability, especially where Paul was concerned; whatever outrageous thoughts he expressed, whatever he spontaneously decided to do, Elowen would continue along her own sweet way. She's her own woman, Jo thought as she went eventually yawning to bed, leaving her parents talking quietly on the terrace. No matter how good things are between them now, Dad will never change that. But then I don't suppose he wants to — it's probably why he's here with her. He's never cherished things that come easy.

★ ★ ★

The days settled down to a routine. They would go down for a long morning on the beach, then one or two of them would form an advance party back to the apartment, stopping on the way to buy food. Occasionally the three adults might manage a short siesta after lunch, before giving in to the children's impatience and moving down to the apartment's pool. Sometimes they went out for a stroll after tea, then it would be time to put Sammie to bed. Teddy, although older, would usually be so worn out by his day's exertions that he wouldn't be long in following.

'I'm going to the market first thing,' Paul announced one morning as they tore into the baguettes. Jo smiled; here was a break with routine, just as she had begun to appreciate it. 'It's best to go early — more choice,' Paul went on. 'We're running low on several things. Your boys eat like horses.' He fixed Jo with a stare.

'Yes, sorry, Dad. They can't help it, they're growing. And you do insist on making them walk everywhere; it sharpens the appetite.'

'First-class exercise, walking,' he said loudly. He threw out his chest. 'Keeps your mother and me fit.'

'I never thought to see the day when you'd walk in preference to driving,' she said. 'Or scrum round the shops and the market selecting your own food either, come to that.'

Elowen laughed. 'You've done it now, darling,' she remarked. 'Come on, boys, help me clear away. I've heard all this before.'

Paul leaned his elbows on the table, squaring up to his daughter in what she thought of as his Mesmer pose. 'We are what we eat,' he began. Can't argue with it so far, Jo thought. 'Simple food, plenty of exercise, avoidance of stress,' Paul continued, 'those are my life rules.' Jo was tempted to ask how the large bottles of wine fitted in — she and Elowen certainly weren't getting through over a litre and a half a day all by themselves. But she didn't; most of what her father was lengthily saying was sound, and anyway she couldn't have slid a word in edgeways. They walked together as far as the market, where Elowen left Paul and Jo to shop while she took the children on to the beach.

'In here,' Paul said, pointing to an arched entrance into the covered, noisy interior; letters cut into the stone said 'Porte Forville'. Jo saw what her father had meant by the market being best early. The stallholders had laid their produce out expertly, and so far the designs hadn't been disturbed by inconsiderate customers buying more of one thing than another. She stopped by a stall just inside the entrance to look more closely.

There were bunches of fresh herbs, and the aromas of mint, coriander, basil, tarragon and parsley. Peppers and aubergines had a gloss like the shine on a fit dog's coat. Do they polish them? Jo wondered. Displays of mushrooms, courgettes, garlic and onions were so similar in size and shape that they would have won prizes at any horticultural show. There were peaches with skins so dark that they matched the raspberries they had been placed beside. Then a wealth of citrus fruits, their sharp smell making her mouth water. Pink grapefruit, cut open to show the flesh, juice running out in steady drips.

'Dad, we've got to have a couple of these.' She turned to look for Paul, who was forging ahead to the fish stalls. Following him, she was sidetracked by the cheese and pâté, pausing to watch a woman carving thin slices from a huge haunch of ham. The ham was still steaming slightly; she thought it had probably been cooked fresh that morning.

She was suddenly transported back to the kitchen of the Provençal farm where she and Ben had worked the summer they met. The smell of boiling ham was in her nostrils, and she could see the farmer's wife, sleeves rolled up above her strong forearms, forcing chicken livers and huge cloves of garlic through a big old-fashioned mincer. The vision was so powerful that she was disorientated; as the inevitable sequel flashed before her eyes — Ben smiling at her as only he could — the colours of the market began to distort and she thought she was going to faint.

She stumbled across to an empty hand-cart behind the stalls and sat down, dropping her head on to her folded arms. *Of course I would think of him here,* she thought wildly, *what else? That woman carving the ham could be our farmer's wife's twin sister. What if it were she herself? Or if the farmer and his sons were over there on the dried herbs stall, nudging each other and saying, that woman looks familiar, wonder what she's done with that nice blue-eyed chap she had with her?*

She felt a hand on her arm. *'Qu'est-ce qu'il y a?'* a kind voice said. *'Vous avez mal?'*

It was the ham woman. She didn't look like the farmer's wife after all. She was frowning at Jo in anxious concern. *'ça va, merci,'* Jo said, trying to smile. 'I'm not ill. *Mais, il fait chaud, n'est pas?* Hot!'

*'Ouf! Oui, oui. Bastien!'* The woman's sudden shout made several people jump, especially Jo, who was nearest. A young man

appeared from the throng, and the woman shot off a long sentence of instructions at him. He ran off to the rear of the pâté stall, returning shortly with a glass of cold water. '*Voilà,*' the woman said, and watched as Jo drank it down. '*Alors, du cognac?*' The young man was proferring a brandy bottle.

'Oh! *Non, non merci,*' Jo said hastily. '*Vous êtes très gentille, Madame. Je suis . . .*' The right way to say 'I'm all right now' eluded her. '*Je suis okay!*' She grinned as the woman laughed and, with a friendly pat on Jo's shoulder, went back to her ham.

I'd better find Dad, Jo thought, there's no knowing what might happen next. She took a deep breath and stood up, relieved to find that her knees were no longer shaking. She looked round for Paul.

He saw her before she had spotted him. 'Look at this, Jo!' she heard him shout, and turned to see him waving a huge fish over his head. 'Did you ever see such a beauty?' Several stallholders were watching him with amusement, although the man whose fish it was appeared less than delighted.

'*Ne touchez pas, Monsieur,*' he said irritably, frowning at his laughing colleagues. But Paul wasn't listening.

'Fish is the thing,' he said to Jo, 'full of

protein and minerals, clean white meat, fresh from the sea.'

'Dad, put it back, it's far too big for us!'

He gave the great creature a considering look. 'Yes, I suppose so,' he said. Regretfully he slapped the fish back on to its slab and the stallholder, glaring furiously at Paul, fussily sponged at it with a wet cloth. 'I'll just borrow that to wipe my hands,' Paul said. With a perfunctory smile he did so; his effrontery seemed to have temporarily knocked the resistance out of the stallholder. That's how we won the Empire, Jo thought.

'Couldn't we have some pâté?' she asked wistfully, steering Paul away from the horrible gasping mouths of the fish. He stopped as if he'd come abruptly to the end of a line.

'Pâté?' he said, glaring at her with furious disapproval as though she'd suggested boiled baby for lunch. 'Have you any idea of the *fat* content of pâté?' The word FAT echoed to the roof high above, causing people to stare. He shook his head at her misguidedness, muttering beneath his breath about people deliberately and wilfully narrowing their arteries and being a burden on the state. Jo, torn between amusement and embarrassment, slipped from his side and went to admire the flowers.

The days went by, typical holiday days.
They would sit on the beach and watch
the children play, or stroll on the Croisette
and observe the fashionable people of Cannes
promenading in their smart clothes. But part
of Jo's mind was constantly with Hal; her
dreams were full of him, uneasy dreams
where she was looking for him and unable
to find him, or trying in vain to put right
a misunderstanding with him, or hurrying
because she was late and she didn't think
he'd wait for her. She would wake disturbed,
and it took longer than it should to shake off
the unpleasant taste left by her visions. It's
strange, she thought wearily, forced awake
by a particularly vivid dream in which she
had been sitting behind Hal on a motor bike,
pressed tightly against him while he tried to
disentangle himself. With all that there is
here to recall Ben, one brilliant moment of
memory is all I've had. Yet Hal, who has
never been here either with or without me,
haunts my mind and won't let me rest. She
lay on her back, missing Hal with an ache
that wouldn't go away.

Elowen asked her quietly the next morning
if she was all right. 'You look a little strained,
darling. Didn't you sleep?'

On the point of saying she was fine, Jo suddenly thought how wonderful it would be to talk. To pour out the anxiety to her mother. 'I had a disturbed night,' she said. She and Elowen were in the kitchen; she could hear Paul outside, supervising the boys as they laid the table for breakfast. 'I — er, I've got things on my mind.'

'Ah.' Elowen managed to make the one syllable full of sympathy. 'I had wondered. We could — ' They were interrupted by Teddy rushing in, dispatched to fetch the butter. Over his head as he burrowed in the fridge, Elowen mouthed, 'Later?' and Jo nodded.

In the afternoon, while Paul was in the shallow end of the pool encouraging Teddy to swim without his arm bands, Elowen said, 'Shall I take you for a walk to the Suquet?'

'What's the Suquet?' Jo asked.

'The old part of the town. Where the clock tower is, up on the hill.'

'Just the two of us?' She met her mother's eyes.

'Oh, I think so. Paul can manage both children, as long as we're not too long.'

They set out along the familiar route to the beach, branching off and climbing a path between buildings of an earlier date than the rest of Cannes. 'It's so different!'

Jo said in surprise. There were no roads, only flights of steps, onto which the front doors of the narrow little houses opened. Here and there old people perched on chairs, watching the world pass up and down. Small shuttered windows were set in the sheer walls; it was old, shabby, and slightly smelly; it had faithfully kept the character of a medieval town. She turned to Elowen, her face breaking into a smile. 'I'm glad you suggested it,' she said.

'We're not at the top yet,' Elowen replied; they had stopped for a breather. 'You may not be so enchanted when you see the final climb up to the clock tower.'

But it was easier towards the top. The steps broadened out into an open space, and across a road paved with huge, smooth slabs, worn shiny by the feet of centuries, stood a wide archway surmounted by the clock. 'It sounds twice,' Elowen said, 'you'll see.' She looked at her watch. 'In ten minutes. It'll strike on the hour, then again four minutes afterwards.'

They went under the arch into the courtyard beyond. 'Do you want to go into the church?' Elowen asked.

'No, thanks,' Jo said. 'Let's sit and look at the view.'

All of the town lay before them. Up

here they were detached from the Cannes of nowadays, untouched by its hurry. To the south was the sea, darkening to navy, its smooth surface interrupted only by the vague shapes of the Îles des Lerins, lying off-shore. Behind rose the foothills and, beyond, the mountains. Elowen led the way to a bench. Jo remarked that you could still admire the view from a sitting position. 'It's a well-managed town,' Elowen agreed, 'even down to arranging wall heights so that you can see over them.'

They sat in silence for some time. Then Elowen said, 'What is it, darling?'

Jo shrugged. Now that the moment had come, it seemed impossible to put her distress into words.

Elowen said gently, 'Is it Ben?'

'Ben?' She was amazed. 'No! Why should it be?'

'Because you were here with him, in the south of France. I wondered if the memories were painful.'

Jo thought of her near-faint in the market. 'There are memories, you're quite right. But they're not painful.' Suddenly she was struck by the thought that her troubles would not have arisen had Ben lived. In order not to dwell on that, she said, 'It's Hal.' Then instantly wished she hadn't.

'Ah,' Elowen said. 'I don't wish to pry, but it hasn't escaped my notice that, apart from the most banal generalities, you haven't mentioned him at all since you arrived.'

'I may not have been talking about him, but I've never stopped thinking of him,' she said. Then: 'It's awful!'

'Oh, Jo.' Elowen took her hand. 'Of course you miss him, but — '

'I don't miss him.' But that wasn't right either. 'Well, I do, but I certainly don't miss the tension.'

'Tension?'

'I don't like what I've become,' she plunged on, 'I'm not good at what I have to be — you know, a housewife, mother, homemaker, all that — and, although I try to fight it, I resent the fact that Hal doesn't have to be it as well.'

'He has to earn a living,' Elowen pointed out gently.

'*I know*!' Then, more quietly, 'I know. Sorry, Mum, I didn't mean to shout. But *I* earned a living, before I got bogged down with domesticity. I hate having to give it up. Give up the writing. The — ' She made herself stop.

'The independence?' Jo nodded. 'Oh, dear.'

Elowen's tone made Jo look at her. 'Don't

60

say it like that! It's not that serious! Is it?'

Elowen was frowning. 'The combination of resenting Hal's career whilst wishing you still had your former independence sounds as if it could become serious, yes.'

'What do I do?' she asked in a small voice.

'Have you talked to Hal?'

'Yes, a bit.' Then, more honestly, 'No. I was angry about him going to Cairo, and I was shitty to him. Sorry.'

'That's quite all right. Go on.'

'I fixed this up — coming to stay with you — without consulting him, and he said I was being unreasonable. I said he hadn't bothered to ask my permission before arranging to bugger off to Cairo, and he said he wasn't talking about asking permission, just about the normal consideration you expect between husband and wife. I told him to stop being a pompous git, and he said I was overwrought. I wasn't!'

Elowen said, 'Oh, darling!' Detecting a slight tremor in her voice, Jo glanced at her; Elowen was struggling with laughter.

'Mum, it's not funny!'

'I'm sorry! It's just the idea of you yelling at Hal and calling him a pompous git.'

Reluctantly Jo began to smile. 'He *is* pompous. Sometimes.'

'They all are. It's part of being male.'

'He was right, really,' Jo said after a moment. 'Wasn't he? About the need to be considerate.'

'Yes. The question is whether or not *he* normally is.'

'You're taking for granted that I am?' Jo asked, amused.

'Are you?'

Jo sighed. 'I'd have said I used to be. Now — I don't know. I seem to get a devil inside me, and I sort of snap.'

'It's not easy, bringing up children. Little ones can be very demanding, and one sometimes yearns for time to oneself. Time to think.'

'Tell me about it!' Jo said fervently. It was wonderful how well Elowen understood. Then: 'You said just now was Hal usually considerate. The answer's yes. He does try to help, only sometimes he's miles away, thinking about something much more interesting than children's meals or clean underpants, and he doesn't notice.'

'Perhaps you wish you too had the freedom to be thinking about something more interesting,' Elowen said.

'How perceptive! Indeed I do.'

'You must talk to him. Make the time, and don't let yourself get — what was his

62

word? — overwrought. No more calling him a pompous git.'

'I'll try.'

The silence extended, and Jo thought they'd said all they were going to. But then Elowen began, 'Darling, I'm in two minds whether to say what I'm thinking, because I may be wildly off the mark.' She turned to look earnestly at Jo. 'Forgive me if I am.'

Jo laughed. 'Oh, Mum, do for heaven's sake go on! The suspense is killing me.'

Elowen laughed too, shaking her head. 'No, this is serious.'

'I know.' She waited for her mother to speak.

'Jo, your father and I wasted years of our lives together because both of us wanted our own way, and neither was prepared to bend,' Elowen said. From nowhere, words popped into Jo's head: *We have followed too much the devices and desires of our own hearts.*

'All I'm saying,' Elowen went on, 'is, don't let it happen to you. In the end you'll come to regret it, and nobody can give you back the years you spend apart.'

Jo closed her eyes. She thought, oh, Mum, I'm sorry. She squeezed her mother's hand. 'I understand,' she said quietly, 'and thank you for saying it. I don't know if I — we — have a problem or not.' But, she added silently, I do have an awful feeling that it's going to get worse before it gets better.

★ ★ ★

The chance didn't arise for a further talk; Jo wasn't sure if she was relieved or sorry. As the days went by and the end of her holiday approached, she found herself wishing she could go back to England with her parents, home to the calm old house which had been in Elowen's family for generations. But then she felt guilty at the implied disloyalty to Hal; how would he feel, if I announced I wasn't coming back? Hal. Oh, I do miss you. She wished he was going to be there to meet them at the airport, but he wouldn't get back till she and the boys had been home a week.

★ ★ ★

When Elowen and Paul saw them off at Nice, Jo found herself being hugged very tightly in her mother's arms. 'Make it all right, darling,' Elowen whispered. 'I think it has to be up to you.' Then the press of people separated them, and it was time for goodbyes, for promises to write, to get together again soon. It won't be that soon,

Jo thought forlornly, thinking miserably of what lay ahead. It takes a huge effort to sort out your problems, and the one person who might have helped is about to be left thousands of miles behind.

She lifted her chin as she led the children through to embarkation, smiling as she turned for a final wave. I'm old enough to sort out my own life, damn it, she told herself. She sat the children down, wondering how she was going to occupy them until the flight left. You're on your own, kid, she thought. From here on in.

# 4

Hal's summer in Cairo had been hot and unpleasant. He hadn't been able to immerse himself in his work as thoroughly as he usually did; somehow the edge was off the fascination. He was suffering from a vague guilty feeling that he shouldn't be there. But I have to, he told himself, this is my work. Coming to Cairo was the next step in getting on with it. But a spectre of unease cast a shadow over all that he did.

On top of the predictable discomforts of high summer in a hot, dirty city teeming with traffic and pushy people, he went down with severe food poisoning. Although he spent most of his time within the air-conditioned walls of his hotel or the museum, at times he ventured further afield. On one such occasion — a trip out to the Step Pyramid at Saqqara — he'd unwisely bought lunch from a market stall.

Goddam it, this shouldn't have happened to me, he thought miserably as he sweated and retched in his hotel bed, clutching a bowl that he was too weak to go and empty. His head felt as though someone was sticking daggers through it, and his stomach was so tender that even the weight of a sheet hurt. Jeez, I used to have tin guts, once. He remembered — and the memory brought waves of renewed nausea — some of the meals he'd eaten in South America. Must be getting soft.

He was still being sick a day and a half later. The hotel doctor gave him an injection from a huge syringe which Hal would have thought more appropriate for a vet, and told him he'd been very silly, 'Another time, you must send for a doctor immediately.' The injection worked like a charm. The relief was well worth the sore buttock.

He wished Jo was with him. On the rare occasions he'd been ill, she'd nursed him with just the right degree of care, understanding when he wanted to be quiet and leaving him alone. Lying with the blinds drawn against the Egyptian sun, eyes closed, he thought of her. But he could only picture her as she used to be. He saw again the bemused and disorientated girl who had come to San Francisco to stay with Ben's parents, the widow whose great weight of grief had yet to be released.

Hal had been involved in that release. One of his most enduring memories was of Jo, her strained face still showing incomprehension, sitting on a West Coast shore under the stars as she told him how Ben had died. Hal had come to recognise that his love for her had been born that night.

He loved her now, he knew that. It was a relief, he had to admit, to be away from her in her present mood; she seemed to have become a restless, prickly creature. And he was grateful for these weeks alone in which to assess, to search for a solution to their problems. But, loving her however she was, he missed her.

* * *

One night he dreamt of Magdalena. He saw her again in her wedding dress, in those swathes of stiff white net she had put on to marry someone else, mummifying her forever beyond Hal's reach. The net became a winding-sheet as his dream vision changed into a scene that his own eyes hadn't witnessed: Magdalena dying, body twisting with the agony of childbirth, crying out his name as she lay amongst white linen that was stained with scarlet. But his sleeping brain made a mistake: in his dream, the dead baby that had insisted on its mother's company into the dark of the grave was no longer the child of Magdalena's husband. It was Hal's.

In the brilliant white of Cairo in the early morning, he could rationalise it all. He stared out over the city, and told himself that the dream, vivid enough to have shaken him awake, haunting enough to fill him with horror and a memory of his old grief, had come because he was tired and ill. The alternative was that he'd dreamt of his lost Magdalena because he was afraid of losing Jo. And he didn't want to think about that.

* * *

San Francisco. Home again. Hal wondered, as the aircraft landed, whether anyone would be there to meet him. He endured the wait through immigration, and the even longer wait for his baggage to appear on the carousel, then set off resolutely for the exit. He'd told himself not to expect anything, then he wouldn't be disappointed. I'll call a cab, he thought, be home in . . . He saw Jo. She was by herself, staring in the wrong direction with a face that gave away a great deal.

He walked up behind her, and tapped her shoulder. She jumped violently, and swung round. She was pale. 'Hi, kid.'

'Oh, Hal.' Her voice was soft, softer than

he'd heard in a while. She threw her arms round him, trying to fit herself around the bulk of luggage he was still holding. With cavalier disregard he let it all go, wrapping her in his embrace and kissing her with the accumulated hunger of weeks.

'Where are the kids?' he asked eventually when they paused for breath.

'Teddy's at school. I left Sammie with Bernard and Mary, we'll have to pick him up on the way home. I thought it'd be nice to meet you on my own,' she added quietly.

He looked down into her face. She had dark rings under her eyes and her skin looked slightly translucent. He thought, we ought to do a whole lot more things on our own. Her eyes had the particular greenness they acquired when she'd been crying. He said gruffly, 'Let's go home.'

★ ★ ★

Over the next few months, Hal felt increasingly like someone being taken to task for giving the wrong answer when he wasn't even sure he'd been set the question. Jo moved like a phantom inside the cloak of her unhappiness, working mechanically through the day's chores as if she'd been wound up and couldn't stop till she'd run right through her programme. Hal was tired and often felt ill; he certainly wasn't equal to the challenge of Jo. The food poisoning had left him drained; wondering if he'd picked up something worse, he went to see the doctor and was made to undergo several tests of varying degrees of embarrassment. To his relief, the doctor said he was fine, but told him to take things easy. Hal didn't mention it to Jo.

For the first time, he was reluctant to make love to her. By evening, when he'd done a day's work in college and spent a couple of hours writing up his 'Minoan thing', he was worn out. She would come to lie beside him on the sofa when she'd finished for the day, curling up against him. Usually she'd be exhausted too, and often fell asleep within minutes of lying down. But one evening he saw a spark of her old self in her eyes, and he knew with dismay that she wanted to make love.

He sighed, and moved away from her slightly. But she closed in on him again, nestling into his shoulder and finding bare flesh above his collar, kissing and sucking gently. For a moment his body responded. But his mind was saying, no. He just wanted to sit there, half asleep, paying minimum attention to the television. He didn't want anything else.

He felt for her. She didn't often make the first move — she hadn't usually had to — and once she'd asked him very shyly if he'd mind. 'No,' he'd said, 'sure I wouldn't mind'. The thought had excited him greatly then, the idea that one day she'd do what she promised and appear before him dressed in her long leather coat, stark naked underneath. But in those days, she'd been able to excite him just by looking at him.

Now, she was trying tentatively to arouse him. She wants me, Hal thought painfully, and I don't want to know. Tenderness for her shot through him, and he took hold of her hand to stop its gentle exploration. 'I'm sorry,' he said. 'I'm bushed.'

He felt her sag with disappointment. For some time she lay against him unmoving, her hand still captured in his. There was nothing he could say to make it right. After a while, she got up and left the room. When he went to bed, she was lying with her back to him. She didn't turn round.

Weeks passed, and she didn't repeat her overtures. There were evenings when he wished she would, when he tried subtly to let her know he'd have welcomed her. Something held him back from approaching her: it would have been unfair. Why should he expect her to be ready for him, just because he wanted her? They were in a stalemate; Hal suffered the bitterness of being unable to reach the person he loved most in the world.

★ ★ ★

Sam was going up to San Francisco for Christmas. He was breaking the habit of more than thirty years, during which he'd spent every festive season with his elder brother Thomas and his wife. It took something important to make him change his ways; Thomas and Eleanor had welcomed him with love that first terrible Christmas after Ruthie had died, and he'd never forgotten. Childless themselves, they'd worked so hard at making it jolly for the six-year-old Hal that he thought he'd suddenly acquired two extra parents. Memories like that didn't fade, Sam reflected, not ever.

In subsequent years, the get-togethers had included other family members; once Thomas had rashly invited their cousin Robert, and Robert's wife Olive had upset everyone trying to organise them. Sam had felt sorry for her kids; the girl was just a baby, but the boy, Max, was five, and had looked like he'd understood folks didn't like his mom. Sam had detailed Hal, eight years older, to look out for the boy. Hal had let Max ride pillion on his new bicycle, and Max fell off and tore his best trousers.

Sam had puzzled over how best to write to Thomas and Eleanor announcing his change of plan. In the end, incapable of working out exactly why he felt he ought to stay with Hal and Jo instead, he simply said Grandaddy wanted to see his grandsons, and that he expected he might be useful now and again to help with the dishes. Perhaps that's all it is, he thought, as he drove sedately up to San Francisco on the Saturday before Christmas. Only Jo looked so tired that weekend they came to visit, and her letters recently haven't sparkled like they used to. I will not say a word, he vowed to himself. But maybe I can do some good.

The boys were sitting on an upstairs window sill, looking out for his car. As he pulled into the drive, he caught sight of excited faces and waving hands, then the two children abruptly vanished, reappearing at the front door. 'He's here!' they yelled, and Sam was beset by sticky hands, warm moist kisses and two hard little heads.

'Hi, boys,' he said, returning their enthusiastic welcome. 'C'mon, you can

74

help me with my bags. But don't look in the trunk!'

Hal appeared in the doorway. He looked thin, and his eyes behind his glasses were deep. Sam looked at him. Oh, boy, he thought. 'Hello, son. How are you?'

'Fine. Good to see you, Dad.' Hal embraced him, then went to help the boys with the luggage.

'Where's my girl?' Sam said, putting his head round the kitchen door. Jo was at the sink, finishing the washing up. She turned at his voice, and Sam thought she didn't look any happier than Hal.

'Sam,' she said softly. 'Welcome.' Then, with flattering but surprising vehemence, 'Oh, I'm glad you're here!'

Sam studied them closely over the next few days. They both took his presence for granted — which he liked since it made him feel one of the family — and he got the impression that, although they were trying to make an effort because of him, the way they were acting wasn't all that different from how it would have been if he hadn't been there. Which was decidedly worrying, because they were both as miserable as sin.

Hal spent a lot of time in his study; he seemed to find it hard to to come out and be sociable at mealtimes and in the evenings.

And Jo, poor girl, was a walking disaster area. Sam watched her as she absently went through her days, lurching from one mishap to the next, unable to keep her mind on what she was doing. She sat watching the rain pouring down, forgetting that she'd just put out washing. Then she bought home the wrong present for Sammie, only realising when she was wrapping it up on Christmas Eve and it was too late to go and change it. Her inattention in the kitchen, Sam thought, was positively dangerous; she'd bitten her lips against the pain when she'd dropped hot fat down her sleeve, and his concern at the enormous blisters on the tender skin inside her forearm had brought tears to her eyes. 'I'm useless!' she'd said, trying to smile at Sam, making light of it. 'What a wonderful housewife I am!'

'Well, yes you are,' Sam reassured her, smiling with her. 'You have a deal to do, and you do it very well.'

But he clearly hadn't been convincing enough. 'Oh, Sam, I don't.' Her eyes turned to him, sombre with sorrow. 'I'm dreadful. I hate doing things badly, and the only work I do is work that I *can't* shine at.' She turned hastily away, pulling her sleeve down over the blisters. 'Supper's ready,' she said dully. 'Would you call Hal, please?'

It's Christmas Eve, Sam thought as they sat over coffee. I am with my son and his family, and I'm beginning to wish I'd gone to Thomas and Eleanor. I'd even have tolerated Robert's Olive. He looked at Hal, who had hardly said a word since he'd reluctantly emerged from his study. Damn it, Sam said to himself, I intend to enjoy Christmas, even if they don't. 'What're you working on, son?' he asked Hal suddenly, bright voice jarring in the prevailing depressed mood. 'You haven't told me what it is keeps you so occupied all day!'

Hal looked up, surprised. He frowned slightly, almost as if he'd forgotten Sam was there. 'Sure. It's — I'm rewriting a paper I did when I was in Mexico. The journal wanted to reprint it, but my thoughts on the subject have changed some since I wrote it. I'm bringing it up to date.'

Mexico, Sam thought. He looked across at Jo, whose face was sharp with pain. 'The money will be nice,' she said, stitching on a quick, brittle smile. 'More coffee, Sam?'

I have to talk to her, Sam thought later, looking at her across the room. She was watching Hal, and unaware of Sam's eyes on her. Hal had his shut-in look; there's no reaching him when he gets like that, Sam reflected. I hope she's not trying too hard, it'll only hurt her to keep failing. He'll come out of it, when he's good and ready.

Sam was more concerned about Jo.

Maybe I ought to be surprised that those old memories linger in Hal, he told himself. Jo sure seems to be — she reacted to 'Mexico' like someone had punched her on a bruise. But Sam knew his son. He'd never met Hal's Magdalena, but he knew she'd scored a scar across Hal that would never totally fade. And Mexico was where Magdalena had lived. Jo had every right to look desolate.

It hurts to see her hurting, Sam realised. He wanted to help her. It had been a sudden impulse to show her Ruthie's photograph, back in the summer, but he'd never regretted it. Jo was now in on a secret nobody else knew, Thomas and Eleanor apart, but that was OK. Something had happened to him since that day, and now it felt like Jo was the daughter he'd lost all those years ago. He couldn't have loved her more had she indeed been his own.

★ ★ ★

Christmas Day went well, better than Sam had expected. The booze helps, he thought; hard to be depressed when you have champagne fresh after breakfast, then a couple of bourbons before lunch and wine with the meal. Now the boys had calmed down, and were quietly playing on the floor with their new toys. The three adults had cleared up, and the kitchen was immaculate, smelling lingeringly of roast meat. Jo, far from her home, had given them a proper English Christmas lunch, which Sam had enjoyed even if it was maybe too soon after Thanksgiving for another turkey.

He went to join Hal, who was watching television. 'Where's Jo?'

Hal shrugged. 'Upstairs, I guess.'

'D' you want to take a walk?'

Hal looked at him sleepily. 'Not much,' he said with a grin. 'I'll stay here with the boys. You and Jo can go, if you want.'

'Right.' Sam went out into the hall, and called up to Jo.

'Coming,' she said. 'What is it, Sam?'

'I'd like some air. Will you join me?'

She looked at the closed door of the living-room. Then her eyes came back to Sam, and there was a warmth in her face. 'Yes,' she said. 'Yes, let's.'

Walks, in Sam's book, took a good two hours and had to be attacked at a brisk pace. He didn't mind where they went, and was quite happy to tuck Jo's arm under his and let her direct them. She brightened up the minute they left the house, and Sam didn't think it was only due to him joking about the huge display of flashing lights on the Christmas tree next door. They talked about music, children, holidays, gradually peeling off the covers till Sam could get down to the subject he really wanted to discuss with her. And — he hoped — she wanted to discuss with him.

They found a seat in a sheltered spot beneath trees, and sat watching a few other walkers who'd tired of being indoors. Intermittent gusts of wind whipped up dead leaves and bits of newspaper, and already the short daylight was fading. Not a time to stay out long, Sam thought. He reached to hold Jo's hand.

She said suddenly, 'He still thinks of her.'

Sam sighed. 'I know.'

'It's because she died, isn't it? She died when she was young and lovely, and he couldn't have her any more, and now he keeps this memory of a perfect woman, untarnished, unattainable on her blasted pedestal.'

'Right.' Sam thought it was best to let it all come out, all the hurt and the anger which she didn't seem able to fire off at Hal.

'It's not fair!' She took her hand from Sam's to push her hair back under her hat. Her face was taut. The everlasting cry of a child, Sam thought, 'It's not fair'. Now what leads us to believe life will be fair?

'No,' he said gently. 'I guess not.'

She rounded on him, working herself up to a fury. '*She'd* have been boring and preoccupied sometimes, and done things like letting cobwebs collect and forgetting to get anything for supper!' Sam nodded sagely. '*And* she'd have got fat and dumpy — and hairy, too, Latin types always do.' Sam nodded again. 'I can't be perfect, any more than anyone can be who you live with all the time,' she railed on. 'Damn it, Hal isn't perfect either, so why should I have to be?'

'I don't suppose Hal expects you to be perfect,' Sam interrupted mildly. It was one thing for her to storm against Magdalena, who was dead and beyond hurt. But he didn't think it was too good an idea for her to go assigning to Hal emotions that he was sure Hal didn't have.

'No. No, perhaps not. But . . . it's just that I know he'd rather have her than me!' Suddenly it all seemed to catch up with her. Rain on the washing, Sammie's disappointed face when he'd opened her present, the pain of the oozing blisters on her arm, and a hundred other annoyances and minor heartaches that happened to everybody but that most people took in their stride. And, far worse than anything else, Hal's brooding detachment. She sat, hands clenched into fists, and as Sam watched she began a despairing moan that tore right through him. Tears formed in her eyes; Sam put his arms round her and pulled her head down on to his chest.

'Don't cry, honey,' he said. 'Don't tear yourself to pieces.' He stroked her head, knocking off her soft woolly hat, his hands smoothing her silky hair. None of these things would bother her a hoot, he thought, if she had Hal's hand on her shoulder, his smile making light of things for her. He wished for a moment she would lean on him instead, but he knew she wouldn't. If no support was forthcoming from Hal, then she'd muddle through on her own. In time she grew quiet. He passed her a clean handkerchief.

'It's all right, I've got a tissue,' she said, fumbling in her coat pocket. 'You'll never get the mascara off your hankie.'

'Damn the mascara.' He pushed the handkerchief back into her hand. 'Tissues disintegrate, all over your face and up your nose.'

She started to laugh, mopping her eyes and blowing her nose. 'You're nearly as bossy as Hal,' she remarked.

'Oh, God. Am I really?'

She looked at him over the handkerchief, a flash of merriment in her eyes. 'Oh, I think so. Although he says he never got the better of you.'

'Someone had to show him he couldn't be chief all the time.'

She watched him solemnly. 'Yes. Quite.' She stood up, cramming her hat back on and stuffing her hands in her pockets. 'Shall we go back?'

'If you wish.' He looked at her quizzically. 'Unless there's more?'

She shook her head. 'Not really, except I wish you could tell me why I hate being a housewife, why I never seem to want to *do* anything any more, and why everlastingly I'm so damned tired.'

Sam smiled, falling into step beside her. 'We'll need to walk to Sacramento and back before I've answered all that.' She chuckled. 'But, Jo ...'

'What?'

'I'll do anything. I'll help, any way I can. You only have to ask.' He caught her eye and held it, wanting to be sure she realised he meant it. 'You know?'

She looked surprised at first. Then her face softened into a smile. 'I know, Sam. Thank you. I just might take you up on that.'

# Part Two

## March – April 1985

# 5

Absenting yourself from home to go to Cairo, Hal thought, was one thing. If you announced you were going to spend four weeks there in the height of summer, people were more likely to sympathise than clamour to come with you. But Crete; now, that was something else. Crete in the spring would be warm but not stifling, green from the winter rains, and free from the crowds that would flock there later in the year. It would have been quite possible to take the family with him. But he didn't want to. He was finding it more and more difficult to work with Jo around, and if they all went away together he could see all too clearly how things would be.

'It's not a holiday,' he said to her. 'I have people to see in Heraklion, I'm invited to stay with one of the country's leading experts on the Minoans, and any time I have left over, when I'm not clambering about on ruins, I shall spend writing before it gets driven out of my head . . . ' He had been about to add, by worrying about you.

She looked up at him. She no longer looks

like Jo at all, Hal thought. He put out his hand to touch her, but she shrugged him off. 'You said you'd take me to Crete,' she said, pain and anger in her face.

'Did I?' He couldn't remember. 'When?'

She regarded him for some moments. 'If you can't remember, there's no earthly point in my telling you.' Her voice was icy. 'It was very important to me, at the time.' She turned away and left the room.

He did remember, the next day when he was sorting through the enormous amount of material on his 'Minoan thing'. There was a file of information he'd amassed in London, and he remembered Jo reading it one afternoon, in his London apartment. Oh, Jeez, he thought, it was the day after she came up to stay with me for the first time. The weekend we became lovers. He raced through the house, looking for her. She was in their bedroom, asleep. He went and sat beside her, and took her hand. I go on hurting her, he thought. And each time, she stiffens up some more, like she's showing me she can take it. He wondered what he would do if she ever let up and showed him she still needed him. He wasn't even sure that she did; she seemed to have found a tough, joyless independence that didn't require love from anyone. She turned over and opened her eyes.

'Hi,' he said.

'Hello.'

'I'm making tea. D'you want some?'

She nodded. 'Yes please.' She put her hands to her eyes, squeezing them shut and pushing her fingers into the sockets.

'Headache?' he asked.

'Mm. I'll have some aspirins with the tea, please.'

He felt dismissed. He went downstairs to make the tea. When he returned, she was sitting at the dressing table brushing her hair. He wished she'd still been lying on the bed; he'd wanted to tell her he'd remembered about saying he'd take her to Crete, and that it had been important for him, too. But she wasn't so approachable, sitting straight-backed and glaring at herself in the mirror. He said nothing.

The short time left until his departure bristled with unsaid things. They were formally polite to each other; Jo offered to help him pack, and said of course she'd take him to the airport; he made an itinerary of his movements and provided contact telephone numbers. It's as if she's my secretary, Hal thought, or the receptionist in a good hotel.

It was a relief, finally, to go. Watching her hurry off from the check-in desk, Hal couldn't suppress the jubilant thought that ahead of him was a spell of blessed freedom away from her.

★ ★ ★

He went to London first, for a couple of days of fact-checking. At a loose end the second evening, on impulse he called Helen Arnold. They had met in a small hotel in Peru; Hal had been running away from the memory of seeing Magdalena marry someone else, and Helen, a retired schoolmistress, was touring the land whose history she'd once taught. They had taken to each other; Helen was the only person, other than Sam, whom Hal had invited to his wedding.

Helen lived in Oxford; hearing her voice, Hal wished she was nearer. Near enough for him to call a cab and go see her. When he explained what he was doing, she said, 'Why are you on your own?' and he'd wanted more than anything to pour it all out.

But he couldn't have done so over the phone, and he had a flight to catch first thing in the morning. 'I'm working,' he said instead. 'It'd have been too complicated, having Jo and the boys with me.'

There was a brief pause, then Helen said, 'I see.'

They talked for another twenty minutes, then she said her supper was ready. He thought he was going to get away without another meaningful comment, but he should have known better.

'You may *think* you prefer your own company,' she said as a parting shot — I don't! he wanted to protest, it's not like that — 'but I think you're wrong.' There was no need for her to go on, he knew what she meant. But clearly she wanted to be sure. 'Remember,' she added, 'I saw what you were like in Peru.'

★ ★ ★

He flew out to Heraklion on a mid-week flight full of retired English. He was served a drink and a meal by a disgruntled stewardess from whom he'd earned a reprimand for continuing to read through her speech about what to do in the unlikely event of an emergency. 'You have to listen, sir,' she'd hissed down at him as she stood over him in an uninflated life-jacket. 'It's the regulations.'

Hal slowly lifted his eyes from a fascinating paragraph about possible interpretations of the Phaistos disc. 'I was flying on aeroplanes when you were still in diapers,' he replied. 'Go tell someone else.'

He was lucky, he thought afterwards, to get any service at all.

* * *

As he flew southwards, his pleasure grew. He seemed to have severed himself from home, from the boys, and most of all from Jo, to become again the man he used to be. It was, he thought, as if going back to London had returned him to the state in which he'd first arrived there, with the intervening years wiped out. When he thought of Jo, it was of the woman she had been then. But he tried not to think about her: he wasn't ready.

Getting to Crete had become a crusade; he had started his 'Minoan thing' backwards, approaching the ancient civilisation by first learning about their effect on other Mediterranean cultures. Only now, when he had found out all he could from elsewhere, was he finally going to their heart. A picture flashed into his mind of a small statue he'd seen in London: it was standing in the Minoan prayer attitude, body straining forwards in supplication and right hand to forehead. With a quiet sigh of satisfaction, he closed his eyes to doze away the remaining hour to Heraklion.

* * *

He had deliberately left his first full day free of appointments: he wanted to go to Knossos, by himself. Leaving his hotel early, he found out from a shop assistant where the bus went from. He was finding it difficult to converse in Greek, but he persevered; he'd been fluent nine years ago, there was no way he could have forgotten it all.

Hal had hoped to avoid the crowds. But as the bus pulled up he saw that already there were five tourist coaches in the car park. In the wide courtyard in front of the ruined palace, three different guides asked him if he wished to join their tour, but he declined. With long strides he moved quickly towards the entrance, blocking from his mind everything but the Minoans. He ran up the steps leading to the Cental Court; the Palace of King Minos lay before him.

A long time later, he emerged from the decorative brilliance of the Queen's Megaron into the open air. He stood for a moment, stretching, shaking free from the oppression that had hit him down in those ancient rooms. Maybe it had just been the crowds, so many of them that, even if you waited till one group had departed, another followed hard on its heels. But there was more. Hal, who had never felt claustrophobic in his life, had suddenly experienced a frightening awareness of the thousands of tons of earth and masonry piled above him. For an instant he'd been terrified, beset with the illogical desire not to escape up into the sunshine but to crawl away into a hole like a snake, to delve yet deeper into the dank earth in some crazy gesture of propitiation.

Near him as he'd stood in the Hall of the Double Axes, an Italian woman had fainted. Hal had watched as her companions fanned her and sent for a glass of water. When she opened her eyes, he exchanged a glance with her. Without a word being said, he knew that she had felt it too, whatever it was. Then she was hurried away to the surface; Hal had followed. The fresh air was good, and the hot sun raised scents of thyme and pine that cleared his head. He sat down, his mind still reeling, and started to record his impressions.

After a while he paused. He watched the flocks of people, divided relentlessly into nationalities and each party being lectured in its own tongue. He smiled; outside the Throne Room, he'd heard some voluble middle-aged French people being berated by their guide: 'How will you understand if you will not listen?'

A short distance away sat a woman, writing busily in a yellow notebook. She was wearing a khaki bush-hat and a baggy white t-shirt. She had a Pentax and bag of camera equipment, and he watched as she carefully detached and put away a wide angle lens, then returned to her notebook. He wondered what she was writing. He felt an affinity with her; in this tumult of humanity, there was another person who wanted to scribble it all down before the impressions faded. She was fairish, quite tall; he imagined she was German, or English.

He had written all he wanted to, for the time being. He stood up, stepped out from the shade of his olive tree into the dazzling sunshine, and went to catch the bus back to Heraklion.

★ ★ ★

All the next week he was busy, with people to meet and lectures to attend. He experienced Cretan hospitality to the full, warmed by the generosity and the kindness. When the time came to leave Heraklion, it was hard to persuade his hosts that he really did prefer to go off on his own, that, although he appreciated the offer of a car, with or without a driver, he was quite content with the bus. They looked at him as if he was mad, shrugging off his eccentricity as typical of the peculiar ways of foreigners.

He sat on the bus heading west along the coast road, happy to be on his own again. He was going to Rethymnon; someone had told him he mustn't miss it. The road was wide and smooth, and he sat back enjoying the scenery, mountains rising steeply to his left, the incredible blue of the Sea of Crete to his right. He thought he saw cloud building up inland, but realised with wonder that it was a higher mountain range.

In the evening, after finding suitable accommodation and spending an hour on the beach, he went out for a stroll. He decided he liked the Venetian architecture of Rethymnon. He sat over a couple of beers at a cafe by the harbour, enjoying the sunset, watching the population on their evening parade. Behind the waterfront were narrow lanes lined with shops and restaurants; he looked forward with pleasure to finding a good place for dinner. The choice was simple: in a street that contained five restaurants in a row, he went for the busiest. The tables were set out under awnings, and lights were hung from the trees; it was an excellent vantage point, and Hal thought he'd spin out his meal and spend the rest of the evening there.

'Please, you mind share your table?'

Hal looked up. The waiter, flying round trying to attend to eight requests at once, was standing by him, a plate in each hand. 'Sure,' Hal said, shifting his papers to make room.

He imagined the waiter was merely planning for future need — the restaurant was filling fast — but a voice said from behind him, 'Thanks. Sorry to disturb you.'

He turned. Standing beside the waiter was the woman he'd noticed at Knossos. He smiled. In retrospect, the incident had amused him — he must be getting middle-aged, if a pretty woman caught his attention merely because she was writing in a notebook. He stood up, pulling out a chair for her. 'You're welcome,' he said.

She settled herself, arranging her large leather bag on the floor, then turned her attention to Hal. She sat with her head on one side, apparently quite unembarrassed. Her hair was reddish, and cut short. What he could see of it around the bush-hat was thick and curly. She wore tinted glasses, behind which her eyes were an indeterminate light colour. Her skin was tanned, and she was tall and curvy.

'Have you finished?' she asked.

'I haven't started yet. They're busy, tonight.'

She smiled. 'I didn't mean eating. I meant staring.'

'No. Have you?'

Her smile became a laugh. 'Fair enough.' She held out her hand. 'Since we seem to have broken the ice, my name's Angela.'

'Mine's Hal.' He took her hand briefly. 'I have a shirt like yours,' he observed. She was wearing a scarlet football shirt that said 'Forty-niners'.

She looked down at herself. 'Is San Francisco where you come from?'

'That's where I live. I was raised in Chicago.'

'I live in Gloucestershire. That's in England.'

'Right.' He could have said, 'I've been to England. I got married there'. But he didn't. He'd been trying to place her accent. Her voice was very like Jo's, but with a faint burr that he couldn't identify. Gloucestershire. Where the hell was Gloucestershire?

The waiter arrived with Hal's order, and asked Angela what she would like. 'Beer, please. And . . . what's that you've got?'

She stared down at Hal's plate.

'Squid.'

'Ah. I'll have dolmades and a tomato salad, please,' she said to the waiter.

'You don't like squid?' Hal asked, smiling.

'Sometimes. Not today — one too many ouzos last night.'

'Good party?'

'No party. I'm on my own. Well, till the weekend. Then, with any luck, Rob arrives.' She left the enigmatic statement hanging, and reached down into her bag for her notebook. While Hal got on with his squid, she wrote several quick pages before the waiter interrupted her with her meal.

'*Efcharisto*,' she said, and began eating.

'What are you writing?' Hal asked. She couldn't write while she ate, and he wanted to go on talking to her.

She delicately ejected an olive pit into her half-closed hand and put it in the ashtray. 'Notes. Background information for my photos.'

He remembered the wide angle lens and the Pentax. 'Is that what you do?'

She laughed. 'I'm an amateur.' Then, defensively, 'I'm bloody good.'

He couldn't think of a suitable response, and there was silence for a while as they ate. Then Hal said, 'Maybe we'll see each other again. I'm collecting background information, too.'

'Background to what?'

'I started out writing an article on the Minoans. I have too much for an article, so I guess it'll have to be a book.'

Angela took off her glasses and polished them on her shirt. Then she looked directly at Hal. Her eyes were a very clear grey. 'Have you got a publisher?'

Hal laughed. 'Good question. I had somebody interested in the article. Now I have to persuade him it makes a much better book.'

'Best of luck,' Angela said.

She had finished her meal. She looked around for the waiter. Hal said without thinking, 'Can I buy you another drink?' She turned to him. She seemed to specialise in long silent glances, and they made Hal feel vaguely guilty, as if he'd been entertaining dishonourable thoughts. He made himself meet her stare.

'No, thanks,' she said. 'I want to write some more before I go to bed.' She went on looking at him.

'What are you doing tomorrow?' he asked. She was glancing at the bill, getting her money out. It was a lucky coincidence to have run into her again. She might be off anywhere in the morning.

'I shall spend a frustrating morning trying to get through to Rob on the phone.'

'I hope you have plenty of small change.'

'I'll reverse the charges. What are you doing?'

Hal felt suddenly happy. 'I have two days' notes to write up. Reckon I'll work out a method of writing on the beach.' He looked at her as she got up to go, an enquiry in his eyes.

'OK.' She lifted a hand in salute. 'Maybe I'll see you.'

* * *

He told himself with monotonous persistence that he wasn't disappointed she hadn't shown up. He'd worked hard on his notes all day, looking out for her. Later, strolling through the lanes before dinner, he had gone on looking for her. He went to the same place to eat, but she didn't come. Walking home to his hotel, he found her standing outside a jeweller's shop, her nose pressed to the glass. 'Gold's cheaper than it is in England,' she remarked without turning round. He wondered how she'd known it was him. 'I'm after one of those double axes, to remind me to be more aggressive.'

'God help us,' Hal said involuntarily. She laughed. 'Fancy a drink?'

'Yes please.'

They walked to the harbour, and sat down at a table overlooking the calm sea. Hal ordered ouzos, and the drinks arrived accompanied by glasses of water and a plate of small snacks. He watched as Angela absently ate her way through all of them. 'Hungry?' he enquired as she finished the last olive.

'Mm? Sorry. Did you want some?'

'I ate already. We'll have some more, with the next drinks.'

'OK.' She sat frowning at the calm water.

'Bad day?' Hal asked eventually.

'Frustrating day. I couldn't get a line to England till this afternoon, then there was no reply.'

'You can try again tomorrow.'

'Yes. I can.' She looked up at him, her expression unreadable. 'He looks a bit like you, actually. He's tall, too.' And you, Angela, Hal thought, sound so like my wife that, here in the half-dark, half-drunk, my senses fuddled . . . 'Are you married?' Angela asked suddenly.

'I am.'

'But not happily.'

'Why should you say that?'

She shrugged. 'Because you're here and she's not.'

Hal sighed. She was a clear-sighted woman. 'Right. We used to be happy. I guess things have got in the way.'

'A familiar story.'

'Are you going to marry your Rob?' He'd noticed she wore no ring.

'I don't know.' There was a long silence. Angela called the waiter and ordered more drinks, and this time she divided the snacks into two. 'You can have the last olive,' she said.

'Thank you.'

She said with sudden ferocity, 'It had to be!'

Hal looked up; she was staring at him coldly. 'What did?'

'The only half-way decent man in the whole of Crete who's on his own, and you have to be married.'

He let the 'half-way' go, and said, 'Well, aren't you?'

She shook her head impatiently. 'No, I just told you.'

'Well, if you're not married you're — 'spoken for', I believe is the quaint English expression.'

She started to laugh. 'Is it? I never heard

that before. Spoken for.' She polished off her ouzo in a gulp.

'I know another Englishwoman who drinks like you,' Hal remarked, remembering an evening with Helen Arnold. 'She said she had a swallow like a navvy, and it was years before I found out what a navvy was.'

'I do not swallow like a navvy! Navvies wear awful vests, and have tattoos, and swear a lot and have big bellies.'

Hal grinned. 'I only said you swallowed like one.'

'Are you referring to your wife?'

'No!' He laughed, then stopped suddenly. He didn't want to think about Jo.

They watched the slow, steady procession of people. Angela's comments, Hal noticed, became more caustic in direct ratio to the number of ouzos she consumed. A party of young Germans passed by, clearly drunk, singing loudly and punctuating their efforts with loud belches and guffaws of laughter. Angela watched them. 'The Master Race,' she said. 'Thank Christ they didn't win the war.' A tall, bronzed, blue-eyed young man came lurching towards their table, knocking into it. He apologised perfunctorily, then, focusing more clearly on Angela, attempted to kiss her hand, saying something in his own language and gazing into her eyes. I wouldn't if I were you, pal, Hal thought. The young man's face wore an idiotic smile of expectancy. Angela smiled at him sweetly, and said, 'Piss off.'

Hal swallowed his laughter and said, 'What did you think of Knossos?' There was no knowing what she might do next, and the young blond god wasn't alone.

She turned to him as the Germans wandered away, her mouth open to protest. Then, apparently changing her mind, she said meekly, 'I was disappointed. If you could arrange a private tour at dawn, or at sunset, or by moonlight, it would be a different matter.'

'I wish I could,' Hal said. 'No whisper down the spine? No fleeting sense that you heard four-thousand-year-old footsteps?'

'No.' Angela shook her head. 'Too many people, too much restoration. Oh, I know,' she went on as Hal began to speak, 'I've read the guide books, I'm sure they did what they thought was best. But you can't get away from the fact that you're looking at the work of Arthur Evans and his team, done at the turn of the century.'

'The fragile aura of long-ago hands finally obliterated,' Hal said.

'Exactly! Is that from a poem?'

'Er — no.' Hal didn't like to admit he'd just made it up.

'What about you?' Angela asked. 'What did you make of it?'

'Much the same. Only . . . ' He'd been about to tell her about his moment of fear underground, but he wasn't sure she'd appreciate it. It was very important, suddenly, that she shouldn't laugh.

'Only what?'

He looked across the table at her. Her face was serious; she was watching him intently, with a small frown of concentration. He thought, what the hell, and told her. 'Then a woman fainted, and the feeling went away,' he finished. He found he couldn't meet Angela's eye. He went on staring at the diminishing stream of passers-by, until he felt a touch on his arm.

'I wish I'd been there with you,' she said, very quietly. He turned to her. Her eyes glistened, their pupils widely dilated in the soft light. In that moment, she looked utterly desirable.

With an effort, he forced a smile. 'Maybe we'll break in under cover of darkness,' he said lightly.

But that wasn't very sensible; Angela smiled and said, 'Oh, yes.' He moved so that Angela's hand fell from his arm.

'One hell of a palace, isn't it?' he said. 'What organisation.'

He was aware of her slight retreat from him. Unbidden, unwanted, the thought flashed into his head, with such a feel for other people's mood, what a woman she'd be to make love to.

' 'Our castle's strength will laugh a siege to scorn',' Angela said, after a moment. 'It must have been a nice life,' she went on, 'provided nobody expected you to somersault over bulls.'

'There are any number of matadors who'll tell you the bull leap is impossible.'

'Yes, I expect you're right. Probably nine out of ten of the dancers impaled themselves. That famous fresco looks as if the bull's horn is going through the woman instead of under her arm.'

'You should try Delphi in the early morning,' Hal said. He was losing the battle to keep the conversation away from emotive topics. 'It may not be the same now, but fifteen years ago, I reckoned I was hearing the oracle.'

She watched him. Then she said, 'Delphi's too far away. But I thought I'd go to Phaestos. They say it's less commercialised than Knossos. I'm catching the bus down to Agia Galini tomorrow.' Her words tumbled out as if she had to get them out before she changed her mind. 'Fancy seeing something of the south side of the island?'

Hal thought rapidly. He had to spend another couple of days in Heraklion before he left, and after Crete he intended to visit the Greek mainland. He started working it out, then stopped. It was academic: he wanted to go to Agia Galini with Angela. 'Sure,' he said.

She looked surprised, but recovered quickly. 'There's a bus that goes direct, leaving at ten-fifteen. Can you make that?'

He smiled. 'Try me. Where does it go from?'

She reached down into her bag for a map, folded to a town plan of Rethymnon. 'There.'

Hal put on his glasses and peered. 'OK.'

Angela got up, stuffing the map back into her bag. 'I'm going to try once more to get through to Rob. See you in the morning.'

'Night, Angela,' he said.

Her tall figure was visible for some time among the shorter local people sauntering home. Running away? Hal asked her silently. You talk to your Rob. It'll be me beside you on the bus tomorrow. He called the waiter and paid the bill, faintly taken aback at the number of ouzos they'd got through. I have to keep on drinking, he thought recklessly. I'm not accountable for my actions when I'm drunk. Leaving the waiter a large tip as if he were buying an indulgence, Hal went home to bed.

# 6

Hal was awake before his wrist-watch alarm went off. He lay in bed in the peace of early morning, full of excited expectancy. And why not? he thought. I'm on vacation, goddam it. Then he got up, had a fierce cold shower and went out to find some breakfast.

Even at seven-thirty, people were about. He crossed the square outside his hotel and walked along the beach; the sea was perfectly still under a sky shot with the last remnants of the orange and pink of dawn. To his left were cafés, their tables set out on the wide boulevard facing the beach. There were already a few customers. Hal, hungry suddenly and attracted by a menu like a sandwich board advertising egg, bacon, sausage and toast, found a table and ordered a full breakfast. Later, returning to his hotel to pack and settle the bill, he found he had over an hour before the bus went. Leaving his bag in the lobby, he set off to look at the Venetian Fortress.

It was well worth the walk. Narrow streets and alley-ways were left behind as the pathway turned into a flight of steps, and there on the headland above the town appeared the golden walls of the fortress, very similar to its counterpart in Rhodes. Hal stood looking through an archway, reminded of the weeks he and Jo had spent in Rhodes. He could hear her voice. 'I'm pregnant,' she'd said, face aglow. Then, touchingly, 'Are you really pleased?' They'd both been almost sure she was pregnant. The visit to the English doctor in the Old Town had been merely for confirmation. Avoiding giving an instant response, he'd said, 'Are *you* pleased? That's more important.'

'Your child,' she'd whispered, eyes filling. 'Of *course* I'm pleased.' He'd often wondered if she'd been trying to convince herself.

Now, in the strengthening sun on another Greek island, he thought how different the pattern of their life would have been if she hadn't got pregnant. He arrested the picture. My child, too; she didn't conceive Sammie all by herself. Then, impatiently: I don't want to think about Jo. Not today.

He moved on around a corner of the great walls, to be presented with a sudden view of the sea. Its deep blue retained the utter flatness of early morning; there wasn't a breath of wind. There came a faint chug, chug of small engines, and two little fishing smacks slowly puttered into view. Their

111

wakes painted the sea with deep vee-shapes of white, extending in diminishing clarity to an impossible distance. Lost in his thoughts, he let the time slip by. He had to run back to his hotel to collect his bag, then sprint up the road to the bus station. A bus was standing with its engine running. The driver, leaning against his door, was putting drops in his eyes.

'Agia Galini?' Hal panted, hoping the driver would say no; the route lead across mountain roads, and the eye-drops weren't a reassuring sign.

'*Ochi*. No.' The driver, blinking furiously, took his arm and led him over to another bus.

Hal grinned. '*Efcharisto*.' He bought a ticket and got on the bus. The first eight or nine rows were full, and she wasn't there. He'd put his glasses on to buy his ticket, and he couldn't focus on the back of the bus.

A voice said, 'Hey, four-eyes, I'm up here.' With his glasses off he could see her, sitting in the second-to-back row. 'The view's better from here,' she said as he approached. 'These seats are higher.' He stood for a moment looking down at her. Then, with a lot of revving, the bus's engine roared into life and they swung out of the bus station. He sat down hurriedly beside her.

The journey was spectacular. Great heights rose either side as they crossed the central spine of the island; the bus struggled up around tight, steep bends, and views opened up into gorges with the glitter of water a very long way below. The grassy slopes were brilliant with flowers. Herds of goats were tended by ruminative peasants, who waved majestically at the bus. The old men wore knee-high leather boots over old-fashioned breeches.

Beside him Angela was writing in her notebook, her intent silence interrupted only by 'Damn!' and 'Oh, shit!' as the bus hit bumps and caused her pen to make wild parabolas. She said, 'Why don't you sit by the window? I'm not looking out, and you are.' They changed over, and she went back to her notes. Hal didn't mind not talking. He was thinking about the mountains, reflecting how unexpected it was that the Minoans, in the midst of these great peaks that soared up to the sky, should have worshipped a deity of the deep earth. It was to propitiate, he thought; this is an earthquake zone. His mind went back to being underground at Knossos. Again the faint echo of terror ran through him, a distant racial memory of what it would have been like to be buried there, fatally interred in choking earth and crushing

113

masonry, when the great quake hit. Someone had told him that the snake was sacred to the Minoans because its shape symbolised the earthquake. A running ripple, the earth moving as if someone were shaking it like a blanket. Help us, Great Mother. He saw in his mind the faïence statues of the Earth Mother, her arms bent down towards the ground as if to soothe. It all made sense.

'Have you clocked the conductor?' Angela said, putting her notebook away. He looked down the bus to the young conductor, standing chatting to a passenger a few rows in front. He had black curly hair and long, almond-shaped eyes that seemed to bend around the curve of his face. He was slight and wiry, narrow-waisted and tanned. 'Pure Keftiu, isn't he?' Angela whispered. 'Could have come right off a fresco.'

'Right'. Hal nodded. Sometimes the past seemed very close.

'Theseus?' Angela said.

'No, Theseus was from the Peloponnese, he wouldn't have looked like a native Cretan. Maybe that's King Minos, reincarnated.'

'I can't wait to see Phaestos,' Angela said with a sigh of pleasure. Me neither, Hal thought. He wondered with a moment's clarity if he would be looking forward to it as much if he wasn't going with Angela.

They reached Agia Galini before noon, and Angela said she was going to find herself a room. 'There are plenty of hotels,' Hal said, looking round. 'Reckon I'll check into one of them.'

She grinned at him. 'No doubt you're richer than I am.' She turned to go, hitching up her bag on to her shoulder.

'Have dinner with me,' he called.

She paused. Then she turned, looking straight at him over the top of her glasses. 'OK.'

He grinned. 'I have no idea where,' he said, answering the question he could read in her amused expression. 'Meet me here, at seven, and we'll take it from there.'

'OK,' she said again. Then she went on down the street.

★ ★ ★

Hal, his mind on other things, went into the first hotel he came to. It was new, with white walls and bright blue paintwork. Green leafy plants grew in terracotta pots. He was shown to a room with a balcony overlooking the street. He unpacked, then went out to buy food at a small supermarket

115

across the street, retiring upstairs with the intention of spending the afternoon writing on his balcony.

I shouldn't drink so much ouzo, he thought some time later. He was still sitting on his balcony, and he had eaten his way through bread and feta cheese, a tomato, a pepper, a packet of nuts and a tub of yoghurt. The bottle of ouzo was half empty. Half *full*, he corrected himself, I'm an optimist. He felt boyish and silly, smiling at nothing. The intention to write was a vague memory; he couldn't summon the concentration. He closed his eyes, comfortable in his chair, feet up on the balcony rail. I could have a swim, he thought as he drifted into sleep. He woke up an hour later, very thirsty. He had a long drink of water — he'd forgotten how dehydrating ouzo was — then put on his trunks and went to look for the beach.

At the bottom of the lane was a small harbour, sheltered by headlands and big enough only for fishing-boats and pleasure craft. A path led off from it, and Hal climbed to the top of a slight rise. The path went on to a beach, but he decided he'd rather swim off the rocks. The sea was surprisingly cold. He came up from his dive gasping, but after a few minutes he got used to it. He floated on his stomach, looking down at shoals of

116

fish hanging quite still, suddenly moving all together in the same direction as if worked by an invisible string. Wish I'd brought Teddy's mask and snorkel, he thought. He'd have loved this, we could have . . . The happy idea stopped short; Hal had deliberately left his family at home.

He swam back to the shore, careful to avoid the sea-urchins. He sat on the warm rock drying off, frowning out over the sea. I'll work, he thought. Couple of hours, then I'll feel better. I'm here to work, I have to stop enjoying myself. He set off determinedly for his room. A *good* two hours, he was thinking, then when I meet Angela this evening I'll . . . That thought also led to guilt. But what can I do? I have no idea where she's staying so I can't cancel dinner. No way can I just fail to turn up. He smiled ruefully; like it or not, the evening was unavoidable.

Trouble is, he admitted, I do like it.

★ ★ ★

Seven o'clock came, and went. He was beginning to think she wasn't going to turn up when she came into view.

'Angela!'

She had almost walked past without seeing him. 'Hello, Hal.' She came to sit beside him. She looked different. There was a soft, absent look in her eyes that Hal hadn't seen before. Like a woman fresh from her lover's bed, he thought, still preoccupied with what she's just been doing. 'I'm late,' she said. 'I hope you haven't been waiting long.'

'Sure, it's OK. What'll you drink?'

'Beer, please.' She sat smiling at him. 'I've been talking to Rob.'

'Ah. You got through.'

She nodded. 'Yes. It took ages. He leaves the phone off the hook when he has a bath, and the silly sod had forgotten to put it back, so I kept getting the engaged tone.' She laughed. 'Luckily he had to phone his mother, otherwise he mightn't have noticed for days.'

'When's he coming?'

'Saturday night. I said I'd meet him at the airport, and it's jolly nice of me considering what time his flight gets in.'

'Which is?'

She grimaced. 'Four-thirty in the morning.'

'That's love for you.'

'Quite.' Her expression faltered. She said quickly, 'I think I'd like an ouzo chaser with this. Join me? I'm buying.'

They sat in silence for a while. Hal felt thrown by seeing a facet of her that was so different. He glanced at her surreptitiously;

her expression was dreamy. 'Come on.' Impatiently he finished his beer and downed the ouzo. 'There are better views than this.'

'Oh!' Angela looked surprised. 'OK.'

He sensed, as they walked off down the lane, that she was back with him again. He was touched, that she was making an effort for his sake.

'Let's sit down by the water,' she suggested. 'I had an ice-cream there this afternoon.'

'What else did you do?'

'Swam and sunbathed. Isn't it lovely?'

'Right. But you have to watch out for the urchins.'

She frowned. Then she said, 'Sea-urchins. Yes.' She laughed. 'For a moment I was thinking of dirty little boys tying cans to cats' tails.'

They sat in the fading light, watching people ambling around the harbour and along the jetty that stretched out into the sea. 'Yours or mine?' Angela asked, breaking the companionable silence. Hal looked in the direction she'd indicated, and saw a fat couple in tight shorts and gaudy shirts.

'Mine,' he said, after considering. 'They have a PanAm bag.'

'But her frizzy perm, sunburn, and the way all the veins stand out in her legs are a dead give-away,' Angela countered. 'That's typical

English abroad. Bet you a hundred drachs they're mine.'

They sat and listened while the couple passed by. Their accents, even to Hal's ears, were unmistakeably British Midlands. 'Good trick, the PanAm bag,' he observed, reaching for his wallet. 'Had me fooled.' He slapped a hundred drachma note into Angela's open palm, grinning.

'Pleasure to do business with you,' she said, folding it and tucking it into her bag.

They joined in with the saunter to the end of the jetty, returning the friendly greetings of local family groups. A week or so here, Hal thought, and you act like a Greek. In a piercing flash he remembered Ben, who had adapted to Greece as if he'd been an expatriate returning at last to his homeland. He could hear Ben's laughter. Jeez, he thought, Jo this morning, now Ben. He shook his head violently; the two images faded, then formed again.

'I'm hungry,' Angela said. 'Shall we go and eat?'

Hal wanted to stay out there with her in the darkening evening. He wanted her vivacious presence to exorcise the ghost of his dead friend. To bring him back into this moment, so that he was no longer haunted by Jo's present distress. I mourn the woman

120

she was, even as I mourn Ben. He was aware of Angela looking at him sympathetically.

'You do look miserable,' she said kindly. 'You need feeding.' She tucked her arm under his and they walked back along the jetty.

★ ★ ★

They chose a taverna in a street set back from the waterfront.

'I'm paying for myself,' Angela said firmly as they sat down. 'Then I shan't be under an obligation.'

'I'm paying. And you won't be.' Hal thought his voice was marginally firmer than hers. 'As you pointed out earlier, I'm richer than you.'

She looked at him for a long moment, then gracefully bowed her head. 'OK. Thanks. I won't order the most expensive thing on the menu, only the second most.'

Hal grinned. 'What's your room like?' he asked.

'All right, as rooms go. What about your hotel?'

'Very comfortable. I have a balcony overlooking the bus stop.'

'Handy if you're late for the bus.'

'The proprietress is charging me a special

121

rate, because I have a double room and I'm only one person. But she warned me I mustn't bring in any *friends*.' He looked darkly at Angela.

She burst out laughing. 'Do you think she'll be sitting up to catch you coming in with some scheming hussy shadowing you upstairs?'

'Probably. But I'm fixing to disappoint her.' He raised his glass of retzina and clinked it against Angela's. '*Kali orexi*. That means *bon appétit*.'

'I know,' she said witheringly, 'I've got the phrase book too.'

He sat back, enjoying looking at her, enjoying being with her. He was glad, after all, that she'd phoned her Rob, that talking to him had made her happy. I am totally under control, he told himself. Not that it matters, because clearly she's not interested anyway. 'Are all your clothes too big for you?' he asked. Tonight she was wearing the white t-shirt she'd worn at Knossos. It had a red flower on the front.

She smiled. 'Most of the ones I've got here are. No point in putting your goods in the window if you don't want to attract buyers.' She shot him a glance. 'I might surprise you, though, yet.'

He thought, maybe I'll surprise you, too.

The food came, and they ate as if this were their first meal in days. They talked incessantly; Hal watched Angela's expressive face, fascinated. A blind man passed, carrying a white stick with a bell on the end. He was selling lottery tickets. Hal thought he knew what was going through Angela's head. But the next moment her face changed; she began telling him, with vivid mimicry, about some weirdo she worked with. 'How does your Rob manage with you?' he asked.

Angela looked wary. 'How do you mean?'

'He has, no doubt, the advantage of long acquaintance and greater intimacy — ' Hal could hear the suggestive echoes hanging in the air as he hurried on, ' — but personally I find it impossible to work you out.'

She smiled. 'I don't think Rob has any difficulty. He just doesn't bother. He's not a great one for working people out, nor for allowing them to do it to him.' Hal sat without speaking, waiting for her to continue, and in the end she did. 'Rob said you have to grow a shell, and keep all your real feelings locked away beneath it. That way they don't bother you.'

'That doesn't make sense,' Hal said analytically. He thought this Rob sounded facile. 'A shell means nobody knows your feelings. It doesn't mean you don't have any.'

She smiled reminiscently. 'Quite. But then my Rob is a very straightforward thinker. He has a mind like a Morris Minor engine.' She looked up briefly, and Hal nodded. 'Efficient, but not terribly complicated.'

'Ah.' He wanted to say, then what the hell are you doing with him? but managed not to.

'Anyway, my shell doesn't do me much good, where Rob's concerned, since he knew me before I grew it.'

Hal watched her sympathetically. He put his hand over hers. 'Should that matter, if you love each other?'

She looked up at him, her face full of vulnerability. Then abruptly her expression hardened and she removed her hand. 'Don't grill me,' she said quietly. 'I've been through it often enough in my own head, I don't want to talk about it with anybody else.'

'OK.' But he couldn't let it rest. He wanted the last word. 'Personally, I reckon you're too valuable to hide yourself under a shell.'

Instantly she replied, 'Yes, and you're married, aren't you?'

He sighed. Final words didn't seem to be his prerogative, tonight. He turned away

124

from her, staring out into the street.

He felt her hand creep back under his. 'I'm sorry,' she said softly. 'I didn't mean to take it out on you.'

He squeezed her hand. 'Sure. I know. Let's have another drink.'

'Great. We'll stay permanently pissed, keep laughing, and not spare a thought for all the complications that await us back in the real world.' He turned back to her. In the low light under the taverna's awning, he thought she looked beautiful.

'Sounds fine to me.'

\* \* \*

They sat hand in hand, hardly talking. Hal felt fatalistic, as if he were being driven to some unknown destiny by forces outside himself. If he tried to think of home, of Jo, of the boys, there was a feeling of displacement, a sense that over there, in that fuzzy cloud that represented home, there were challenges to face, fences to take that he wasn't sure he could clear. Whereas here, in this Cretan light that put everything into sharp relief — OK, he thought, I know it's night, but I'm cut — it all seemed so simple. Attract, want, desire, take. The theme ran through all the myths — no god or goddess

125

ever held back from going all out for what they wanted. But mortals weren't so selfish. So fickle. Or were they? He didn't know.

'Phaestos tomorrow?' he asked eventually.

Angela had been staring into space, her eyes glassy. 'Yes.'

'Want to go together?'

'Yes.'

'Then we'll go find out about the buses before we go to bed.' Before we go to bed. He didn't regret the double meaning, although he hadn't intended it.

'OK.' Angela got up, still holding his hand. They walked up to the bus stop and consulted the timetable.

'Eight o'clock too early?' Hal asked.

'No. I'll meet you here, just before eight.'

'Right.' He stood facing her. She put her hands on his chest and, standing on tiptoe, kissed his lips. He watched her go, then went back to his room.

★ ★ ★

He lay awake long into the night, restless in the wide bed which had more than enough room for two. What's wrong with me? he thought angrily, I never have gone for casual sex but I'm lying here burning for some woman I've known only days. Hours, in terms of the time we've actually spent together. Christ, he thought, punching his pillow with a balled fist, I only hope she has the sense to keep heading me off.

What's this Rob like? Does he care for her like she deserves? God, she's so . . . Stop it. Stop thinking about her.

He gave up on sleep. Searching through his books for something to distract him, he put on his glasses and made himself concentrate on a biography of Arthur Evans.

# 7

Hal woke in time for a quick breakfast in his hotel's cool dining-room. While he ate, he read through a summary of the notes he'd collected on Phaestos. It's going to be a working day, he thought. I'll make sure of that. Upstairs collecting his camera, he saw Angela coming up the road. He leaned over the balcony and whistled to her, and she looked up.

'You've got seven minutes,' she called. 'I shan't ask the driver to wait if you're not there.'

'I will be,' he replied.

It was as well they were early; the bus, carrying just themselves and two other passengers, pulled out three minutes before the hour. 'But he honked his horn first,' Angela said. 'A warning of imminent departure, I suppose.' She dropped her voice and whispered, 'Do you think that pair's going to Phaestos too? I'd hoped we'd have it to ourselves.'

'No, I reckon they're going to the beach,' Hal said. 'People don't take beach mats to archaeological sites.'

'Oh, are they carrying beach mats? I didn't notice.' She sat staring at the other passengers, two thickset girls in jeans and grubby t-shirts. She leaned nearer to Hal to whisper again. 'Wherever I go, I keep coming across pairs of dykes,' she confided, 'and they all seem to be Dutch. Or German.'

'I think those two are, too. Dutch or German, I mean. You're probably the better judge as to whether they're dykes or not. Being a woman, I mean,' he added hurriedly.

Angela smiled. 'I don't think I'll bother. One shouldn't make assumptions about other people's sexuality.' There didn't seem anything he could reply, so he kept quiet.

The bus dropped them off at the junction with the main road to Heraklion. The conductor said there would be a connection up to Phaestos in five minutes. 'Is that a Greek or a rest-of-the-world five minutes?' Angela wondered.

'It won't make any difference to me, I'm not wearing a watch.'

Angela was humming softly. She looked happy. In the sunshine at the beginning of a perfect day, Hal wished the moment could go on for ever. The bus arrived, and trundled them up to Phaestos; the two German girls didn't get off. Hal and Angela found themselves climbing the gentle slope up to the site entirely alone.

'Told you they weren't coming here,' Hal said.

Angela sniffed. 'That's being wise after the event,' she observed.

Hal reached for her hand. 'Right.' They bought tickets, and went on to the site. It's true, Hal thought immediately, it's quite different from Knossos. With a smile of relief, he lifted Angela's hand to his lips to kiss it, then let it go. 'D'you mind if we go round independently?' he asked.

'Not in the least,' she said. 'Better, really, because then we shan't influence each other's impressions.'

'Right. Don't leave without me.' He blew her a kiss and started to descend the narrow steps into the amphitheatre.

Phaestos made up for the disappointments of Knossos, Hal thought, plus two hundred percent. He didn't need to refer to his guidebook; the relevant information was already in his head. He forgot about Angela, forgot about Jo, the boys, everything; some indefinable time later, exhausted by the heat reflected off the stones, throat parched, he went to sit in the fragrant shade of a pine tree. He caught sight of Angela, at the opposite end of the Central Court. She was no longer alone; one of the guides had joined her, and the two had their heads together in animated conversation. Hal watched as they wandered slowly through the great ruined palace, stopping for Angela to take photographs. He noticed with amusement how frequently the dark Cretan touched her. She didn't seem to mind; on the contrary, Hal reckoned, she's enjoying it.

Eventually, another custodian called out to Angela's companion, and he left her to return to the tourist pavilion. She looked around for Hal, caught sight of him under his tree and came to join him. 'Oh, that was wonderful!' she exclaimed. 'Move over, I want to sit in the shade, too.'

'Who's your friend?' Hal asked.

'He's terrific! He's been here twenty-six years, he's told me masses of fascinating stuff. He says we have to come at sunset, because that's when the gods walk. Oh, Hal, isn't it fabulous?'

Her enthusiasm was an extrovert version of his own. 'It sure is.'

She was getting out her notebook. 'We'll have a beer in a minute,' she said, 'up there in the pavilion. But I must make some notes before I forget what was what.' He peered over her shoulder. She sure found herself the right guide, he thought. He'd reckoned he knew all there was to know about Phaestos, but after a moment he got out his own notebook and began copying from hers. She realised what he was doing, and he heard her laugh softly.

'You don't mind, do you?' he asked, not pausing.

'No, not at all. It's not my words I'm writing, it's his.' She nodded in the direction in which her friend had disappeared. 'I think he ought to be a poet. What a lovely man.'

Hal finished writing. He gave her a nudge that sent her off the edge of the rock they were sitting on. 'Stop sighing after him and buy me a beer,' he ordered. She picked herself up and collected her bag.

'You're just jealous,' she said. 'OK, come on.'

★ ★ ★

Hal could see, as they sat over their beers, that she was looking out for her friend. But he didn't reappear. 'Ah well, never mind,' she said philosophically.

'Maybe he was a god, descended just to make your day.'

'He did that, all right. But I took his picture, and he took mine, so that should prove he was real.'

'Not necessarily. You might be the only

woman in Gloucestershire to have a photograph of Zeus on her wall.'

'The Asterousia Mountains,' she said dreamily, pointing with her beer glass towards the south east. 'They're called that because the skies are so clear here that the stars are always brilliant. But you probably knew that.' She smiled at Hal, who hadn't known it at all.

A short time later, the peace was broken by the arrival of two coach parties of tourists. Hal saw Angela's face fall. 'It had to happen,' he said consolingly, 'we've been in sole possession for the last two hours. Us and your pal, Zeus.'

She didn't answer. They sat in silence, watching the file of people spill out and mill all over the site. They were English, and someone had to be asked to switch off his portable cassette player. The men wore shapeless shirts with sandals and socks; most of the women wore shorts.

'Will you look at them,' Angela said bitterly. 'Jesus, the women abandon their underwear when they leave Gatwick.' Hal looked where she was pointing. Two women, both well into their sixties, were clambering up rocks in strappy suntops and abbreviated shorts. He had to agree, it wasn't a pretty sight.

'It's the holiday spirit,' he said tolerantly. 'You get it all over the world.'

'No you don't!' Angela sounded quite angry. 'Greek women in Bournemouth wouldn't giggle about like teenagers with their great breasts flopping about all over the place and half their buttocks falling out of their shorts, they've got too much dignity.' There were shrieks of excitement as the party's Greek guide put his hand on someone's bottom. Then they were all rounded up to be shown over the site, and some of them formed themselves into an impromptu Conga line and started singing.

'It's like something out of Play School,' Angela said. 'Let's go, we haven't got a dog's chance of picking up any more atmosphere, not now.' She stormed off down the path, but Hal could still hear her muttering to herself. He paid for the beers, and went after her, catching up with her by the bus-stop.

'Give it a rest, huh?' Hal said. 'They're enjoying themselves.'

'I know. I don't know why I'm so cross about it.' She kicked up pebbles with her toe. Then she took off her glasses to wipe them on her t-shirt, and Hal was surprised to see she had tears in her eyes.

'Come on,' he said, touching her arm. 'I'll buy you lunch, when we get back.'

They sat a long time over lunch, but both of them were more interested in drinking than eating. Hal wondered how long it was since he had been sober for an entire day. Angela was quiet and preoccupied; Hal was obsessed with the thought that this was all going to end because he had to go back to Heraklion tomorrow. Or the next day. The purpose of coming to the south of the island had been accomplished; he'd been to Phaestos. There was no reason to stay. Later, they wandered arm-in-arm down to the beach. They lay down in the shade of the rocks and went to sleep. Hal woke up, immediately aware that Angela was no longer lying beside him. He sat up, looking round. She was at the water's edge, sitting on a rock with small waves breaking over her feet. He went to join her. 'I'm going to Athens,' he said dismally.

She went on looking out to sea. 'What for?'

'I need a rest.'

'Huh! You won't get much rest in Athens.'

'I know. I'm not staying there, I'm going on to a very quiet island which I'm told is deserted in April, except for the inhabitants.'

She nodded. 'Have fun. Or perhaps fun isn't what you're after.' He had no answer.

After a while he said, 'What'll you and your Rob do?'

She shrugged. 'I don't know. Hire a car, I expect, and get to some of the places you can't reach on the bus. And I'd like to walk the Samaria Gorge, if Rob brings his trainers.'

'You'll have a good time together.'

She sighed. 'Half good, anyway. He'll be full of remorse for the first few days because of his shitty wife.'

'I see.'

She turned to him, scowling, then resumed her contemplation of the horizon. 'No you don't,' she said with quiet intensity. 'His shitty wife no longer lives with him, she buggered off with someone else. But he feels he should keep himself lily-white so that he can go on being the injured party. And, of course, in case she decides to go back to him. If anyone knew he had me up his sleeve, they'd think Rob hadn't done too badly after all. And she'd divorce him and claim half the house.'

There it was again, Hal thought, that clear-sightedness that cut right through the self-deception. But it seemed to hurt her. 'I'm glad you appreciate your own value,' Hal said. 'You are too good to be kept up any man's sleeve.'

She looked surprised, then pleased. 'What a lovely thing to say.' She leaned towards him and kissed him lightly. Emotions warred in him: desire because she attracted him so strongly, compassion because she was a fighter and he wanted her to win. And, again, the recurrent feeling that he was running off down a dangerous path.

She was resting her head on his shoulder, and he couldn't resist the temptation to put his arm round her. She relaxed against him. 'When I make enough money,' she confided, 'I shall buy a little place at the back of beyond and live by myself, taking photos of stonechats and weasels and occasionally exchanging a word with the milkman. Then I'll buy a cat — oh, and a goat — and everyone will refer to me as that dotty woman at the end of the lane.'

Hal kissed the top of her head. 'Don't do that,' he said quietly. 'Don't give it all up. Sure, relationships are difficult. We all know that. But it'd be a waste to shut yourself away.'

She didn't reply.

They went on sitting on the shore until it eventually got too cool. Then slowly they walked back to the town. 'I don't think I'll want to eat tonight,' Angela said. 'What about you?'

'No, OK,' Hal said. 'What shall we do, then?'

'Drink. Drown our sorrows.'

'OK.'

'I'm going to have a hot shower,' Angela said as they came to the turning that led up to her room. 'See you later?'

'Right.' Hal wanted to suggest something nice that they could do, something to cheer them up, but his mind had gone numb. 'Meet you at the seat where we sat yesterday, in an hour.'

She nodded, and hurried away.

★ ★ ★

This is our last night, Hal thought as he went into his hotel. It hurt to think of leaving, but he knew he was going to. He must. I'll tell her, tonight. Will I tell her why? He stood irresolute at the foot of the stairs. He could hear the proprietress, talking and laughing with friends in the room behind the reception desk. He could smell cooking. He went to tap on the door. The proprietress looked up, smiled and came out to him.

'I'm leaving tomorrow,' he said in Greek. 'Probably early, so I'll pay you now, OK?'

'*Ne, ne.*' She delved in a drawer behind the desk and took out Hal's passport. He handed

138

her a bundle of notes, which she swiftly counted and put in her pocket. She turned the pages of Hal's passport. 'American,' she observed.

'That's right.'

She smiled brightly, then said, 'I hope you will come again.'

'Maybe one day.' He didn't think it was likely.

He went slowly upstairs and began sorting through his things, folding and packing unenthusiastically. I don't want to go, he thought, I want to stay here. With Angela. He had a shower, then got dressed. He picked up his wallet from where he had flung it on the bed. He stood for a moment, looking down at the two pillows side by side and the crisp sheet turned neatly down. Then abruptly he left the room, slamming the door behind him.

Angela was sitting on the seat by the harbour. She smelt of a perfume he didn't recognise, and she was wearing a v-necked short-sleeved jumper that revealed quite a lot more of her than he'd yet seen.

'You putting your goods in the window?' he enquired.

'I told you I might surprise you. Actually, everything else is in the wash. There are t-shirts dripping all over my floor, so it's just as well there's no carpet.'

'Oh.' He'd had his laundry done by someone in the hotel; he didn't think he'd say so.

'I tried to phone Rob,' she said, 'but there was no reply. He's probably working late. Not that it is very late, in England.' She sounded sad.

'Well, you'll be seeing him soon,' Hal said.

'I know. But it always cheers me up when I talk to him.'

Hal nearly asked why she needed cheering up, but he didn't. He imagined he already knew. Maybe I should talk to her Rob, he thought flippantly. Might work for me, too.

'We can't sit here all evening,' he said after a while. 'Let's go eat.'

'I'm not hungry.'

'Me neither. But we have to eat, or otherwise we'll turn into alcoholics.'

'I don't want to be an alcoholic, I've seen photos of what it does to your liver.' Hal didn't want to think about his liver just then. It probably looked like one of those sponges he'd seen for sale in the market.

'You're making me feel sick,' he said. 'We'll have to have another drink so I feel better.'

'Let's talk about something sensible,' Angela suggested as they were shown to a table.

'I was under the impression we had been,' Hal remarked.

'I meant something like astronomy, or anthropology, or . . . '

'Does it have to begin with 'a'?' Hal asked as she ran out of steam.

She lifted her eyes to his. 'I don't give a damn. I just want to stop thinking about . . . everything, and I thought a lively intellectual discussion about the possibility of a tenth planet in the solar system, or what the other side of the moon looks like, might . . . ' Hal began to laugh. 'Oh, shut up!' she exclaimed. '*You* think of something!'

'Tell me some more about yourself. What do you do? Where do you live?'

She sighed deeply, leaning forward on to the table, her chin in her hands. 'I told you where I live. Gloucestershire. As to what I do — a bit of everything.' She looked brighter suddenly. 'I've just done a course of evening classes in car maintenance. You should see me change a set of brake linings, I was the fastest in the group.' Hal smiled. 'Why are you smirking like that?'

He shrugged. 'Because I like to see you enthusing about something, it makes your eyes shine.' Her face changed again, and he realised what he had said. And my intention was so good, he thought; he'd hoped that talking about real life — life back home — would remind them both they had a lot to be happy about. A lot to lose. He'd meant his comment to sound lighthearted; somehow it had come out sincere.

She told him about Gloucestershire while they ate. She lived in the Forest of Dean. In exchange he told her about his travels in South America, which was about the only topic he could think of that didn't lead to Jo. It was a relief, in some ways, when they got up to go.

He took hold of her hand as they left the taverna. 'Take a walk down to the end of the jetty with me,' he said.

She nodded.

They walked slowly, pausing to look in shop windows, taking their pace from the other sauntering couples. They'll all still be together tomorrow, Hal thought. He hadn't found the words yet to tell Angela he was going, but he had an idea she already knew. There was nobody else on the jetty. They stopped at the far end, looking out over the sea.

'Where would you get to if you swam due south?' Angela asked.

'Libya.'

'Would it take long?'

'Yes. You'd need a boat.'

'And here we are without one.'

Hal looked up at the sky. 'Moon's up,' he remarked. 'It's paling the stars.'

'It's worth it. I like moonlight.'

'Moonlight becomes you,' Hal said tritely. He heard her laugh. 'What?' he asked.

'Nothing. It's just that you've said more nice things to me in the space of however many days than . . . ' She broke off. Hal watched her. In the dim light, her features were invisible, but the way she stood gave away what she was thinking.

'Angela,' he said.

She turned to him, and he reached out his arms. She closed in to him, and her body against his was firm and curvy. I'm doing this to help her, to console her, goddam it, he thought, it's not desire.

But it was. Without either of them seeming to make the first move, a joint magnetism drew them into a kiss. Such a soft mouth, such a warm tongue, Hal thought, to say those bitter things. He was drowning in her, his head reeling with the power of her attraction. For a moment he felt it

143

was inevitable that they sleep together, and his body leapt in fierce eagerness for her. Then the thought hit him: that's just what she needs, another man using her beddable body for one single, brilliant night.

Because that's all it could be.

Isn't it?

Very gently, he pulled out of kissing her. Holding her head in his hands, he held her against his chest.

'No good?' she said quietly.

'Jeez, you have to be kidding!' He almost laughed. 'Can't you tell? Hell, Angela, if we'd gone on with that . . . ' He stopped short. Why talk about it, when there was no way they were going to do it? He put his hands on her shoulders, pushing her away so he could look at her. She's so lovely, he thought, her hair curling round her face and her eyes full of moonlight. He wanted to say, if we'd met another time, if I'd — we'd — been free, if I didn't have my buried heart full of someone else. But he kept quiet. He thought — hoped — that the regret was probably hurting him more than it was hurting her. 'I'm paying you a compliment,' he said softly.

'Oh, yes! The compliment of finding me totally resistible.'

'Angela, don't. It's taking all I have to

resist at all, when at this moment you're everything any man could want. But that's this moment.' He shook her slightly, as if trying to shake his words into her. 'You know?'

Her eyes stared back into his, her face twisting gradually into its habitual cynical expression. Then slowly she started to smile. 'What would you do if I threw myself into your arms and went on kissing you?'

He looked at her, studying her face. For a moment, he really didn't know if she was going to do it or not. Then he felt the tension slowly dissipate. He said, 'You know as well as I do what I'd do.'

She nodded. Then she turned away and walked quickly back along the jetty.

He didn't go after her. He gave her half an hour, then he went back to his hotel, an ache in his heart. He stood for a long time on his balcony, until eventually the streets were quiet. Then he finished his packing and went to bed.

★ ★ ★

He was going to catch the morning bus to Heraklion. Before he left, he took a walk around the town, but he didn't see her. He went along the jetty, busy this morning with happy people. The mood of last night returned; he felt an enormous sorrow for what might have been. He went to the taverna where they'd eaten, and ordered a beer. He asked the waiter if he'd seen Angela, but he shook his head.

'She went out early,' he said.

Hal said quickly, 'How do you know?'

The waiter shrugged. 'She stay in my cousin's house.'

'Where is that?' He pointed down the lane, giving directions. 'Thanks,' Hal said, 'thanks a lot.'

He felt vastly relieved: I can leave her a note. I won't have to disappear without a last word. He found a sheet of paper and wrote swiftly, not having to pause and think; it came from the heart.

*'I'm leaving today, going back to Heraklion. I'm sorry to go so suddenly, without seeing you to tell you goodbye. Especially after last night.*

*You are a terrific companion. You talk, think, laugh and kiss like a sexy angel. No doubt you also make love like a sexy angel. I wish things had been different, so that I could have gotten to find that out.*

*I have one hell of a lot of sorting*

*out to do. No way would it be right
to involve you.*

*Good luck, Angela — hope your Rob
makes it. He is a lucky son of a bitch.
You tell him so, from me.*

*Hal'*

He wanted to give her something. Across
the road in a jeweller's shop he saw little
gold charms, including some of the Minoan
double-headed axes. He hoped she hadn't
already bought one; he didn't think so. It
would have shown in the revealing neckline
of the top she'd worn last night. With an
effort, he blotted the memory from his
mind.

He chose an axe, on a fine gold chain.
He sealed it in an envelope with the letter
then, following the waiter's directions, found
the house where Angela had her room.
Yes, he was told by a woman washing the
steps, Angela was still staying there, but she
was out. Hal realised he didn't even know
Angela's surname.

'Will you make sure she gets this?' he
asked the woman, holding out the envelope.
'It's very important.'

'*Ne, ne,*' the woman said, getting laboriously
to her feet. Beckoning to Hal, she led the way
inside to a cluttered kitchen. She reached

into a cupboard and held up a British passport. 'Angela,' she said, opening it and pointing to the photograph.

Hal smiled. 'Right.' He watched as the woman closed the envelope inside Angela's passport and returned it to the drawer.

'Thank you. *Efcharisto poli*,' he said, and left.

★ ★ ★

The bus arrived. Hal got up from the bar and went to claim a seat. As they rattled away, he thought with painful regret, back to the real world.

# Part Three

## April – May 1985

# 8

April was half over, and Jo was lonely. It seemed that Hal had been absent for ever; she began to think he'd always be thousands of disinterested miles away, an itinerant husband who came home now and then, no more a central part of her life.

His departure had been accomplished so smoothly. No histrionics, no unreasonable scenes. Only once had she been stung to protest: as she'd sat sewing a button onto one of his shirts, he'd ruffled her hair and said lightly, 'Shame you're not unattached. Shame you're not packing and coming with me.' The moment was etched into her brain. She'd looked up at him, almost hating him in that second, wilfully ignoring the real regret and affection that had prompted his somewhat tactless remark.

'But I'm not unattached, Hal.' Her voice was icy. 'And I have no idea why you're so sure you'd like me if I was. You're forgetting — you've never known me unattached. You met me too late.'

He stood for some time, his face sad as he watched her. Then briefly he rested his hand

151

on her shoulder and said quietly, 'I know.'

She'd instantly wanted to re-run the scene, to take back the angry words. More than that she wished with a sudden huge yearning that she could be unattached, just for a while. Just for him. No, she corrected, for both of us.

★ ★ ★

During the first endless week of Hal's absence, she worried because other people seemed to have been noticing the discord between them. It troubled her deeply, especially when the other people were her mother and Sam, both of whose opinions she valued highly. 'Don't let it happen to you,' Elowen had said. And, 'Make it all right. It has to be up to you.' Why, Mum? Jo asked silently, knowing she could never put the question. There was a growing independence in her, the belief that she should solve her own problems. Not a child, are you? So why go bleating for help? Why lean on other people? And anyway she knew intuitively that Elowen was right.

Sam, at Christmas, had obviously been aware that things between Jo and Hal were bad. The memory of his kindness made Jo feel happy, briefly. He'd seemed to know when everything was twisting up inside her so tightly that she wanted to scream, and he'd always managed to alleviate the tension. Poor Sam, she thought, smiling faintly, it must have been like spending Christmas under Krakatoa.

And I went on about Magdalena, as if I'd been trying to see how awful a thing I could say, and still got no more than a nod in response. Now Magdalena's a scapegoat, if ever there was one. Or is she? Jo had fallen so deeply into the quicksand of her own circuitous thinking that she no longer knew. Have I made something out of nothing? she wondered. Now that I really do have a problem, is Magdalena just a convenient peg to hang it on? Or is her memory a real threat, one that might disturb even our most idyllic times? No. I'm not, she told herself firmly, enough of a fool to chuck away a good marriage because of Hal's love for a woman who's dead and gone. There's too much of a fog between us, she thought. It's so thick that I am quite unable to tell him why I'm so unhappy.

I'm not so sure I even know myself.

★ ★ ★

One day she managed to have nine hours entirely on her own. Edmund went to a friend's house after school, and Sammie spent the day with Edmund's grandparents; Bernard and Mary MacAllister treated the boys with the same easy, tolerant love, and Sammie was as much a grandson as their own son's child.

The freedom went to Jo's head. I have to have more! I feel brand-new! But she was guilty, too, because the absence of her beloved children had felt so good. She tried to make it up to them by being more attentive, till she realised there was nothing to make up; they'd both enjoyed it as much as she had.

Tentatively she began to wonder if she might repeat the exercise. It'd mean using people, she realised. That went against her firm belief that you didn't make use of people's affection by asking them favours. It also violated her determination to work it all out by herself. But I have to do *something*! she cried silently on a morning of bitter disappointment: an airmail letter had dropped on the mat, and she'd rushed to pick it up, convinced it was from Hal. It was from Helen Arnold. Hal had sent postcards to the boys. Hers must have got lost somewhere between Crete and San Francisco.

'How would you feel about having Teddy to stay for a while?' she asked Mary diffidently, trying to sound casual.

Mary said, 'Would you let us have him? Really?'

Jo wondered, with a pang of self-dislike, why she'd only made the suggestion when it suited her. I could have proposed it for their sake, ages ago, she told herself crossly. She knew how much the MacAllisters loved to be with Edmund, how much of a consolation he'd always been for them. At almost eight, he resembled his dead father more than ever.

* * *

There, she thought as the arrangements progressed, I'm halfway there. Well, they say even murder is easy after the first time. With self interest driving her on, she picked up the phone to call Sam.

'Sam, is my credit still good?' she asked him as soon as he answered. She didn't want the usual exchange of pleasantries — it would be hypocritical, when she was ringing to ask such a major favour. Sam might think she'd been buttering him up.

There was a slight pause, then he said, 'Sure, Jo. What is it you want?'

'Could you come up here to take care of Sammie while I go away?' It took him longer

155

this time to reply. When he did, it wasn't exactly what she'd expected.

'You're sure it's the right thing, to go after him?'

She let out her breath with a sigh of relief. She hadn't had to explain: Sam wasn't only with her, he was ahead of her. 'I'm not going after him. I have to be alone. I can't see where I'm going all the time I'm here. There's too much else to think about.'

'I'll come,' Sam said. 'I'll come with pleasure.'

★ ★ ★

Jo would never have believed she'd do it.

Never have thought she'd leave her two children, one of them not yet three, with other people. Yes, they were grandparents, close blood relations, almost as involved with her children as she was. But they were still other people. She wondered what it'd be like, for the first time in eight years, without a child to care for. I should think, she thought, elation suddenly building up and bursting out of her, it'll feel bloody marvellous.

But the next day she was smitten with guilt: how will the children react to having me absent as well as Hal? Poor little Sammie, he'll think he's been abandoned. And Teddy won't even be in his own home, but cast out among strangers . . .

I'm going daft, she said to herself, firmly crushing the picture of her boys as pathetic waifs thrown into the cruel world to fend for themselves. I'll be imagining them up chimneys next. Selling matches in the snow without any shoes on. The change'll do them good — it's high time I let them know I'm human too, and need a break occasionally.

She wondered where to go. She imagined herself staying with her parents, in Cornwall. Or going to some Mediterranean holiday resort, to lie in the sun and do very little all day. Neither plan appealed; she knew she couldn't be with her mother without her troubles being discussed, and, tempting though it was, this wasn't the time for talk. And she wasn't keen on a holiday, either. In her present mood, she doubted whether she'd enjoy sunshine and indolence. She wanted something to do, something that was just for herself.

She dreamt one night of her Hawkhurst house. Of Copse Hill House in the spring, daffodils in the grass, sunshine on the warm red brick. Waking, she wondered why it had taken a prompt from her subconscious to make her see the obvious. The house had been empty since the last tenants returned to Japan a month or so ago ('Jolly good bet, Japanese,' her property manager had remarked, 'all that taking their shoes off saves your carpets,') and there was every reason for Jo to make a visit home to inspect her property. *Every* reason, she repeated to herself as she raced to look up the property manager's phone number.

'Yes, the house could certainly do with some decorating,' Mr Tallis said when he'd stopped being surprised to hear from her, 'especially outside — it was a hard winter. But that's what we're here for, Mrs Dillon! We can see to all of that for you, there's no earthly need for you to fly all the way home.'

'No, it's all right. I have to come to England for other reasons.' That's true enough, Jo thought. 'I'd like to see the house, and I can put any necessary work in hand while I'm there.'

'You really don't need to — it seems a shame to come back and then have to get yourself involved in decorating,' Mr Tallis persisted.

'I'm not necessarily going to pick up the paint-brush myself,' Jo said gently. This conversation could go on for ever, and it was costing her money. 'I'll be home in a week or so. I have keys. I'll contact you when

I've decided what I'm having done.'
'Oh!'

Jo thought she might have sounded sharp. 'That's fine, then,' she concluded sweetly. 'Thank you for looking after everything so well.' Then, with excitement: 'See you soon!'

★ ★ ★

The days until her departure were busy with preparations. She did load after load of washing, caught up in an illogical treadmill of having to get everything clean. She pulled herself up short when she found herself packing a winter coat for Edmund. He's only staying with his grandparents for a couple of weeks or so, she thought, he's not leaving for good.

By the evening before her flight she was sick of the complicated arrangements, too tired from her efforts on the boys' behalf to care much what she packed for herself. She decided to take the absolute minimum. She went up into the attic to look for a suitable suitcase. Hal had taken the only smallish one; the others were far too big. Then she caught sight of Hal's rucksack in a corner, covered with cobwebs. She pulled it into the light, and a huge hairy-legged spider ran out of it. She brushed at the faded green material, peering at the luggage labels still tied to it: Mexico City. Lima. San Francisco. And, scrawled in black ink on the inside of the top flap, *H S Dillon. No Fixed Abode.* The very writing expressed weariness; Jo wondered at what point on his travels Hal's mental state had fallen so low as to drive him to that moment of despair.

Holding something that belonged to Hal brought him very close; briefly she felt her unhappiness lift. Then she thought, he went away to South America to isolate himself after Magdalena. Now he's gone to Crete to isolate himself from me. She laid her head down on the rucksack.

'I'll borrow this, Hal,' she said aloud. 'I don't think you'll mind.'

\* \* \*

They all went to see her off at the airport, although she wished they hadn't. Bernard carried her rucksack, and Mary said several times, wasn't Jo travelling light, and was she sure she was taking enough? I'm not going to get irritated, Jo told herself, she's doing this for me. Even if she *is* pleased about it. Mary looked faintly surprised when Jo suddenly gave her a bear-hug and a kiss, but she returned the embrace with equal warmth. 'You enjoy yourself, honey,' she said, patting Jo's cheek. 'We all need a rest, now and again.'

'Feed yourself up some, too,' Bernard added, patting her arm.

Jo grinned. 'Right. I will.' She knew she wouldn't, but he meant well. She bent down to the boys, holding them in a brief intense hug. 'Be good, chaps.' She fought to control the wobble in her voice; Sammie's upturned face was dubious with the threat of tears, and Edmund looked touchingly earnest.

'I hope you have a *really lovely* time, Mummy,' he said.

His pluck tore at her. And he looked so like Ben. 'I will, darling.' She made herself smile. 'I'll send you a postcard, lots of postcards.'

'Great! We can put them with our ones from Daddy.'

Daddy. Hal. She was trying not to think about Hal and his bloody postcards. She still hadn't received one. 'That's a good idea!' she said. The strain was increasing. 'Now I think — '

'C'mon, boys.' Mary picked up the cue. 'What's it to be? Milkshakes or ices?'

As he was led away, Sammie screeched, 'Both!'

Sam caught her eye as the children

161

retreated with the MacAllisters towards the exit. He smiled at her understandingly. 'You have to go, you're out of choices,' he remarked.

'Yes.' She took a deep breath. 'I hope it'll work out all right.'

'It won't, all by itself. But I reckon you'll know what to do when the time comes.'

She sighed. 'I wish I could believe that.'

He took her by the shoulders, shaking her gently. '*I* believe it,' he said quietly. 'Doesn't matter that you don't, one of us having faith'll be enough.' He pushed her gently away. 'Go on. I'm not hanging around here any longer, the kids'll drink my milkshake.'

'Oh. Yes, of course. Don't forget to look in the fridge, I've left you — '

'*Go on.*' He pushed slightly more firmly, smiling his smile that made him look like Hal. 'Skip the chat, I've heard it all, already.'

She stood looking at him. 'Goodbye, Sam.'

'Goodbye, Jo. Good luck.'

★ ★ ★

Flying by herself was tremendous, Jo realised, propping up a new novel behind her tray of food. She couldn't remember the last time she'd been able to read while she ate.

And, later, it was wonderful to stroll along

to the lavatory without one of the children immediately deciding they needed to go too, and could you hurry Mummy 'cos it's urgent. And no nappies to change! She remembered the last time she'd flown with Sammie; nine people had come and rattled the lavatory door while she desperately tried to clear up a momumental poo that had overflowed Sammie's nappy and run down inside his trousers. What *were* you meant to do with a dirty nappy and a plastic bag full of used baby wipes? Jo had handed the detritus apologetically to a steward, which, Hal had remarked, wasn't a good move since the steward had been about to serve dinner. But he'd entirely agreed with her when she'd said crossly that people who designed aeroplanes ought to be made to travel on them with toddlers, just to see for themselves how inadequate the facilities were. 'I'll write to the chairman of the airline,' he'd said. 'We'll send him the diaper, tell him there was no place to chuck it away.'

Later the lights went down. She curled up across the empty seat beside her and slept, waking to the smell of coffee. After breakfast she spent a luxurious ten minutes freshening up and putting on some makeup. Then England was beneath her; in her precious solitude she walked in the peace of her own thoughts.

★ ★ ★

Nobody knows I'm here, she realised as she boarded a train at Gatwick; not a soul in the world knows exactly where I am at this minute. The thought increased her sense of freedom, and she found herself smiling brilliantly at the man opposite. He flashed her a surprised grin in return, and Jo hastily looked away, reaching into her bag for her book. Sorry, mate, that wasn't what I meant at all. She tried not to laugh.

She hurried up the platform at Victoria. Hal's rucksack sat comfortably on her shoulders and, restless after the long flight, she decided to walk to Charing Cross. The afternoon was sunny, and people were looking happy. Back in her own country after more than three years, Jo felt happy too.

By train to her local station, by taxi to Copse Hill House, and the memories were crowding in. The greenness of England astonished her; she'd forgotten how thick and lush it was. And it was only April! The roads seemed minute, after San Francisco. Suddenly she remembered Hal, arriving at her house that first time after struggling down by car from London. She could appreciate now just how strange everything must have seemed. 'They're quiet roads,' she'd said. He'd given her his what-the-hell-are-you-talking-about glare, and said, 'Maybe, but they're so damned narrow.' She asked the taxi driver to drop her in the road, and she waited until he was out of sight before walking up the drive. She made herself keep her eyes downcast till she was right at the front door, then she looked up.

She'd always loved this house. She had come here after she'd lost Ben; here in this enfolding countryside, in the peace of woodland and fields, she had found the strength to dig herself a new furrow. The house had given her its support; never had she entered it without a sense of homecoming and relief. It was *her* home. She had moved there accompanied only by Edmund, then hardly more than a baby. She had changed the house a little, grafting onto its strong character something of herself. Then Hal had come here — had come to find her — and now the house held something of him, too.

She stood for a long time looking all around her. The house's mellow old bricks were rounded at the edges and comfortably settled, giving the air of a broad back bent by the weight of years but still standing firm. The paintwork was in need of attention, but not seriously enough to spoil the house's charm. Although the lawns needed mowing, someone had cared for the garden; roses had been pruned, edges of flower beds were straight. Nothing I can't put right in a few days, Jo told herself. Then, thinking piercingly of Hal, ain't nothing I can't handle.

Quickly she got out her key and opened the door. She stepped into the hall, and the familiar smell of the house hit her. Funny, she thought, you never notice that your house has a smell when you're in and out every day. But when you go away for any length of time and then come back, it's so strong, and it belongs so uniquely to your house, that you wonder why you don't notice it always. What is it? Can't be anything of mine, because I haven't been here for years. It must be just the house, and what it's made of — an amalgam of wood, and stone, perhaps overlayed by hundreds of years of flowers in vases and polish laboriously rubbed into the floors. She wandered through the ground floor rooms. Kitchen, clean and tidy, but more battered than she remembered. Living-room, which someone had painted a bright yellow — she didn't like it at all. And the furniture had been moved round — it didn't look like her room any more. This, she resolved, is where I'll start. I told Mr Tallis I wasn't going to do it myself, she remembered. Well, I was wrong. It's my house. It's had enough of other people's input.

She went slowly upstairs. Her bedroom. She'd decorated it when she'd moved in, and it was flowery, pastel-coloured. Don't think I like that anymore, she thought. I want cream and beige, and some dark, strong colours to flash out as contrasts. Ideas flew through her head; her enthusiasm increased by the minute. 'I'll unpack,' she said aloud, 'then I'll make up the bed and fix something to eat. Then I'll make a list of all I want to do.'

Her list grew vast. Running through it when, much later, at last it was finished, she began to laugh. Realistically, she was going to have to find help, unless she was prepared to stay here up to her armpits in paint for the entire summer. 'I'll get someone for the exterior, and maybe get them to do up the kitchen, too,' she decided, speaking out loud again; she felt so welcome that it seemed quite natural to talk to the house. 'But I'm going to do the living-room and the bedroom myself. OK?'

It certainly felt OK. She went to bed tired, but full of excited anticipation. It occurred to her that she had come away to rest, and she wondered what her family would say if they knew her rest was going to include giving her house a facelift. 'But that will be a rest, won't it?' she said into the friendly darkness. 'All on my own, starting and stopping when I like, free to finish a job even if it takes me till midnight, with no interruptions for meals, no need to tell absent-minded people to watch out for the wet paint or the jar of white spirit on the landing. Equally free to say, it's a lovely day, sod the painting, I'm going out walking.'

She turned over, so happy that she couldn't stop smiling. And it's only the first day, she thought as she settled down (I think I'll buy a new duvet, this one smells musty). I've got days, weeks even, ahead. She didn't even want to think beyond that; part of her cure, she'd decided, was to live purely in the moment. Shouldn't be difficult, with such an exacting timetable.

'Thanks, house,' she said quietly. 'Thanks for having me back.'

# 9

Jo slept for eleven hours, waking to find the sun streaming across the floorboards and the clock saying nine-thirty. She lay for a while, realising that, if anything, she felt even more positive than she had done last night. In addition she didn't feel tired any more; she was full of vitality, eager to get on. She had a shower, pleased that she'd remembered how to light the boiler and set the central heating and hot water controls. She had breakfast from the iron rations she'd bought on the way home, then put on Hal's old waxed jacket and set off to walk to the village.

It took her forty minutes, and made her conclude that although the walking was good exercise — and enjoyable, with spring burgeoning all around — it was far too time consuming; she'd have to hire a car. She went into the post office to consult the *Yellow Pages*, then picked up a Ford Escort from a place just round the corner. She decided to drive into Tunbridge Wells to buy decorating materials.

The lovely thing about being on your own,

she reflected as she drove along, is being free to scrap the plan you've made for the day, if a more appealing alternative comes along. Here I am, on my way to get paint, and brushes, and perhaps a new duvet and some bedroom furnishings too. And all I came out for was something for lunch.

She stood in the paint shop for half an hour, deep in thought, imagining how various colours would look in her living-room and hall. She knew she wasn't up to papering; she'd enliven plain-coloured walls with new curtains. She went to look at curtain materials, and by the end of the morning had made up her mind. Maybe I should sleep on it? she wondered over a half-pint of lager and a sandwich. No. I want to get on with it. *Now.*

On the way home, she decided she'd call in to see her neighbour. Jenny had been a friend in need when Jo had lived there alone, and they had exchanged Christmas cards ever since. Jo liked the idea of dropping in unexpectedly; she left her car in her own drive, then went next door. But the house was shut up; there was no response to her knocking. She went across to the neighbours on the other side. What was their name? They came for a drink on Christmas morning, and the wife left her cardigan . . . She stopped in the middle of the road. That line of thought led directly to Hal.

He had arrived unexpectedly on her doorstep a couple of days later, with a stuffed zebra under his arm. She had thought he was Mrs Watson (*Watson*, that was their name), collecting her cardigan. She closed her eyes, picturing him. He'd looked even taller in the hall of her low-ceilinged house. She felt a tremor of remembered excitement: she had been on the verge of falling in love with him, and his proximity had made her so nervous. She opened her eyes. Hal's not here now, but it's all right. I'll manage.

She rang the Watsons' bell, which performed an electric version of Big Ben striking the half hour. The front door opened, and the diminutive figure of Mrs Watson appeared in the narrow gap allowed by a security chain. Security? Here? Jo thought. Well, she always looked the nervy type. And maybe Hawkhurst is less safe than I recall.

'Yes?' Mrs Watson said. 'Can I help you?'

'It's me,' Jo said, feeling foolish. 'I used to live next door.'

'Good heavens! So you did!' The door slammed in Jo's face, and for an amused moment she wondered if Mrs Watson had decided she wanted nothing further to do with her. But then the door opened again; Mrs Watson had merely been taking off the chain. 'Hello, dear! It's Mrs MacAllister, isn't it?'

'No, not any more. I . . .'

'Yes! You married, didn't you? That nice American, the tall man who used to smile sideways.'

'He still does.' Fancy Mrs Watson noticing that. And, what's more, remembering it as her overriding impression of Hal. It isn't mine, Jo thought. She must have kept catching him in a good mood.

'We thought you'd gone to America,' Mrs Watson was saying.

'We did. That's where we live, only I've come home to see about the house — it needs some attention. After all the tenants, you know.'

'Indeed I do.' Mrs Watson fixed her with what Elowen called an old-fashioned look. 'There was a family from — Scotland, I think it was. Or Wales. And, really, the language! The husband was trying to start the lawnmower — on a Sunday, too — and quite honestly Mr Watson almost had to have words with him. Not like your nice American.'

'Hal'll be pleased you remember him so

172

fondly,' Jo said with slight irony. Mrs Watson seemed determined to see the best in Hal. You should hear him sounding off at *his* lawnmower, she thought. I bet he can outswear some tenant from Scotland. Or Wales.

'Oh, but what must you be thinking of me, keeping you standing out there!' Mrs Watson released her stranglehold on the door and opened it more widely. 'Do come in, I'll make some tea.'

'Well, I — yes, that would be lovely.' Jo went in. It was the last thing she wanted, but, she thought fairly, I did come knocking on her door.

★ ★ ★

'What happened to Jenny and Tom?' she asked as Mrs Watson poured tea. They were sitting side by side on a small cretonne-covered sofa, surrounded by tables of knick-knacks, photographs and little vases of dried flowers. Jo, used to her own furnishing style that bordered on the sparse, felt cramped, terrified of sending something flying. Where would Hal put his legs? she thought with a smile, imagining him folding himself in among the clutter. Mr Watson, she remembered, was almost as tiny as his wife.

173

'They're still there,' Mrs Watson replied. 'Jenny's away at the moment — her mother's ill, and she usually stays with her during the week.'

'What about Laura?' She had been at playschool with Teddy. She'd have gone on to primary school now.

'She stays with a friend when Jenny's away. They're all here at weekends, though. Poor Jenny, she does look tired.'

'I bet.' Jo remembered Jenny saying in a moment of frustration that her mother was a cross between Hitler and Sherlock Holmes, and Jenny's husband Tom had added that his mother-in-law was less endearing than either. I must see them, Jo thought. 'Tom's living at home, though?' she asked.

'Yes, dear. Oh! I know! We've asked him to a little supper tomorrow night — perhaps you'd like to come too, if you can find a babysitter?'

Babysitter? Jo frowned. Then she realised, amazed at how totally she'd managed to put her family out of her mind. 'No need for that, I'm on my own,' she said. 'Hal's gone to Crete to do some research for a book he's writing, and I've left the children with their grandparents.'

Mrs Watson's eyebrows shot up towards the careful curls across her forehead. She's going to take back the invitation, Jo thought. 'Writing a *book*.' She made it sound a very dubious thing to do. 'I see.' She fixed Jo with a look, and Jo could almost hear the line of thought. 'Oh, well. Very nice for you, I'm sure, to get away on holiday.'

'I'm not really on holiday,' Jo pointed out. 'I'm going to decorate the house.' I'll bloody well have to, now. She'll come and check.

'Of course.' Mrs Watson was smiling her approval. Puritanism lives, Jo thought. 'About half past seven, for eight, tomorrow?' Mrs Watson said as she got up. Jo took her cue and got up too, careful to avoid the spindly occasional table on which she'd put her empty cup.

'Lovely,' she said, adding politely, 'It'll be so nice to see Mr Watson again.' She got the suggestion of another look, then she was shown to the door.

★ ★ ★

She set to work with frenetic energy, racing through all the mucky preliminary jobs. She washed walls, rubbed down woodwork and filled in cracks in the plaster until, by evening, the living-room and hall were ready for painting in the morning. I'll find someone to do the exterior, tomorrow, she

175

thought, and get some tapes to listen to while I work.

She went to bed early with a cup of cocoa, and read another few chapters of her novel. Hal, she thought fondly, wouldn't have approved of either; he didn't like chocolate and never read novels. Suddenly she laughed; the freedom to do exactly what she liked was going to her head.

She made an early start the next morning, and got the undercoat on by ten o'clock. While it dried she went into the village to find a decorator; a card in the paper shop led her to somebody called Reggie Pickett. Reggie was an amiable man, willing to tackle the list of tasks she proposed; she engaged him on the spot. She also parted with twenty-five pounds, which Reggie said he'd need for materials. Jo could hear Hal saying sceptically, you'll never see him or your cash again, but she didn't let it bother her. 'I'm back in trustworthy old Hawkhurst, Hal,' she said aloud as she drove home. 'We're not all quite as cynical as you.'

She put the first coat of matt on the living-room before lunch, and Reggie gratified her faith in human nature by turning up in an incredibly filthy old van just as she was finishing her coffee and sandwiches. He refused the offer of coffee, but said he didn't mind if he had a cup of tea instead, three sugars please and not too much milk.

'I'll make a start out there, then, love,' he said, putting his cup in the sink.

'OK, Reggie. I'll be in the living-room, if you need me.'

He sang out, 'Righty-o-oh!'

★ ★ ★

During the afternoon, she realised with amusement that Reggie was one of those people who just had to be making a noise. If she was within earshot he'd talk mercilessly at her, not appearing to mind if she replied or not. She adopted the tactic of nipping away while he paused for breath; when he noticed she was no longer there, he would stop talking and begin either a shrill whistling, or else a surprisingly accurate rendition of highlights from *South Pacific*. It seemed to be his favourite musical. He would accompany himself with various tappings and drummings, on whatever surface was to hand.

She finished the living-room, and stood in the doorway admiring it. The new paint was cream with a touch of apricot; it looked warm, and brought out the red in the bricks of the fireplace. I'll do the curtains next, she thought, then this room'll be finished, and I'll have a comfortable refuge while I'm doing the rest. She lifted the corner of a dust-sheet and had a look at the curtain material. I could start this evening, get them tacked, and — then she remembered she was going out to dinner. I won't have to cook, she thought with relief. Painting was tiring, and she knew she wouldn't have bothered with a proper supper. She went outside to see if Reggie would like a cup of tea.

' . . . neee-ver — let — her — go!' he was warbling, coming down his ladder one step per note so that he descended while his singing rose to its climax. Noisy or not, Jo thought, he works fast enough; all the woodwork on the front of the house had been done. 'I give it a good rub-down and I done one lot of undercoat,' Reggie said, 'but I'll do another in the morning, you want a good covering. Nice, innit, that white?'

Jo had forgotten the Kentish tendency to put an 'o' in the middle of 'white', so it came out 'woit'. 'Yes,' she agreed, 'I think it's nicest, against the brickwork.'

'Loverly old house, this one,' Reggie said, patting the wall affectionately and assuring himself of Jo's everlasting approval. 'I've always liked the looks of it. Glad to see you're taking care of it. Rent it, don't you?'

Jo wasn't sure if he really meant rent, or whether he was actually asking if she let it. 'I live in America,' she said, answering in a roundabout way; she'd sound patronising if she corrected him. 'We do, that is — my husband's American. So we let the house to tenants while we're away.'

Reggie whistled in through his teeth. 'Risky business,' he said darkly, as if she'd confessed she and Hal were drug smugglers. 'Farmer up the road had tenants, in one of his old cottages.' He leaned towards Jo. 'They had a party, and their mates walked off with two of the chairs.'

'Oh, dear!' Jo said, trying not to laugh. 'Well, we've been lucky so far, all seems to be present and correct.'

Reggie looked up at the house. 'Doesn't do to take chances,' he remarked. Jo wondered how many chances he'd taken in his life. 'You be careful.'

'Yes, I will.' He's quite right, she thought, and I'm wrong to think he's silly and small-minded. 'Tea?'

'Tea'd be grand.'

* * *

Reggie went home after his tea, and Jo ran a hot bath and lay in it for half an hour, her

179

mind busy with planning what to do next. Living-room curtains first thing tomorrow, then a clean-up, and a vase of flowers in the fireplace — lots of daffodils in the garden. Then what? Bedroom, I think — that'll mean another trip into town, for paint, new bed linen . . . She slid down in the hot water, almost asleep. I feel good. I feel *great*.

She was ready at seven-thirty, but thought it would be disapproved of to arrive at the Watsons' dead on time. She fetched the postcards she'd bought for Edmund and Sammie, and wrote appropriate messages. Thinking about the boys made her miss them. I could phone, she thought, it'd be lovely to hear them. But it'd be upsetting for them. Or it might. Then Sam and the MacAllisters would have the miserable task of comforting them. On the other hand, they may be having such a whoopee time with their respective grandparents that being called to the phone to speak to their mother would be just an interruption. She smiled. I won't risk it.

She wandered into the living-room, wrinkling her nose at the strong smell of gloss paint. She perched on the end of the sofa, looking round with satisfaction. For the first time that day, her mind wasn't busy. As if he had been waiting for this moment, Hal came crashing into it.

'Oh, Hal,' she said. 'I can't think about you. Not yet. Not *now*. I'm going next door in a minute, and this is my big chance to make them realise I'm not as loopy as they thought.' The Watsons, she remembered with embarrassment, had witnessed some of her weirder extremes of behaviour over the years; she was convinced they'd thought she was peculiar. 'I'm going to be normal this evening. An ordinary person.'

But he was still there. He was smiling at her, that familiar half-smile which Mrs Watson remembered so fondly. 'Hal,' she whispered. Then, wiping away the tender expression she could feel on her face, 'Oh, bugger off, Hal!'

\* \* \*

At twenty to eight, she knocked on the Watsons' door. Mr Watson admitted her; the security chain had been left off in her honour. 'In here,' he said, leading the way to the amazingly cluttered sitting-room. 'Mother's in the kitchen, just putting the finishing touches. Tom's already arrived. You remember Tom, don't you?' He watched her with a twinkle in his eye. 'In you go — I must see to Mother.' Then he burst out, 'We didn't tell him you were coming!'

'Oh!' She stood in the doorway. Tom, hearing her come in, turned round to see who it was.

'Bloody hell!' he said. He shot to his feet and, lurching against a small shelved stand, sent assorted objects all over the hearthrug. She hurried to help him gather them up, picking a careful path between flowers, china animals, a small plastic model of Westminster Abbey and something that looked like an up-ended spectacle case.

'It's OK, they're dried flowers — there's no water in the vase,' she said under her breath, poking the stems back into the little pot. 'Is that broken?'

Tom was holding a silver frame with a photograph of a drooling spaniel. 'No, don't think so. But I'm covering it with peanutty finger-prints.'

'Here.' Jo lifted her skirt and pulled out a fold of petticoat, giving the frame a quick rub.

'I always said you were forward,' Tom remarked. 'Are your knickers white and lacy too?'

'No, plain M&S cotton.' She handed him the frame. 'Put this back on the whatnot, before Mr Watson comes back.'

'On the what?'

'The thing you just knocked over. It's called a whatnot.'

'Ye gods,' Tom muttered, doing as he was told.

'They won't notice a thing,' she said, eyeing the rearranged objects.'

'Don't you believe it. Mrs W sets them out with a set-square and a protractor, we haven't a dog's chance of getting away with it.'

He sounded really worried. Jo was trying not to laugh. 'Could we stand in front of it?'

'Not all evening, they'd think it was odd. I'll have to — ' Abruptly, he broke off. 'Damn the whatnot! I haven't even said welcome home!' He hugged her, kissing her cheek. 'Aren't you in America?'

'Not at this precise moment. I'm doing the house up.'

'On your own?'

'Yes.'

'I always said Hal was a jammy bugger.'

'Even more of a one than you thought. He's in Crete.'

'There you are, then. Jen's with the *Obergrüpenführer*.'

'Yes, I heard. Is it anything serious?'

Tom shrugged. 'Don't think so. But Jen says she'd rather suffer being with her than sit at home and worry.'

'Poor Jenny. How's Laura?'

'Fine. She's on Reading Level Two.'

'That really is terrific, Tom. I'm so glad.'

'Oh, shut up!' He gave her a good-natured push.

'Stop it!' she hissed. 'You'll have the whatnot over again.'

The door opened; guiltily Tom and Jo sprang apart. Mr Watson came in with glasses of raisin-coloured sherry, and Mrs Watson came in behind him. As if by ESP, her eyes went directly to the stand Tom had sent flying. 'Here we are,' Mr Watson said, 'and here's Mother.' Jo made a mental note to ask Tom if in fact the Watsons had any children — somehow it didn't seem likely — or if 'Mother' was a sort of courtesy title, like cooks in the old days always calling themselves 'Mrs'.

'Sherry, dear,' Mrs Watson said, passing her a glass and then turning her attention to the whatnot. She moved the photo of the spaniel an inch to the right, and altered the angle. Jo knew perfectly well that Tom was trying to catch her eye, but she didn't dare look at him.

'This *is* kind of you both,' she said, smiling widely. 'It's so thoughtful to have invited us, isn't it, Tom?'

184

'It certainly is.'

'Well, I know how one is when one's on one's own,' Mrs Watson said. 'Such an effort to cook a proper meal, just for one.'

Jo was about to say she always found it an effort to cook a proper meal, but thought the remark might be misconstrued. And it would without doubt have set Tom off on something even more flippant. She turned to Mr Watson, who was asking her about the house. 'It'll look even better in a week or so,' she said, 'when I've finished decorating it. But considering how many tenants have been in and out, it's not too bad at all. And I — ' She stopped, realising it hadn't been tactful to mention the tenants. Mr Watson sniffed, and Jo remembered that he'd almost had to remonstrate with some Scotsman, or Welshman, about language not suitable for the Sabbath.

'I liked the Japanese ones best,' Tom said, manfully coming to her aid. 'The husband was a mad keen golfer — do you know, Jo, playing here was the first time the poor little sod had actually set foot on a golf course? They have to queue up in Japan for about a million years before they get a game — he told me they play most of their golf in great netted-off areas like airship hangars.'

Jo had seen Mrs Watson's face at hearing

her former neighbour referred to as a 'poor little sod'; her expression clearly said it was a bit much, even if the man had been a tenant. Jo didn't think she could hold in her laughter much longer. 'Excuse me, I must just pop upstairs before we eat,' she muttered to Mrs Watson. She closed the sitting-room door behind her and flew up the stairs, great snorts of laughter shaking her. Oh, God, she thought, I'm enjoying this!

★ ★ ★

Mrs Watson had cooked a very nice meal, and Mr Watson shared a bottle of red wine between the four of them. Then they had a cup of coffee, and soon after that the Watsons began yawning and looking with exaggerated delicacy at their watches.

'Goodness, is that the time?' Jo said, in one of the lengthening gaps in the conversation. 'I really must be off — I have to be up early in the morning to make my curtains.'

Tom stood up hurriedly. 'And I must go, too,' he added. 'Work tomorrow.'

'Oh, dear, must you? Yes, I suppose you must,' Mrs Watson said, answering herself before anyone else could. 'Let me see, did you have coats?'

'No, I didn't,' Jo said. 'I didn't come far.'

The Watsons stood together side by side in the hall, like a reverse receiving line. Jo shook their hands. 'Thank you both so much,' she said.

'Yes, thank you,' Tom echoed.

'I do hope you'll come and see the house, when I've finished,' she went on. 'Then I can repay your kindness.'

'That's right,' Mrs Watson said. 'Good-night, now.'

'Good-night.'

Jo and Tom turned to wave when they reached the gate, but the front door was already shut. There was the sound of bolts being shot across; they both started laughing. 'Ever felt really welcome?' Tom said.

'Oh, stop it, they'll hear.' Jo looked back anxiously at the house; the lights were going out. 'Look,' she said, fresh laughter breaking out, 'they're dashing off to bed in case one of us goes back for something.'

'Ooh, I do feel pissed,' Tom said. 'A glass of wine and a thimbleful of sherry and I'm anybody's.'

'We're so ungrateful!' Jo said as they walked off down the lane. 'It was nice of them to ask us, wasn't it?'

'Yes, it was. Only it was their turn — they never had Jen and me back after that New Year party we had, and old man Watson was out of his tree on my booze.'

'You put too much brandy in the punch,' Jo said. 'I lost my shoes, and Hal trod on my toes.'

'I was dressed as a nun,' Tom said reminiscently. 'Remember?'

'Of course. Hal thought you were bonkers.'

'Bet he didn't say bonkers. Bet he said I was screwy, or an asshole, or a motherfucker, or one of those other choice pieces of American popular vocabulary.'

'I have no reason to believe that Hal thinks you're an asshole,' Jo said.

'I am, all the more for that. I'm just about to ask his old woman if she'd like a nightcap with me.'

'His old woman'd love one. She thought you were never going to ask.' Tom put his arm companionably across her shoulders as he ushered her into the house. She hugged him. 'You're fatter than Hal,' she observed.

Tom stood and looked at her. 'Quite honestly, Jo, I can't think of a reply to that. I think I'll go and find some glasses. What would you like to drink?'

'A cup of tea, please.'

'Bollocks.'

'OK, I'll have brandy.'

He returned with glasses and a bottle. 'Here,' he said. 'Happy days.'

'And to you. Hope Jenny breaks out of Spandau soon.'

'Me too. I miss her, and Laura. I need someone to laugh with, otherwise it all builds up and I let it out in the wrong places. Like tonight.'

'I noticed.'

'Did it matter?' He looked at her earnestly.

'No. Not in the least. And if it did, would you mind?'

'Not much. Have some more brandy, and we'll drink to our absent spouses.'

'Our absent spouses.'

'Jammy old Hal,' Tom said reflectively, after a while. 'He nearly hit me, once.'

'Did he? Why?'

'It was when you'd scampered off to Rye without him. He seemed rather anxious to find you, only Jen had ordered me not to tell anyone where you were.'

'I remember.' This was getting dangerously near to things she didn't want to think about. She had thought she'd lost Hal, when she'd gone to Rye. But she hadn't. Not that time.

'Sorry, I didn't mean to make you sad,' Tom said kindly.

'I'm not sad.'

'If you say so.'

She looked up. She'd thought before what

a warm smile he had. 'You're a nice chap, Tom,' she said.

'Yes, I probably am.' He was very near her, sitting on the floor in front of the sofa on which she was sprawling. He turned round to look at her. 'I could kiss you,' he said softly, 'which seems a lovely idea, especially after the laughter and the brandy. But on the other hand, I really would be a motherfucker then, wouldn't I?'

'You'd probably be an asshole, too. Shall we just have a little one, and not tell them?'

'Yes.'

He leaned forward and gently touched his mouth to hers. She'd never kissed anyone with a beard before. She felt illogically glad that Tom had a beard, because kissing him was so different from kissing Hal that she couldn't for one moment think this was Hal, even if she was half-cut. She pulled away before she began enjoying it. 'I'm going to go home, Tom,' she announced, 'because if I have any more — of either you or your brandy — it might end in tears.'

'I shall see you to your door,' he said, getting up.

In the hall he said, 'Hal once kissed Jenny there, so now we've evened the score.'

She turned to smile at him. 'Then we'll

have another one for luck.' She kissed him lingeringly. 'Just watch me home from here, Tom — you needn't come with me.' She went through the gap in the hedge and opened her front door. Tom, still standing on his doorstep, waved.

'Good-night,' he called. 'I'm saying it loudly, then all the neighbours will know you've finally gone home.'

'With my honour intact!' she called back. 'Night, Tom.'

# 10

In the morning, Jo was very glad she and Tom had been sensible. Sensible, she thought. What a wonderfully descriptive, parental sort of word. Sensible shoes. I do hope you're going to be sensible. Well, we were sensible, and I can look forward to seeing him again, with or without Jenny, it doesn't matter. Nothing happened, except we had a lot of fun.

'Back to work, house,' she said as she got up. 'Reggie's coming to get on with the outside, and I'm going to make the curtains.' She had breakfast, made a cup of tea for Reggie as soon as he arrived, then settled herself at the dining-room table to get going on the curtains. Sitting with the steady *tch-tch-tch* of the sewing machine lulling her thoughts, she was reminded suddenly of sewing curtains for the little flat that she and Ben had moved into when they were first married. She paused, staring out of the window; she could hear Reggie somewhere near at hand, loudly announcing to the world in general that he was going to wash that man right out of his hair.

Ben. Thinking about him doesn't hurt as much here as it did in France. In fact, it makes me happy. Picturing him, having him on my mind. House, you really do me good. Here I am, head full of my Ben, dead and gone these seven years, and all I feel is gratitude that he was mine, for a while. She sewed on, smiling, her mind far away.

Eventually she was interrupted by the sound of approaching whistling. 'I'll do the gloss coat s'afternoon,' Reggie said, appearing at the window. 'Coupla days to do the back of the house, then on with the kitchen.'

'That's fine,' Jo said. 'I'm off to town to get some stuff for the bedroom later, but I'll wait till you come back, then I can leave the house open.'

'Righty-o-oh.' He turned to go, then, with a slightly bashful smile, said, 'Right peaceful here, innit? Can't think when I've enjoyed working on a place so much.'

She looked up. 'Yes, it's peaceful. I'm glad you like it.'

'Oh, I do that.' He leaned confidingly in through the window. 'I was telling my Sheil — that's Mrs Pickett — there's something about your house.' He went off, breaking into the opening bars of *Bali Hai*. Jo thought, it's not only me, then.

193

Smiling, shaking her head, she went back to her sewing.

★ ★ ★

The days went quickly by, and by the end of the week, Jo and Reggie had completed Jo's schedule of work. They made a leisurely tour of inspection of the outside, then went into the house.

'Have I done OK?' Jo asked, watching Reggie scrutinising the paintwork in the bedroom.

'Not bad, for an amateur,' he said, grinning back at her. 'Them beams are a picture. Nice to see them in the plain natural wood, without paint. Didn't oughter have black paint, beams. Nor any paint, come to that.'

'Yes. I like them this way.'

'Wood's too pretty to be covered up. You done the colours nice.'

Jo thought so, too. In this room, the paint was the colour of clotted cream; the furnishings, too, were predominantly cream, with touches of tan and yellow. The flowers and the pastels had gone; the room was no longer noticeably feminine.

They inspected the rest of the house, then Reggie packed up his van and Jo settled up with him. Then, since he'd been such

194

an important part of this renovation of her house, she ran back inside, coming back with two bottles in her hands. 'Which do you like, gin or whisky?' she asked him.

He grinned. 'I like 'em both.'

She laughed. 'OK, have them both! There's an inch or two out of the gin, but I don't suppose I'll want any more of it. I'll be going soon.' She didn't think she'd realised it until that moment.

'Very civil of you,' Reggie said.

'You're welcome.'

She watched him drive away. Her mind was racing.

★ ★ ★

Later she asked the Watsons to tea, and showed them the newly-painted house. They stayed to admire it for half an hour — Mrs Watson said wouldn't it be nice when Jo had put all her knick-knacks out again — then said they must be off.

She saw them to the door, then put on her boots and went for a long walk.

★ ★ ★

When she got home, she decided to telephone Helen Arnold. She told herself it was a sudden impulse: in fact, she knew it had been prompted by thinking about Hal. Hal would have phoned Helen, if he'd gone with Jo to England. And a letter had arrived from Helen, shortly before Jo left San Francisco.

Won't it be fun, Jo thought, looking in her address book for Helen's number, to telephone out of the blue? She'll have no idea I'm here!

Helen's voice said, 'Hello, Helen Arnold.'

'Hello, it's Jo. Jo Dillon.'

'Jo! Well, what a lovely surprise. How are you?'

'Fine, fine, everyone's fine. I was just calling to thank you for your letter.'

'It's a kind thought, but really there was no need. Writing would have been cheaper.'

'Oh, it won't cost much.' She was just working out how to break the news that she wasn't in San Francisco when Helen interrupted.

'You're in England, aren't you?'

'Yes!' She waited for the surprised delight, but it didn't come.

Helen said, 'I see.'

No you don't! Jo wanted to say. Nobody does. *I* don't. 'I'm at Copse Hill House,' she said. 'I've been decorating.'

'I expect there was a considerable amount to do, after your tenants.'

Why are we talking trivia, when it's not what either of us is thinking about? 'Yes, quite a lot. It looks much better now.'

'When do you go home?'

Jo thought, I *am* home. Faced with the question of her return to San Francisco, she realised just how reluctant she was to go. 'I'm not sure.'

There was quite a long pause. Then Helen said, 'He phoned me from London.'

'Hal?' *Of course* Hal, dummy.

'Yes. He was about to set off to Crete.'

'He's researching for a book.'

'Mm.' She's going to have a go at me, Jo thought, tell me Hal has to make these trips, that it's essential for his work. She's Hal's friend, not mine, she's bound to see it his way. God knows why I even bothered to call her, I should have — 'Jo? Are you still there?'

'Yes.'

'For what it's worth, he didn't sound very happy. And I told him I thought he was wrong to go off on his own.'

'Did you? But I thought you'd be on his side!'

'Not at all. I don't know him very well — not nearly as well as you do — but I did meet him at a particularly relevant time of his life. He was very low.'

'I know about Magdalena,' Jo put in, in case Helen thought she had to be diplomatic and not give away Hal's secret past.

'I'm sure you do. It seems to me, Jo, that Hal has a fundamental belief that he's happiest on his own, whereas — '

'Tell me about it!'

' — Whereas in fact,' Helen sounded as if she was smiling, 'he can only be happy alone when someone's there in the background for him. Someone to go home to.'

'One day I might not *be* at home.'

'That, of course, is up to you. I suppose what I want to say is, don't imagine he left you in San Francisco and arrived in London without a backward glance.'

'Oh!' It was exactly what she had imagined. 'He didn't?'

'No. Actually,' there was that lift in the voice again, 'I'd say he sounded a lot lower than you.'

'I've been working on my house,' Jo said. 'It's done me good.'

'I can tell,' Helen said wryly. 'And I can guess why, too.'

Can you? Jo thought. I wish you'd tell me. 'It looks nice,' she said.

'I'm sure. When am I going to be allowed to inspect it?'

'Oh — I don't know. I'm not sure how

much longer I'll be here.'

Helen laughed. 'I didn't expect an immediate invitation.'

She said no more. She asked about the boys, and told Jo she was off to Tuscany in May. As they said goodbye, Helen said, 'See you soon.' It's what people *do* say at the end of a call, Jo thought. Isn't it? But, settling down to sleep, something about the conversation with Helen was still niggling at the back of her mind.

★ ★ ★

The next day was Saturday. Tom had said Jenny was coming home for the weekend, and Jo went round in the morning to see if she was about. Jenny came to the door in a dressing-gown, looking tired.

'Hello,' Jo said. 'Are you too worn out to make me a coffee?'

'Yes. You can do it yourself, and make me one while you're at it.' Jenny led the way through into the kitchen, then gave Jo a hug. 'It's great to see you. How's the decorating going?'

'All done. You must come and have a look.'

'You wouldn't like to do this house, too?' Jenny sat down at the kitchen table, gazing round at the walls while Jo filled the kettle.

'Not much. But you could get the chap I had — his name's Reggie Pickett, and he can sing all of *South Pacific*.'

'I might do that. *I'm* certainly not doing it. God, I'm exhausted! I didn't get home till nine last night, I had to take Mum for a hospital appointment.'

'How is she?'

'Ha! She's fine. Bloody well should be, she's had me, two nurses and a doctor running round after her. She's worn me out — she's a dreadful patient.'

'Oh, I'm sorry. What's the matter with her?'

'She had a cold, then pneumonia, pleurisy and bronchitis. Tom says she's got chronic hypochondria, he says we should confiscate her medical encyclopedia.' She grinned up at Jo, looking more like herself.

'Will you have to stay with her for much longer?'

'No. She wants me to, but I'm leaving it to the nurse now. I've told Mum I have to be here. Tom's going to say he's got bubonic plague and needs me more than she does.'

Jo brought mugs of coffee to the table. 'How's Laura?'

'Great!' Jenny's face softened. 'She's starting riding lessons. It terrifies me — she keeps wanting to gallop.' They talked for some time, catching up on each other's news. Then Jenny said, 'I'm pleased you're coming back. It'll be nice to have you next door again, both of you. *And* your boys.'

Jo looked at her in great surprise. 'I don't know that I am coming back.'

'Don't you?'

'No. Why do you think I am?'

'Because you've done your house up. And why do you keep saying 'I'? What are you proposing to do with with Hal?'

'He's gone to Crete to research a book.' I'm sick of saying it.

'So you decided you'd have a break too, and you flew back to your precious house.' Jenny hesitated. Then, as if she'd made up her mind to go on, added softly, 'where you sorted yourself out before.'

'I . . . ' Jo stopped. God, she's right. Of course she is. And that was what Helen was driving at, too. My house gave me strength before, and it's doing it again.

'You just said you've finished the decorating.' Jenny stirred her coffee vigorously. 'What are you going to do now?'

Good question, Jo thought. There was silence in the kitchen; she could hear the hall clock ticking. She glanced at Jenny, who was staring intently down at her cup.

What *do* I want to do? Go back to San Francisco? No. Stay here?

Yes. But not yet.

Not till Hal's here too.

But he, as I keep telling people, is in Crete. Researching a bloody book.

She drained her coffee too quickly, burning her throat. Then she stood up, restless suddenly. 'I'd better go and say hello to Tom.'

'OK.' Jenny looked at her for a moment, her expression amused. Then, smiling, added: 'He's gone dead keen on you, all of a sudden. He says your sense of humour is emerging, now you've stopped being so anxious.'

'Oh, does he?'

'Yes. Go and find him, he's in his potting-shed.'

Jo had the distinct impression that there were a lot of things Jenny wasn't saying. She's made me think, Jo realised. Damn it, she's virtually made me come to a decision. Was that what she intended? She walked down the garden to Tom's shed.

'I've come to say good morning to the Asshole,' she said to Tom's back, putting her head round the door.

Tom straightened up. 'Just as well it's me in here,' he said. Then: 'It's good having you around. When are you all coming back?'

'You too! Jenny just said it'd be nice to have us next door again.'

'Well, isn't that why you've been doing the house up?'

She shrugged. 'I have no idea.' She picked up a flower pot and put it down again. 'We'll see.'

'Careful, that's Bill and Ben's house you're fiddling about with.'

'Sorry.'

'Hope you do come back. You and the Jammy Bugger.'

'It'll be both of us or neither.' I hope, she added silently.

Tom made a face. 'That's a relief. We don't want any more of your stormy passages.'

'We'll try not to be an inconvenience to you.'

'Just as long as you don't start throwing things.'

'I don't imagine it'll come to that. Come and have a look at the house later, you and Jenny.' She turned to go. 'I've given her the name of my decorator chap, she says your kitchen needs doing.'

'Oh, God, does she? She was quite content with it till you went and did yours.' As she set off up the path, she heard him call, 'Troublemaker!'

203

★ ★ ★

She made herself lunch, then went out to work in the garden. She decided to cut the grass; the mower obligingly started at the second attempt.

Jenny and Tom came to look at the house, and she gave them a cup of tea. She told them she couldn't offer them a drink because she'd given her whisky and gin to Reggie Pickett.

As they left, they promised to keep an eye on the house till she got back.

★ ★ ★

Alone in the kitchen, she sat for a long time.

Then she went out to the hall and sat on the stairs, the phone on her lap. Rummaging in her bag, she found the number of Hal's hotel in Heraklion. He'd given her several contact numbers; he always did, whenever he was away, in case of emergencies. This, she thought, is the first time I've ever used one. Is this an emergency? I suppose it is.

She had waited patiently until now to call; he should be in his room at seven in the evening.

'Hello.' His voice made her rapid heartbeat even faster.

'Hello. It's me.'

'Jo? What's up, kid?' He sounded strained. Anxious? Of course, Jo thought, he would be. He'll be thinking there's a problem.

'Nothing's up. Everyone's fine. At least I assume they are. I'm in England, I've left the boys with Sam and the MacAllisters.'

There was a long, costly silence. Jo could hear Hal thinking, hear his brain racing to work out what this meant and throw him up an answer. 'You're at home?' he asked. Funny that he should call this house home. It was just how she'd been thinking of it all these days.

'I am.' She paused, trying to calm her breathing. 'I've been decorating — there was quite a lot that needed doing. I got a chap called Reggie to help me, he did the outside and the kitchen.' Why am I going into such detail? 'It looks great now.' She took a deep breath. 'But I need a holiday. I thought I'd come out to Crete.'

Quick as a flash he replied, 'No point. I'm not staying.' Her heart seemed to flutter, making her feel sick. But then he said, 'I'm going to Athens tomorrow, then I'm going out to one of the islands.' There was an aching pause. Then he said — and she hoped she was only imagining the reluctance — 'You could join me there.'

She let out her breath. At least he hadn't said don't come. 'OK,' she said casually. 'Can you send me directions?'

'When are you planning on leaving?'

She thought quickly. 'Monday. Or Tuesday.'

'That soon?' He sounded horrified. 'No time for me to write, I'll tell you now. Unless you want me to wait for you in Athens?'

It was what she'd been about to suggest. But it sounded as if it was the last thing he wanted. 'No, no, you carry on,' she said gaily. 'I'll manage.' So she wrote down to his dictation where to get the bus, the destination she had to look for, the place where the ferry left from and, at last, the name of the island where she was bound.

'Kea,' Hal said. 'K — E — A.'

* * *

She booked herself on a Monday night flight to Athens. Not wanting company — even Jenny and Tom's — she went out in her hire car most of Sunday. She spoke to Mary MacAllister on the phone, saying with a cheeriness which, she was sure, Sam would have seen right through that she was going

206

out to Athens to join Hal. Mary asked if she wanted to speak to Teddy; Jo could hear his laughter in the background.

'No, best not,' she said. It wasn't easy. 'I'll send another card in a day or two. Will you tell Sam I'm no longer in England? Oh, and give him and Sammie my love? I'll try to phone him from Greece.'

'Sure, no problem,' Mary said. 'Give our love to Hal.'

★ ★ ★

On Monday she phoned Mr Tallis at the property management agency, and asked him not to let the house again till further notice.

Now why, she wondered, putting the phone down, did I do that? I'm keeping my options open, she answered herself calmly. That's all.

She took her hire car back in the afternoon, enjoying the walk home to the house. She wondered if the spell of fine, sunny weather was contributing to her reluctance to leave England. She packed Hal's rucksack, tidied the house, then, far too early, called a taxi to take her to Gatwick. But it's best to leave, she told herself. There's nothing more I can do.

I don't want to go, I wish I could stay here.

But I can't.

* * *

The flight left at ten-fifteen, and would arrive in Athens some four and a half hours later, ten to four in the morning local time. Sitting in the departure lounge with two hours of waiting ahead, she wondered why she'd chosen a night flight.

She got out her book, but it was hard to concentrate. Persevere! she ordered. I don't want to think about Hal, and me, and where it's all going, but I don't seem to be able to help it. I've been on vacation, and now I'm going back. I'm picking up the reins again, and tomorrow I shall have to start doing some serious thinking.

But tomorrow is another day. She smiled suddenly, then as quickly stopped. Another Scarlett O'Hara quotation had flashed into her head: *'tomorrow I'll think of some way to get him back.'* But then, she thought, I haven't lost him.

Have I?

# 11

Hal arrived in Athens in the early evening. He felt in limbo, in transit between one world and another. The large amount he was drinking added to his sense of confusion, but he hadn't the self-control to stop. He didn't think he was ever really drunk; just not quite sober, so that he kept a barrier between himself and the real world.

He sat in Syntagma Square, downing a succession of drinks until late into the night. The city buzzed and hurried around him, but he was turned inward, with little sense of where he was. He thought perpetually of Angela, still tender and hurting from cutting himself away from her.

He recollected with shamed horror his confusion at hearing Jo's voice on the phone the previous evening, in his hotel in Heraklion. Her call had interrupted him in the middle of an erotic daydream, and he had felt as shocked as if Jo had walked in on himself and Angela, locked together in his bed in the throes of their violent initial passion. And, now that Jo had calmly announced she was coming out to join him, he faced the prospect of reunion with her. Today was Sunday, and he had three days to sort himself out before she'd be with him. No, two, he corrected himself; she said she was leaving Monday night, so she'll get down to Kea Tuesday. He closed his eyes, rubbing at them with his knuckles in despair. While in Athens he'd planned to visit the archaeological museum, which he hadn't been to in years, but his concentration was shot to pieces and he reckoned it'd be a waste of time. I should have said I'd wait for her in Athens; we could have gone on to Kea together.

I could call her.

But he didn't.

★ ★ ★

Before he left Athens the next morning, he went up to the Acropolis. It was a pilgrimage; he walked up streets he'd walked with Ben in an early morning fourteen years ago, and, remembering Ben's cheerful company, momentarily he felt lighthearted. He climbed to the Parthenon, leaning on the ramparts to stare out over the city.

Immediately below, small houses crouched, jumbled together, huddling in the shelter of the towering walls of the Acropolis like fungi in the shade of a huge oak. Further away, there were stately shuttered residences, domes and towers. And, high above the tallest rooftops, the jutting shape of Mount Lycabettus. Behind him a flag fluttered, and he laughed briefly at the memory of Ben, disgruntled and complaining because Hal had dragged him out of bed just to see a bunch of Greeks greet the dawn and put up their flag. He could hear Ben's voice, quite clearly. He walked slowly down through the Plaka, deep in thought. He made his way through busy streets to the place near the museum where the Sounion bus went from. The timetable said there would be a bus in twenty minutes. Time for a beer, he thought.

He dozed for the first part of the journey, his tall body wedged uncomfortably in a seat made for shorter people, his head bouncing against the window as the bus progressed slowly south-eastwards out through the Athenian suburbs. Then he sat watching the sea, his mind in retreat.

The bus ended its run at Sounion, and most of the passengers got off to visit the temple of Poseidon. Hal, not in the mood, turned his back on the magnificent headland and got on another bus down to Lavrion, to catch the ferry for Kea. He was in luck;

today the once-a-day service left in just under the hour.

By the time the ferry sailed, Hal was exhausted. He lay down along a seat on deck, his head on his bag, and went to sleep. He thought that probably somebody would wake him when they got to Kea. But he didn't much care.

★ ★ ★

The island of Kea turned out to be so attractive, so peaceful, that Hal's spirits lifted.

An elderly man with a long grey moustache was waiting on the quayside for the ferry, anxiously watching the disembarking passengers as if searching for a homecoming child. He approached Hal. 'You have room?'

'No,' Hal admitted.

'You want room? Very clean, by the harbour?'

'OK, I'll have a look.'

The old man led the way a short distance along the waterfront, then turned into a narrow alley. He indicated a flight of whitewashed steps, courteously standing back for Hal to precede him. At the top was an open balcony overlooking the street and the harbour, and opening off it were several french windows, all shuttered. 'You are only one?' the man asked, jingling keys in his hand.

'No,' Hal said. 'My wife will be joining me.' My wife. It sounded odd.

The man nodded, and, taking hold of Hal's arm, took him along a corridor to some more rooms. 'Here are better rooms, with bathroom,' he said. He opened a door, and Hal looked inside. Twin beds, cupboard, dressing-table, and a minute bathroom with shower, lavatory and basin. It looked fairly basic. Hal had noticed, as the ferry berthed, that there was a hotel at the far end of the waterfront, but it hadn't shown any signs of life.

'Is the hotel open?' he asked.

'*Ochi*. No. Hotel is being repaired. It will open in June.'

'*Endaxi*.' This'll do, Hal thought. Looks like it'll have to. He asked how much, and grinned at the man's reply. Nobody could have called the price anything but reasonable.

Later he went out to look around the town. It didn't take him long, since it consisted solely of the waterfront, curving for a mile or so around a small bay with a beach at the far end. Along the front were several little bars and a taverna, and behind these, in lanes burrowing back towards the hills, were streets of whitewashed houses. He sat for a while on the quayside watching a tall-masted yacht tie up. After observing the comings and goings for half an hour he reached the conclusion that, the yacht people apart, he was probably the only tourist in the town. Suits me just fine, he thought. Peace and quiet, and a pace of life that's so slow it's almost in reverse.

★ ★ ★

In the morning, he had breakfast in a bar and thought about what to do with himself till Jo arrived. He was disinclined to work; he wanted to look around the island. But it'd be nicer for Jo if they did that together. I'm getting lazy, he thought. I've been in Greece too long, I have an overdose of the 'avrio' attitude. He sat over his coffee, already on nodding acquaintance with some of the local population. A grey-robed priest was looking for one of the town's two taxis to take him on some mission of mercy, and Hal's eyes followed him in and out of several bars, hearing him call out, 'Stavros!' Eventually an overweight young man emerged from a doorway, a cigarette in his mouth, pulling on an incredibly stained cardigan.

Acknowledging the priest, he strolled over the road to his taxi, pausing for an almighty hawk and spit on the way. Hal was pleased he'd finished eating.

'Now I have to work,' Hal said aloud to a grey cat washing itself under the table. He strolled back to his room, stopping on the way to buy provisions from a shop on the waterfront. He wondered if the proprietor had just had some bad news; he'd seldom seen a more glum expression. 'And I'll take a bottle of ouzo, too,' Hal said as an afterthought as the man totted up his purchases. That earned a reaction: the man's dismal face lightened for a moment into a conspiratorial smile.

Hal took possession of the table and chair on the balcony outside his room, and was soon immersed in his work. It never fails, he thought much later, stopping to straighten his back, standing up to gaze out over the water. I'm going to sell this book. I'm going to give up lecturing and write books for the rest of my life.

★ ★ ★

He went to the taverna in the evening, where he got into conversation with the harbour master and Kea's solitary policeman. Back in his room, he worked until late into the night, writing under the unsubtle glare of the naked bulb hanging from the ceiling. Couple of hours tomorrow, he thought as at last he gave in and went to bed, ought to see this part finished.

He refused to think further ahead than that; Jo would be with him some time within the next twenty-four hours, and he had no idea how it was going to be between them. I'll tackle it when it happens, he thought. He remembered her once telling him that he should trust to his intuition, and not be so analytical. OK, so that's what I'm doing now. Then, smiling to himself as sleep began to pull him down: this is one hell of a time for experimentation.

★ ★ ★

Jo arrived in Athens when the night was still pitch-black. Her watch, advanced to local time, told her it was just after four am; the airport seemed dead. Everything was shut except the toilets, and there were only a few dozen people about. There were taxis outside, but she didn't have anywhere to go. Not until day arrived. She sat down on an upright chair, put her feet up on Hal's rucksack and began to read.

By six, her chair had become so uncomfort-
able that she'd decided she'd rather do
anything but go on sitting on it. She
went outside and found a taxi, and, after
checking the notes she'd written down to
Hal's dictation, asked to be taken to
Syntagma Square. Hal had told her she'd
be able to get breakfast there. At six-thirty?
she wondered, as the taxi took her swiftly
into the city centre. She looked around her,
at a long row of shops that all seemed to
be selling lamps. They were shuttered, dark;
Athens appeared to be still fast asleep.

There was slightly more activity as they
swung into Syntagma Square, but it wasn't
what she'd have called hectic. I'm probably
greatly favoured, she thought, I don't suppose
many people get to see Syntagma Square
when there are only a handful of cars in
it. Hal said that it's so thick with traffic the
fumes are making the Acropolis fall down,
and that it's a good job the Elgin Marbles
are safe in the British Museum. At least, I
think that's what he said. She remembered
going to the British Museum with him. He'd
had a flat in Bloomsbury. They'd gone there
afterwards. They'd made love for the first
time, on big cushions in front of a spitting
gas fire.

'Syntagma,' the taxi driver called, bringing

her back to the present. He stopped at a corner, leaping out to get her rucksack out of the boot.

'Thank you. *Efcharisto*,' Jo said. He smiled at her charmingly, and bowed courteously when she added a hundred-drachma tip to the fare.

She watched him drive away, for a moment daunted; it was six-forty in the morning, she was all alone in a huge city which she didn't know, in a country she'd never been to before. Then she thought defiantly, I've been to Cyprus, and I've been to Rhodes. I like the Greeks, they're friendly. Kind to strangers, especially women on their own and in need of a bit of chivalry. I shall do all right.

She strolled around the square and meandered along nearby streets, filling in time until the first pavement café opened up. She got out her map of Athens, and worked out where she was and where she had to get to for the bus to Sounion. She wondered what time the ferry to Kea left, and for an instant felt anxiously that she ought to get down to Sounion — no, Lavrion, Hal said the ferry goes from Lavrion — as soon as she could. Then she thought, no. If I miss it, I can go tomorrow. There's bound to be somewhere in Lavrion I can stay overnight. And Hal will just have to wait. She had a sudden stomach-dropping feeling, as if she were descending in a ferociously fast lift. She was getting used to it; it had been happening repeatedly since she left England, every time she thought about being with Hal again. It only came when she wasn't actually doing anything; all the time she was engaged in the actual business of travelling, she'd been too busy to dwell on where all this effort was taking her.

She heard the loud rattle of a shutter being raised. A beautiful aroma of coffee wafted out from somewhere, and she heard steps behind her. 'You want have breakfast?' enquired a cheerful voice.

She turned, and saw a white-aproned waiter wiping tables. He gave her a welcoming smile, pulling out a chair for her. She smiled back, grateful not only for his polite greeting but more so for his timely interruption of her thoughts. 'Yes, please,' she replied, taking off her rucksack with relief and sitting down. 'Continental breakfast for one, and a lot of that lovely coffee.'

While she ate, the city came to life. The pace quickly shot up to maximum, and the traffic thickened as she watched. By the time she'd finished, Syntagma Square sounded and smelt like a racetrack for vehicles past the first flush of youth. Breakfast had lifted her spirits; she'd had toast, honey and coffee, and it came accompanied by a glass of orange juice and a mysterious piece of cake which she didn't think she'd ordered but assumed must be a part of what was understood by 'continental breakfast'. She settled the bill, and then had another look at the map.

★ ★ ★

I think I'm getting the hang of it, she thought later as the bus stopped and started through the suburbs of Athens. She had recognised Syntagma Square in the distance, spotted the Acropolis and Mount Lycabettus. She sat clutching her ticket, sitting tensely upright. She'd been clenching her jaw; her head was beginning to ache. Relax, she told herself. It's silly to be anxious now, I'm well on the way. I've done the difficult part, it's easy from now on.

But she knew the true cause of her tension, and there was nothing she could do about it. Pictures of Hal came constantly into her mind, and before she could control her thoughts she kept finding herself deep into involved mental conversations with him. Why am I so worried about being with him again? Because, came the relentless reply, you think he's trying to break away. Then why did he say to come out and join him, why was he prepared to give me exact directions for getting to where he is? Because you forced his hand. No I didn't, I just said I was coming out to Crete. Oh, yes, and wouldn't it just have made the shit hit the fan if you'd got to Heraklion and found him gone!

Perhaps he'll have left Kea. Perhaps I'll find a note pinned to the harbour wall, 'Message for Joanna Dillon: your husband has gone to Turkey'. Or Israel. Or India. Stop it. If he's not there — and it's hardly likely, unless he's had a brainstorm or someone's given him a frontal lobotomy — I shall have a pleasant stay and then go home again.

I said I needed a holiday, didn't I? Well, I'll have one. With him or without him. Her thoughts were pulling her down. With a huge mental effort, she made herself switch off. Looking at the passing scenery left too much room for her mind to wander out of control; she got out her book and began to read.

The Kea ferry left that day at six in the evening. Jo was relieved she hadn't missed it, but wondered what she was going to do in Lavrion for the next three and a half hours. Wandering away from the ticket office, she stood on the quay, looking out over the smooth navy sea to where she thought Kea lay. Hello, Hal, she said in her head. Do you know I'm here, on the quay at Lavrion, talking to you? Can you feel my presence?

She worked out how long it was since she'd seen him, surprised to find it was only just over three weeks. She wondered why it seemed so much longer. Because, she answered herself sadly, for so many months we might as well have been an ocean apart, even though we were living in the same house. She walked slowly back into the town, and found a pavement café where she sat down and ordered a beer. What am I going to do?

She closed her eyes, thinking back over the past weeks. She pictured Copse Hill House, and felt a glow of happiness, experiencing all over again the security of knowing it was there, it was hers. And, after her and Reggie's efforts, it was looking its best. She held on to the happiness, trying to analyse why it made her feel so good. Is it simply because it's mine? No. There was something else, an insistent thought that she was aware of holding off. Ben. Something to do with Ben, with the house having been her healing refuge after she lost Ben. She let her mind run free, and the answer slowly rose to her consciousness: the house got me over Ben, so I know it can get me over Hal.

But she didn't want that thought. No. Send

it away, don't think it in case it comes true. What do they call them? — self-fulfilling prophecies. But they come about because subconsciously you make your actions fit the scenario you've envisaged. And I am *not* going to do that. 'Positive thinking.' She said the words softly aloud. And less of the advanced metaphysics. I feel good because I've had a fortnight on my own, my mind's been on holiday, free to run all over the place like a young dog let off the lead in a woodland full of wildlife. I've had peace, with nobody bothering me and nobody dirtying houses and clothing and making God-awful messes for me to clear up, only to have everything filthy again the moment my back's turned. I've been purged, she thought. I've put my house in order, in both a practical and a symbolic sense. I'm all right again.

The realisation fell softly on her like a blessing. I am, I really am all right. She smiled gently, full of wellbeing. I've had a period of absence from what was worrying me, and now that I've come back to it, it doesn't seem so bad. In fact, the things that were concerning me so deeply have diminished, so much so that I've been casting around for something more, something big enough to justify such anguish.

What's it all been about? she wondered, tentatively testing her new confidence. And why am I so sure that it's OK to run to Hal? I'm not running to him — she disliked the phrase — out of desperation, to hang myself back around his neck like an albatross. I'm going to him because, although I can manage without him, I'd rather manage with him.

The house had reminded her of their happiest times together. She wanted more than anything to recapture that happiness. I do love him, she thought, I love him with all my heart. She had remained in control of her conscious thoughts at home; she'd been so busy, the days filled with such positive work, that it had been easy. But, as in Cannes, her nights had been full of Hal. She might be able to *manage* without him, yes. But there was a pushy, forceful part of her psyche that wasn't going to allow her to get away with thinking she could be happy without him.

You ran after me once, Hal, she thought. You came to the house to find me, but you did also actually run after me. You came to Rye, and you said you'd lost one woman you loved, you weren't going to lose the other. Now it's my turn to come after you, for much the same reason.

She stood up. She had over an hour to fill before the ferry went, but she had to move, had to take an actual step forwards while her courage ran high.

I do hope, Hal, she thought as she set off for the harbour, that I find as willing a welcome in you as you did in me.

# 12

For a very long time on the voyage to
Kea, it was impossible to see any point
for which the ferry might be heading. Jo
watched as they sailed past a couple of
insignificant humps of island, mere rocky
outcrops, apparently uninhabited. The long
shape of Kea gradually filled the horizon, but
it looked as deserted as the smaller islands;
no sign of roads, churches, cultivated land.
Then she saw a solitary house, and a track
that wound away into the hills. Where are
we going? she wondered. Perhaps this isn't
Kea; there's no sign of a town, a harbour
— nothing.

Unexpectedly the ferry began to make a
turn to starboard, and it slowly rounded a
headland into a bay that had been invisible
until that moment. A lighthouse stood on
a promontory; a small fishing boat was
puttering along slowly under its shadow,
making heavy weather against the cross-
currents off the rocks. The white wake of
the ship showed that they were continuing
to steer gently to the right, and suddenly
signs of habitation came into view. First

a collection of houses, shuttered but well-maintained. Then a beach in the distance, a few cars, and a bus. A long line of low whitewashed houses, and at last, tucked right away in the inside curve of the bay, a stone jetty and a small harbour. People, lots of them, waiting with baskets and parcels to board the ferry.

Perhaps, too, some of them were waiting to meet it. Jo was assaulted by another of the going-down-in-a-lift feelings, this one strong enough to bring a light sweat to her skin. Part of her wanted to go on being in this suspended moment of waiting for something to happen; she almost wished she could arrest time so that she stayed forever on a ferry about to dock, the sun on her back, a sweet fresh breeze on her face. But that, she thought with a smile, would mean something fairly drastic happening to the laws of physics.

It was too late to turn back. She went to lean on the stern rail, watching as the ferry reversed up to the slipway. The stretch of water between ship and land lessened inexorably, and ropes were thrown to men on shore. The ferry came to a standstill, and its rear door crashed to the ground with a rattle of chains. Jo was fighting the frantic urge to let her eyes search everywhere at once. She hadn't seen Hal yet. Has he come to meet the ferry? She made herself scan the quayside methodically, carefully studying the crowd of dark, unfamiliar faces.

He wasn't there.

She heard a low whistle. Her knees shook, and she felt sick. She looked in the direction of the sound. Hal was standing on a wall, above and behind the activity on the quayside. For a long moment he stared at her, his face expressionless. Then he raised his hand, palm facing her. It was almost a gesture of peace. She waved back, then turned from the rail to run below. She picked up the rucksack, waited while a lorry reversed off the car deck, then walked down to meet him.

They approached each other slowly across the few yards of quay that separated them. Hal reached out to take the rucksack from her.

'Hi, kid.'

'Hello, Hal.' He didn't look very well, for someone who had been in Greece for nearly a month. Perhaps he really has been working hard — too hard, she thought. His dark eyes were bloodshot and heavy-lidded, as if he hadn't been sleeping. She felt nervous and disorientated. 'Um — where are we staying?' she asked, falling into step beside him.

'It's not far. I have a room on the waterfront. Not the Ritz, but it's clean and it's cheap.'

'Oh.'

They went on in silence. She was very aware of the space between them. Hal hadn't kissed her, hadn't touched her. But then why should he, she thought, angry with herself for being so sensitive.

'Here,' he said, pointing to steps. Jo went up, then stood back as Hal went to open a door. The room seemed very small. She thought, we shan't be able to get away from each other. Then she wished her instinctive reaction had been anything but that. Hal put down the rucksack.

'That's mine,' he observed.

'Yes, it is. I've been travelling light. I didn't think you'd mind if I borrowed it.'

'Sure. I don't.' He stood in the open doorway. Jo had no idea what would happen next. What would I feel if he came right in, locked the door, took me in his arms and carried me across to one of these narrow little beds? She realised, with a shock of surprise, that she didn't really want him to do that.

Staring at him was becoming awkward; she bent to open the rucksack. 'I think I'll unpack,' she said. Her voice sounded a lot brighter than she felt. 'I wouldn't mind a shower, actually. I've been in the same clothes since this time yesterday, I'd like to wash them out then put on something fresh.' She looked up at him. He closed his eyes for an instant, and she thought he looked worse than ever.

He swallowed, then said with an apparent effort. 'OK. I'll go have a beer. Come along when you're through.' He moved out of the doorway, pulling the door closed behind him.

'Where?' Jo asked.

He waved a hand. 'That way, along the waterfront. I'll look out for you.'

She listened to his steps going away. Then she sat down on the bed that hadn't been slept in. Single beds, she thought. Appropriate, for near-strangers. She felt incapable of thought or action. She sat for some time, then slowly got to her feet. She arranged her few clothes in the wardrobe beside Hal's, and put her sponge bag next to his in the little bathroom. Then she took off all her clothes and went to have a shower.

★ ★ ★

Hal walked quickly away down to the bar. Beer wouldn't do; he ordered a brandy.

'Did your wife arrive?' the barman asked. Hal cursed himself for having told him Jo was coming. Then he thought, what the hell.

'Yes,' he said. The barman said courteously that he looked forward to meeting her. Hal didn't answer.

He took his drink to a corner table. He closed his eyes, his mind full of troubling images. Angela, walking away, her shoulders stiff with tension and hurt. Jo, the eagerness on her face in the instant she'd spotted him masked suddenly by a different expression.

My wife seems like a stranger; she's unapproachable and cool. And, oh, God, why had she had to say that about putting on clean clothes? Her voice had suddenly merged into Angela's, and Hal had heard Angela say, 'I thought I'd start with all clean clothes when I meet Rob.' She'll have met Rob by now. How're you doing, Angela? Is your Rob a stranger, too? He swallowed the brandy and ordered another one. He could think of no way to make things better. He only hoped Jo could.

★ ★ ★

She took a long time over her shower, then towelled and combed her wet hair until it was only damp and put on some makeup. She

231

dressed, then looked at herself in the mirror. I have to go now, she thought. I'm out of choices, just like Sam said. The thought of Sam gave her courage. Sam has faith in me, she thought. Here I go, Sam.

She locked the door behind her, and walked across the balcony and down the steps, hurrying along the alley to emerge on to the waterfront. She turned right, away from the quay; she could hear music in the distance. It wasn't far. Hal was standing outside a bar, a glass of beer in his hand.

'In here,' he said. 'What'll you have?'

'I'd like beer, too, please.'

Hal nodded to a man behind the bar, who came across and shook Jo's hand. 'I hope you will have a happy time,' he said in English. He smiled at her warmly, and for the first time she felt like any other wife arriving to join her husband, cheerful at the prospect of a holiday together, making plans, discussing what to see, what to do. She turned to look at Hal, and almost laughed aloud; he didn't look cheerful at all. In fact, he looked as if, far from discussing his holiday plans, he was about to make arrangements for his own funeral. The barman brought her beer, and another one for Hal.

'Cheers,' Jo said.

'*Eviva*,' Hal responded tonelessly, not looking at her.

She watched him drink half a glass, straight down. She thought in a blinding moment of insight: he's tight!

Her mind raced in confusion. She felt distinctly alarmed, wondering what was wrong, that Hal should have drunk so much that it showed. He had a cast-iron constitution — she was used to him being the only one at parties and dinners who still seemed sober at the end of the evening, yet he never noticeably held back. What's the matter? she thought anxiously.

Then suddenly she felt betrayed.

And very angry: how *dare* you meet me pissed!

She studied him. The lines that ran from his nose to the corners of his mouth were very pronounced, and he had a sort of pallor underneath his tan that made him look slightly spectral. His eyes were deep, lined underneath with grey rings. Her anger left her as quickly as it had come; she thought, I don't think I've ever seen him look so miserable.

She wondered what to do. It wasn't a good feeling, to realise that her arrival didn't rate in his top ten of joyous experiences. A part of her wanted to take the direct approach, demand furiously what was the matter; I've come all this way to be with you so why the bloody hell can't you start looking as if you're pleased about it? But a greater part of her was rapidly filling with sympathy for him.

She reached out her hand and put it on his. He didn't move; he was still looking away from her. 'You look tired,' she said. 'I am, too. Shall we eat early, then turn in? I'd like nothing better than a good night's sleep.' I'd like many things better, she thought ruefully. But Hal had turned to her, and he had the ghost of his half-smile. If Mrs Watson could see you now, my darling Hal, Jo thought, and she wanted to laugh. But she didn't, because Hal's look of gratitude was making her heart turn over.

'Right,' he said. His smile grew, and he added quietly, 'I'm sorry, kid.' She didn't ask what he was sorry about. It didn't seem the moment. He moved his hand and took a firm hold of hers.

'It's OK,' she whispered. But she wasn't sure he heard.

★ ★ ★

They went next door to a taverna. Jo was very hungry, and craved a proper meal; she seemed to have been existing on pre-packed snacks or toast and coffee for days. As Hal led the way to a table, she looked at other diners to see what they were having.

'Where's the menu?' she asked, sitting down beside Hal.

'There isn't one.'

'How do we know what's available, then?'

He smiled briefly. 'Use your eyes.' He pointed through an open hatchway at the end of the room, where a very large grey-haired woman was stirring a vat of spaghetti. 'Looks like spaghetti tonight.'

'Funnily enough,' Jo said with dignity, 'spaghetti was just what I was going to ask for.'

They had another couple of beers while they waited, and then the proprietor brought them two huge plates of pasta with a thin layer of sauce on the top. He put down parmesan cheese, a basket of bread and a bottle of retzina, wished them '*Kali orexi,*' and left them to it.

Jo watched him return behind the bar and pour himself a drink. His face was divided by a great bar of droopy black moustache, and he had deep, soulful eyes. She wondered if faces in this part of the world fell naturally into mournful lines, or whether there had been some local catastrophe recently; a shopkeeper who had nodded a greeting to Hal as they passed had worn the same doleful expression. Just when I feel like being cheerful, too, she thought, and turned with a sigh to her meal.

Spaghetti must be more soporific than I'd suspected, she thought with amusement some time later; their empty plates had been cleared away, and Hal's eyelids were drooping. She watched him surreptitiously. He sat with his arms folded, long legs stretched out in front of him under the table, eyes slowly closing. She wondered if anyone else had noticed. She looked around the taverna; people at other tables were talking quietly, or watching the television in the corner. Nobody was looking at Hal. Some of them — admittedly, the elderly ones — seemed nearly as sleepy as him, so perhaps it was acceptable behaviour here, like Arabs burping as a tribute to a good meal. When she turned back to Hal he'd gone, eyes shut and head gently nodding. She watched for a few moments to see which way, if any, he was going to tip, ready to put out a hand to him if he seemed in danger of falling off his chair. But he lolled forwards rather than sideways; deciding that, for entertainment value, staring at someone asleep was on a par with watching paint dry, she turned her attention elsewhere.

A couple of men came in with a bag of fish. They went through into the kitchen and, presumably, asked the old woman to cook their catch. I wish I understood the language, Jo thought. She loved hearing Hal talk to people in Greek. The men sat down nearby, and soon their fish reappeared. They can't eat all that, she thought, then watched as they did so. One of the men offered the discarded heads to a small grey cat, but before it could decide whether or not to trust this gesture of human magnanimity, the proprietor came and shooed it away.

A man in a dirty pullover carried a crate of provisions through into the kitchen, and the old woman unpacked tomatoes, lettuces, peppers and trays of eggs. I could have done with a salad, Jo thought. Too late now, and with Hal asleep, I'd never manage to explain. She looked at him again, but he was still well away. She smiled. What a wonderful reunion. So much for the pent-up excitement.

A plate of eggs was brought to the table behind her. Five fried eggs, just that? she thought in surprise. She waited to see what the rest of the meal would be, but nothing else arrived. She wondered what effect five fried eggs would have on the digestive system. Had they heard of roughage? And what about the cholesterol?

She was aware of a movement beside her. Hal's eyes were open, and he looked faintly surprised. No, you couldn't really call his eyes open, Jo thought, they're just not quite as closed as they were. She wanted to laugh. Everything felt so peculiar — dreamlike and unlikely — and she couldn't take the situation seriously. She thought she must be slightly drunk too. Tipsy. That's what I am. Tipsy. She reached for the bottle of retzina and topped up her glass. I've got a fair bit of catching up to do.

Hal cleared his throat and sat up. 'Er — d'you want coffee?' he asked her.

'No, it might keep me awake,' she said wickedly. 'Do you?'

'No, I don't either.' He looked at her, frowning slightly. She thought he probably wanted to ask the perpetual question people ask when they've just woken up from an unscheduled doze: 'How long have I been asleep?' She decided not to tell him.

'Shall we go for a walk before we turn in?' she suggested.

'OK.' He crossed over to the bar to pay the bill, then they went out into the quiet night.

It was cooler than she'd expected. She shivered slightly; she hadn't brought a coat. Hal took off his jacket and wrapped it round her. She was surprised; she hadn't thought he'd be sufficiently aware of her to have noticed she was cold. She looked up at him. 'Thanks,' she said. His eyes stared into hers, and she couldn't read his expression. She had no idea what was going on in his head, and she wondered why this wasn't throwing her into a panic of uncertainty. All she felt was a mild curiosity. What *is* the matter with him? She put out her hand to take his. 'My hands are cold, too,' she said quietly.

'Right. We won't walk far. To the end of the beach, and then back again.'

They walked hand-in-hand, slowly. Neither of them spoke; the only sound was the whisper of the sea. Peace, she thought. It's saying, peace. Amen to that.

Hal was aware that he should be asking her interested questions about the things that normal couples talked about. How are the children? and, d'you think they'll be OK with the grandparents? and, did you remember to arrange for us to be picked up at the airport? But that world — home, children, ordinary daily life — seemed impossibly far away. The person he'd been when he was there didn't seem to exist any more. He realised dimly that he should concentrate on the present. He and Jo hadn't managed to make it work, back home. Now they were here, on their own, and maybe this was a second chance.

He resolved to drink less. That way, he'd be better able to control the wandering of his thoughts. And his thoughts kept wandering back to Angela. I have enough to think about right here, for God's sake, he reflected, thinking of the amused look in Jo's eyes when he'd woken with a start in the taverna. There's something different about her, he thought. It's as if she's less — involved, as if things don't have the power to upset her like they did. But that wasn't quite right. He frowned, trying to bring his thoughts into sharper focus. She doesn't feel detached, she seems — benign. He shook his head. This was something he had to tackle sober.

'Come on, we'll go home,' he said, wheeling her round.

'All right.' He was sure he could hear that amusement in her voice again. What the hell was it?

He wanted nothing more than to be in bed, drowsily falling asleep. But as they neared their room, his mind went ahead to all that lay between him and that happy moment. He wondered what Jo was thinking, whether she envisioned them making love. The uneasy mood that had lain between them for so long didn't permit him to say — as he very much wanted to — lie down beside me and hold me till I go to sleep. He wanted the closeness of her, but that was all. He didn't think he knew how to ask for that. They reached the foot of the steps leading up to their balcony.

'Go on up,' he said. 'I'll walk on to the end of the quay, there's not much room for two people to get ready for bed at the same time.' For a moment he saw her face falter. Something in him responded, and he almost put his arms around her. But he thought, and what then? Tomorrow. It'll be better, tomorrow.

She ran up the steps, and he heard the key click in the lock. Then the door closed, quite forcefully. Oh, God, he thought. He went to stand on the wall where he'd watched the ferry come in. He'd thought, before Jo arrived, that he'd know what to do once she was there. But he didn't seem to be any good at acting intuitively.

He stood for a long time, thinking about tomorrow. We'll keep busy, and I'll keep sober. We'll hire a motor bike, and we'll explore the island. There'll be things to see, things to talk about. Maybe it'll be like starting again. His head was clearing. In a mood of determined truthfulness, alone with his thoughts in the darkness, he faced the question he'd been running away from. Do I want to be here, with Jo? Or would I rather be back in Crete with Angela?

There wasn't a straightforward answer. When the hell is there? he thought bitterly. Angela was still with him, hunger for her still flared through him when he thought of her. Until it dissipated, he had no room for any other desire.

But it will dissipate, he thought, I'll make sure of that. Angela had been a part of a dream; he was still in it, but it was fading. Even if he wanted to preserve it, he couldn't. Not now that Jo was here. If we'd met another time, Angela, he thought, then without a doubt we'd have made it, and I should have got to love you like I love Jo. We were out of time, and you'll never know how sorry I am.

It slowly dawned on him what he'd just thought. *I should have got to love you like I love Jo.* But he hadn't been aware of loving Jo; during this recent, troubling time, she'd been merely an impediment to what he wanted. But that's why, he realised, angry, disturbed that he hadn't thought it out before. She came between me and my baser nature — between me and Angela — *because* I love her.

It wasn't an answer, it wasn't a neat

solution that was going to make everything all right in the morning. But, Hal reflected as he walked swiftly back, it was a start. He went quietly along the passage to their room. No light showed around the door, and it would have done had there been any to show; every time he went in or out, Hal amused himself with the thought that there wasn't a lot of point in securing a door which had a gap beneath it you could almost put your hand through. As always in Greece, his perfectionist soul was distressed at the shoddiness of the workmanship. But the irritation always slipped away, after a while.

He closed and locked the door behind him. Jo had opened the window over the alley, and some washing hung on the line outside. Again, the sight brought Angela to mind. He acknowledged her — he couldn't bring himself to ignore her — then, firmly, he made himself think of Jo.

Why did she go to England? he wondered as he cleaned his teeth. She said Copse Hill House needed some decorating, but she has her Mr Tallis to look after that. And leaving the kids with Dad and the MacAllisters — jeez, it's all I can do to persuade her to let *me* look after them while she takes the car to the stores. And, having gone to

England, what the hell made her suddenly announce she was coming out to join me?

He shook his head; he had no answer.

He turned out the bathroom light and went to stand by Jo's bed. She lay curled up on her side, her back to the room, and she had his jacket across her shoulders. He listened to her breathing for some time; she was, he decided, sound asleep. He leaned down to tuck his jacket gently behind her, and, brushing aside her hair, kissed her lightly on the forehead.

'Goodnight, kid,' he whispered. Then, surprising himself with the realisation: 'I'm glad you're here.'

# 13

When Jo woke up in the morning, Hal was still asleep. She lay watching him, reading many different things into his sleeping face and then dismissing most of them as pure fancy. She got up and had a shower, then quietly dressed and made her bed. Then she got out her diary and brought it up to date. That's it, I'm ready for the day now, she thought. I wish Hal would wake up.

She went across to the window, leaning her elbows on the metal rail. Where the sun had caught it, it was already hot. She looked down into the alleyway below. She could smell freshly-baked bread, the appetising aroma making her stomach rumble. She fetched a towel and tried to waft some of the fragrant air into the room.

Hal opened his eyes. 'What the hell are you doing?' he asked.

'Trying to arouse your appetite with the smell of bread. I'm ravenous.'

He grinned. 'After that terrific meal I bought you last night? I don't believe it.'

She put the towel back on a chair. 'How much money have you got?' she asked.

'Not much. How about you?'

'Forty-five drachmas. You can only bring fifteen quid's worth into the country, and I got through most of that yesterday. We'll have to go to the bank.'

'There isn't one here. You'll have to go up to Kea town.'

'I thought this was Kea.'

'No, this is Korissia. Kea town is inland, up the hill. Its proper name is Ioulis, but they seem to refer to it as Kea.'

'Oh,' Jo said. Then, going over what he had said, 'What's this 'you'?'

'You're up and dressed. I'm only just awake.'

'All right. How do I get to Kea town? Can you walk?'

'No, you take a cab. Go and lean on that big grey diesel Mercedes parked across the road, holler '*Stavros!*' a couple of times, and with any luck, a fat man in a stained cardigan will materialise.'

'OK.' She delved into her bag for purse, cheques and passport. 'Twenty-five pounds' worth?'

'Yeah. I have some dollars, you can change fifty of them, too.' He leaned out of bed to reach his wallet, tossing it to her. 'The bank's in a hardware and grocery store. Through the archway, up to the right and it's on your right. *Trapeza* is Greek for bank.'

'*Trapeza*,' she repeated. 'But it'll be written in Greek letters, won't it?'

Hal wrote it out in Greek for her on a piece of paper. 'You'll have to learn the language,' he remarked. 'It'll make our travels in Greece much easier. I'll go find us some breakfast when I get up. See you in the bar at the end.'

She ran down the steps feeling lighthearted and happy. The morning was clear and brilliantly sunny; things appeared to have improved without either herself or Hal actually having done anything. Maybe he just needed a good night's sleep, she thought. The sovereign remedy for everything from a death in the family to a headache.

She crossed the road and found the taxi. She was just gearing herself up to start yelling for Stavros when one of the row of men sitting at the cafe opposite did it for her. In a few minutes, Stavros appeared.

'*Kalimera*,' Jo said.

'*Kalimera*.' He nodded slowly in reply.

'Can you take me to Kea town?' He nodded again. 'Then back here?'

'*Endaxi*.' He opened the door for her.

They drove off along the waterfront, turning left round behind the beach and then forking right inland. Stavros said something to her, in Greek with a few English words, one of which was 'man'. She concluded he was asking where Hal was.

'He's still in bed,' she said, miming sleep by putting her face against her hand and emitting a snore. Stavros laughed.

It was only a short run to Kea town but it was all uphill; she was glad she hadn't had to walk. Stavros waited while she found the bank and got the money; a fat man sitting in an armchair changed Hal's dollars for drachmas and then cashed Jo's cheque, after having glared at it suspiciously for a good half-minute. While he counted out a bundle of dirty notes, she picked up a slim guide to Kea; since it only cost the equivalent of about seventy-five pence, she bought it.

★ ★ ★

Hal was pouring out a cup of tea for her when she joined him in the bar. The sun was already hot, and it was quite warm enough for sitting outside.

'Toast'll be here in a while,' he said.

She handed him his wallet. 'It's all still there,' she said. 'Just the same except quite a lot of dollars are now drachmas.'

'Great. How d'you fancy hiring a bike today and looking round some?'

'A bike?' She thought of the climb they'd had in the taxi to get up to Kea town. 'Isn't it a bit hilly, for bikes?'

'I meant a motor bike,' he said patiently.

'Oh! Yes, that'd be lovely. I've never ridden a motor bike. Have you?'

'Yes, years ago. Reckon you don't forget how.'

'And you could hardly call the traffic a hazard.'

He grinned at her. 'Right. I'll go find us one, after we've eaten. The hire place is up the road.'

'We could get some food and drink, then if we're out in the wilds and get hungry, we'll have it with us.'

'OK.'

'Shall we take swimming things?'

'Sure.'

'Oh! I got this.' She handed him the guidebook. He put on his glasses and began to look at it.

'It has a map,' he said. 'That'll help.' He looked up and grinned at her. His eyes seemed to have lost their puffy redness, although it was hard to tell behind his glasses. But he looks happier, she thought; with or without his glasses, I can see that.

They finished eating, and Jo got up. 'I'll go and get some food and pack it,' she said.

'Right. I'll go get the bike.'

★ ★ ★

She sat on a seat on the waterfront, the picnic, a bottle of water, a small bottle of ouzo, their bathing things and a towel beside her. She heard him coming before she saw him, then began to laugh as he came into view. He grinned back. 'I know,' he said. 'But they don't come any bigger.' His legs looked absurdly long, and he was sitting so far back on the bike's seat that she didn't see how there was going to be room for her.

'You'll have to move forward a bit,' she said, attaching the picnic and the bottles to the carrier on the back. She got on behind him, hitching up her skirt, and he shifted out of her way.

'Better?'

'Not much. But it'll do.'

'Ready, then?'

'Yes.' He revved the throttle till the engine whined and let in the clutch with a jerk. Jo flung her arms round his waist.

'Don't cling on!'

'Well, don't lift it off the ground like that!' She unwrapped her arms, but closed her thighs against his instead. It made her feel more secure; it's like riding a horse, she thought. It'll probably give me stiff muscles by tonight, I haven't ridden for ages.

'OK?' Hal said over his shoulder.

'Wonderful!'

They took the road towards Kea town, from where the map showed another road leading off south-westwards to join the coast further down. As the gradient became steeper, the bike made heavier and heavier weather of the climb.

'You'll have to get off,' Hal said. 'Don't reckon it'll take both of us to the top.'

'OK.' She hopped off while they were still moving, thinking what a neat feat it was, but then Hal stalled the engine and had to stop anyway to kick it back into life.

'See you at the top!' he shouted, and was gone in a whirl of dust and a peace-shattering noise of small labouring engine. She smiled, and started to walk. After a moment she heard a car approaching. Turning, she saw that it was Stavros's grey taxi. He bipped the horn and waved to her through the open window, and she saw him do the same to Hal a bit further up the road. When she caught up with Hal, she was laughing.

'What?' Hal asked, grinning.

'I think you just passed your A-level

in being a Greek male,' she said. 'This morning when he took me up to the bank,' she nodded in the direction of Stavros's slowly-dispersing cloud of dust, 'he asked me where the tall skinny fellow was and I said you were languishing in bed. Now he's seen you sailing happily up the hill on your bike while your woman walks behind. You're probably a total god in his eyes now, he'll tell his grandchildren about you.'

'Thanks,' Hal said modestly.

'You've cracked it, Dimitrios!'

His face changed. He stared at her intently. '*What* did you say?'

She couldn't think for a moment. 'Oh — it was something Ben used to say, when things were going very well.' She watched his face. He looked very serious and withdrawn, as if his thoughts were suddenly far away. After a moment, he shook his head.

'Right. Come on, get back on and we'll hit the road.'

★ ★ ★

Hal drove on down the empty road, temporarily oblivious to the beauty of abundant spring all around. 'You've cracked it, Dimitrios'. It hadn't been Ben's phrase: originally, it had been Hal's. He remembered with total clarity the first time he'd said it. He and Ben had been deep in the Peloponnese, and Hal had noticed how well Ben was adapting to the local way of life. Somebody had just taken him for a Greek, and it had made Hal laugh because it was exactly what he'd been thinking.

'You've cracked it, Dimitrios,' he'd said, 'that guy thought you were a local, he just asked you if the bus had gone yet.'

Ben must have liked the expression. Hal felt surprisingly moved by that. The month they'd spent in the Peloponnese that summer had been the last time he'd seen Ben, and he remembered the trip perfectly. Having his own phrase come back to him now, via Ben using it to Jo and her using it to him, linked the three of them, across time, even across death.

I'd thank Ben for that, Hal thought, if I believed the dead maintain an interest in the living. For an instant, affected by his emotion and by the powerful atmosphere of the deserted island, he almost thought he did.

He became aware of Jo sitting behind him. She'd been humming softly earlier, before he'd made her get off and walk. But now she was silent. He hoped she wasn't worrying over what had made him

withdraw so abruptly. He reached back and
stroked her thigh; her skirt seemed to have
ridden up a very long way. 'Want to swim?'
he enquired.

'Oh! Yes, that'd be lovely.'

They bounced down a track leading to a
stretch of beach. A shuttered hut and some
chained tables and chairs indicated it might
get busy in summer; today it was empty.

'Where is everyone?' Jo wondered, dis-
mounting.

'There's a man digging in his garden.' He
pointed. The man noticed, and waved his
spade at them.

'Damn, you've made him look!' she
protested.

'Does it matter?'

'Yes! I was just about to get into my
bikini.'

'Go behind the rocks.'

'Are you going to swim, too?' she called
out.

Hal, remembering Crete, knew how cold
the sea was. Taking off his shoes, he said, 'I
might.' He watched as she came back across
the sand. Her bikini fitted her beautifully:
taking in her generous breasts, neat waist
and long, well-muscled legs, he realised, with
a faint shock of physical pleasure, that he'd
forgotten how good she looked.

'What are you staring at?'

'You. Come on, let's get our feet wet.'

They walked down hand-in-hand to the water's edge, and a wave lapped up round their ankles. Jo gasped, and took a pace back up the beach. She looked up at him sheepishly. 'We could give it till after we've eaten, couldn't we?' she said. 'It might warm up a bit.'

He laughed. 'Sure. Whatever you say.'

The peace was absolute. It was as if they were the only people on earth. He thought, I'm happy. Jeez, I'm really happy.

Later they spread the towel on the sand and sat down to eat. Jo unpacked the food; she'd bought a bag of olives, and they flicked the stones in a semicircle behind them.

'We'll come back one day,' Hal said. 'There'll be an olive grove here which they'll name after us.'

'Mm.' She seemed deep in thought. He imagined she'd tell him sooner or later what she was thinking about. She did. 'You can really see the appeal of the old religions when you're somewhere like here, can't you?' she said.

'You sure can. Which one in particular?'

'Oh — I was thinking of bulls. It seems totally logical to venerate the bull as the epitome of strength, and vitality, and fecundity. They used to spread the bull's seed on the ground, didn't they, to make the land go on being productive?'

'Right.' What's she been reading? he wondered. Probably one of my books on Crete and the Minoans.

But then she said unexpectedly, 'When I was little, my grandmother gave me a book of myths. There was one about bull worship.' That puts me in my place, Hal thought, duly chastened. 'There was a prince called Theseus, from Troy, and —'

'Athens,' Hal corrected.

' — this prince from Athens,' she shot him a look, 'got sent to Crete, to King Minos, with a group of other young people. They were meant to be sacrificed to the Minotaur, to keep it sweet so it didn't get angry and cause earthquakes, only Theseus was a hero and he killed the beast, then they all escaped.'

'I heard,' he said drily.

'There was quite a lot about bulls and sacrifice,' she went on, ignoring him. 'Of course, it didn't actually go into biological detail, I found that out later, when I read the grown-up version. The Minotaur,' she leaned closer to him, dropping her voice confidingly as if there were hoards of people around to overhear, 'was the result of Queen

Pasiphae's union with a bull. She had this dummy cow, to attract the bull, and she hid inside it and the bull impregnated her. Can you imagine?'

He was on the verge of laughter, wanting to tell her it was only a myth. But she was still very close to him, so close that he could see the fine gold down on the upper curves of her breasts. He felt a surge of desire, as if the ancient perverse passion of a legendary queen had reached out and touched him. Aroused him. He was about to put his arm round her, pull her to him to kiss her. But, unaware, she had moved away.

'Fascinating, isn't it?' she said. He studied her profile; she was gazing out to sea, a dreamy expression on her face.

'Sure.' He pulled his thoughts under control. 'The Theseus legend is big business in Crete. You can almost believe it, when you're in the palace where it happened.' It was the first time he'd mentioned Crete. He sensed a sudden tension between them.

After a pause, she said, 'Was it good?' She was still gazing ahead of her. He waited, but she didn't turn round. The moment ached with suspense.

He said simply, 'It was good. While it lasted.' Then she looked at him, eyes fixed to his so intently that he thought he would have to turn away: But then she smiled very slightly.

'I'm glad.'

He couldn't think what to say. He said nothing.

'Let's go,' she said, getting to her feet in a quick graceful movement. 'I'm thirsty, and you've drunk the last of the water.'

★ ★ ★

She started humming again as they drove off. He felt as if he'd just been put to some test and, against the odds, had passed.

He pointed out to her the flowers that lay like daubs of poster-paint in the grass. Everywhere there was greenness and vitality, a sense of growth that sent the blood pounding. The arid heat of summer was still weeks away; moisture from the winter rains had softened the air, and the land still smelt freshly laundered.

'Like drops of spilled blood, aren't they?' Jo said close to his ear, pointing to the poppies.

He nodded. 'Yeah. And what about the Tyrian purple ones.'

'What purple?'

'Tyrian. They made a dye from it for the exclusive use of kings and queens. If anyone else dared use it they were put to death.'

'Why?'

'Um — probably because it was in short supply.'

'And they made it from those flowers?'

'No, they made it from the murex shellfish.'

'So what's it got to do with these flowers?'

'Absolutely nothing.' He heard her laugh. She said something he didn't catch. It sounded insulting; he heard the words 'pompous git'. He didn't ask her to repeat it.

'Poached eggs,' she said, as they free-wheeled down a hill.

'How's that?'

'The daisies, the ones that point their faces to the sun. They look like poached eggs. I fancy an egg.'

'You can have one for supper.'

'OK. Let's have dinner at the same place tonight, they serve them up in multiples of five there.'

He smiled. Going out to dinner with her — even to a taverna which only had one dish and didn't bother with a menu — was a nice prospect. So was the thought of taking her back to their room afterwards.

He said, 'Whatever you like.'

259

# 14

They roamed the deserted roads and tracks, revelling in the solitude. Passing back through Kea town, they stopped to sit in the shade and drink a couple of ice-cold beers. Hal, thinking back to his resolution not to drink, reflected that it didn't really matter as long as Jo did, too. And, he thought, watching her finish her glass and calmly replenish it out of his bottle, she seems to be getting the taste for it. They watched a youth unloading crates of bottles from a donkey and carry them up a flight of steps.

'Doesn't he know donkeys can climb steps?' Jo said.

'He probably has a kind heart.'

She smiled. 'It's nice to see kindness to animals. It's quite rare, isn't it, outside sentimental places like England.'

'You can afford to be sentimental about your animals when your kids always have plenty to eat,' Hal said. 'Otherwise, it's a question of priorities.'

'Yes. I know.'

A smartly-dressed couple emerged through the archway, looking anxiously around the square. The man's beige linen suit was crumpled; the woman's cream silk dress, which, Hal thought, said 'Paris' as clearly as if she wore a label, had dirty marks on the seat.

'*Il n'est pas ici,*' the woman said, walking with obvious discomfort to look over the low wall down to where the road from Korissia climbed the hill. She was wearing high-heeled shoes. Hal looked down at Jo's worn sandals; her bare feet were filthy. He smiled.

'*Il a dit, une demi-heure,*' the man said, joining her. Their voices grumbled on, and they kept looking at their watches. The man approached Hal and Jo.

''Ave you seen our taxi?'

Hal heard Jo laugh. 'Stavros,' she muttered.

'No,' Hal said, 'we haven't.'

''E said, 'alf 'our, 'e would be 'ere to collect. But . . . ' The man made an expressive Gallic gesture.

'I should have a beer,' Hal advised. 'Could be a long wait.' The man bowed stiffly, and returned to his wife. Their backs were eloquent with disapproval.

Jo leaned close to Hal. 'They think you're letting the side down,' she said. 'Civilised nations ought to insist on punctuality, and not indulge this southern sloppiness.'

Hal took her hand. 'I think you're right.'

He turned to look at her. Her nose had gone pink and her hair was wild from motor bike riding. 'Not that you look particularly civilised,' he added.

'Nor do you. The sleeve's coming off your t-shirt, and you need a haircut.'

'I don't want to be civilised. I like it out here in the wilderness with you.' Her face lit extraordinarily. She leaned over and kissed him.

She pulled away, still looking at him. Then she said softly, 'Me, too.'

They had another couple of beers, then rode on. Jo, who was feeling drunk on sunshine, happiness and beer, didn't care where they went, but Hal wanted to look at some old monastery he'd noticed on the map. But the journey seemed to go on for ever — I wish I'd never shown him the map, she thought, I might have known he'd find some old place he just had to see — and every time they rounded a bend, it was only to see the road extending up and down for a few more kilometers.

'Do you think it's worth it?' she asked Hal, leaning her face against his broad back.

'Yes. We've come this far, we ain't turning back till we've seen it.'

'All right.' She relaxed. Biking was better, she thought, since, by trial and error, Hal had discovered another, lower gear; 'I just knew it had to be there somewhere,' he'd said triumphantly, when five minutes' curse-ridden fiddling about at the foot of an interminable incline had at last resulted in a different, higher-pitched engine note. If Mrs Watson could hear you now, Jo had thought as the echoes of some very colourful language floated away on the air. But it had been worth it; she no longer had to get off for the hills.

'There it is!' Hal shouted suddenly, making her jump. She peered round his shoulder to have a look. White walls surrounded some low buildings, and a small tower topped with a red-painted dome stood over the entrance.

'There don't seem to be many people about,' Jo said doubtfully. The place was deserted.

'They'll be having a siesta,' Hal replied knowledgeably.

'Do monks have siestas?'

'Everybody has siestas.'

They approached the entrance on foot. A heavy brown-painted door was shut tight against them. Hal went to see if it would open. As soon as he rattled the iron door-handle, an invisible ravening hound on the other side erupted into ferocious paroxysms of barking.

'Good God!' Hal said, leaping back and dropping the handle with a thump that sent the hound into further frenzy. He turned to Jo, looking slightly ashamed.

'Guess I didn't want to see the monastery anyway,' he said.

'Nor did I,' she agreed loyally. 'When you've seen one, you've seen them all.'

He came and put his arm round her, leaning against her. 'I'm bushed,' he said. 'We'll go find somewhere quiet and have a siesta of our own.'

'Like the monks.'

'Right.'

'I expect it's all the driving, making you tired.'

'Sure. Nothing to do with the three and a half bottles of beer.'

'It was four.'

'No it wasn't. You had a half of one of them.'

'Oh.'

They went slowly back along the road, looking out for a place to stop. It's all so thorny, Jo thought. You couldn't possibly lie down on that scrub, it'd be like a bed of nails. The sea was a long way below, and the few tracks leading down to it looked very doubtful. They'd almost come to grief once already, when Hal tried to do a wheelie and hit a pothole. Jo reflected that she didn't want to spend the rest of the holiday with anything in plaster. Or anything of Hal's in plaster. She began to giggle. Perhaps Hal had been right about the disputed half-bottle.

'There's a beach,' Hal said, pointing ahead. 'Looks like the road's back by the sea again there.'

The bends unwound, and they found that he was right. They stopped by the road, spread out the towel on a stretch of sand and went to sleep.

Jo awoke to find Hal trying to take the towel from beneath her.

'What's the matter?' she asked dozily.

'We have to get the bike back by five,' he said, 'and I have no idea how far away we are.' She sat up, dazed. Hal reached down and pulled her to her feet. 'I know,' he said, 'I interrupted you in the middle of a fabulous dream.'

She smiled up at him. 'Yes, you did. And I'm not telling.'

They set off, weaving a slightly erratic course. Hal veered from the crown of the road towards the side, and Jo let out a yelp as he swerved into some bushes. 'That was my *knee*,' she complained, rubbing at the bit that had born the brunt. 'I've probably got about seventeen thorns in it now.'

'Sorry,' Hal said. 'I'm still half-asleep.'
'Now's a fine time to tell me.'

★ ★ ★

The man at the bike-hire place didn't bother
to consult his watch when Hal returned the
bike. We didn't have to hurry after all, he
thought. The man asked if they'd had a
good day.

'We had a terrific day,' Hal replied. He
paid what he owed and departed. Jo had
gone on ahead to get them a cup of tea,
and he wanted to be back with her. She'd
just told him an extremely rude joke, and
he wanted to hear if she had any more. He
could see her as he walked towards the bar,
sitting with her knee up picking at it.

'It's at least seventeen thorns,' she said.
'Have you got any tweezers?'

'Not with me. I have some in my bag.'
He put on his glasses and inspected her
knee. 'I don't see any thorns,' he said after
a while.

'You're blind as a bat. Run your finger
over there — ouch, don't press so hard!'

He saw what she was complaining about.
He managed to extract most of the thorns
between his finger and thumb nails, laying
them neatly in a row on the table. 'You'd

better wash it well,' he said solicitously. 'It might swell up.'

She raised her eyes to his. 'A girl can live in hope.'

He watched her. Several thoughts ran swiftly through his head. He winked at her. 'Have another cup of tea, kid.'

They returned to their room, and Hal lay on his bed and read while Jo had a shower, calling out progress reports on how much her knee was hurting. And her sunburnt nose. And her thigh muscles.

'I'm beginning to think you're regretting your day,' he remarked.

Her face appeared around the bathroom door. 'Not entirely,' she said, then closed herself in again. They had discovered that the shower soaked the entire end of the bedroom if they didn't firmly close the door. He smiled. He had been going to take a shower too, but it was so comfortable lying where he was that he thought he'd postpone it till later. Then they could go eat all the sooner.

'I'm hungry,' he called.

'Ten minutes,' she called back. 'Twenty at the outside. Do you want to go on and be having a beer? Another beer?'

'I shall go watch the ferry come in,' he announced. 'I don't want to miss the big excitement of the day.'

'All right.' She opened the door. She'd finished with the shower. 'Funny, isn't it, how you adapt. In Lavrion it looked like a piddling little ferry-boat. But here, where everything's relatively further down the scale, it's like watching the QE2 sail in, with Marine bands and bunting and streamers.'

'They only have streamers when a ship's leaving,' he said pedantically. 'So that the strips of paper can gradually tear apart and fall into the water as the ship sails away.'

'Better save yours for the morning, then,' she said.

'Shall we go back to the mainland, tomorrow?' he suggested on impulse.

She considered. 'I suppose we've seen Kea now. All right, I don't mind.'

'I'll check the timetable, see what time it leaves in the morning.' He got up from his bed, pulling a sweater from his bag. 'You'll be wanting my jacket again,' he said. Then he blew her a kiss and went out.

★ ★ ★

'Seven o'clock,' he said as she came to join him in the taverna a little later. 'We'll have to be up early.'

'I did my packing just now.' She smiled

268

at him in satisfaction. 'I can't get over how lovely it is travelling light. How far could we go, do you think, with just a change of clothes and a sponge-bag?'

'Everywhere.' He grinned back at her. 'I can kiss goodbye to my rucksack, then.'

'Yes. I'll buy you another one, if you like.'

He looked over to the kitchen. There were several different pans of food cooking tonight. 'Looks like we'll have a choice,' he said.

'We've proved our staying power with the spaghetti. We're now old and valued customers.'

'Pity we're leaving tomorrow.'

The mournful proprietor invited them to look at what was available. They thought they'd have some of everything, and ended up with moussaka, bean and potato stew and a big mixed salad. 'Don't you want your five eggs?' Hal asked.

'I've gone off the idea.'

'I always said you were fickle.'

'Not fickle,' she said thoughtfully. 'Faddy, maybe, but not fickle. Let's have some more retzina,' she added enthusiastically. 'I've only had half a bottle so far.'

'And you've been in Greece for two days. We'd better have quite a lot, then.'

He wondered later where she'd heard all the jokes. She remembered a whole lot more, as the retzina loosened her up.

'Who have you been under the table with?' he enquired.

'Tom,' she said. 'Not right under it, just a little way.'

'Right. I thought I'd heard the one about the constipated Welsh miner before.'

'He says I'm showing a sense of humour, now I've stopped being so anxious.'

Hal mulled over that for a while. It raised several interesting points. 'I thought you always did have a sense of humour,' he said eventually. 'But I agree about you being less anxious.' He decided to let drop the question of which table she and Tom had been half-under. He didn't think he had any right to question her behaviour. 'There's something different about you, kid.' He stared at her intently across the table, and she stared right back.

'Your eyes are slightly crossed,' she observed. 'I've never noticed that before.'

'It's yours that are crossed,' he replied, amused. They were; it made her look like a Siamese cat. He'd always loved Siamese cats.

'Why am I different? Is it just the boss eyes?'

'No. You've been different all day, and your eyes only crossed with the second bottle of retzina.'

'What, then?'

He considered. He couldn't put it into words. Not yet. And he wondered if he'd really want to, if he were sober. 'I don't know. I'll have to work on it.'

She leaned back, and yawned hugely. 'Sorry,' she said. 'It's all catching up with me suddenly. Shall we go?'

'OK.'

She put her arm round him as they left, her head dropping in an affectionate, familiar way onto his shoulder. He noticed several interested glances, which at first he took for amusement. Then he realised that nobody except him knew how much she'd had to drink. They think we're going off to bed together, he thought. They're probably glances of envy.

They ambled along to their room, and he felt a slight regret that they'd be leaving the next day. Strange, how quickly a place became home when you were travelling and not staying anywhere for more than a few days. Jo went into the bathroom, and he heard her vigorously cleaning her teeth.

'Reckon I'll take a shower,' he said as she emerged.

She smiled at him over the towel she was using to wipe her face. 'All right.'

The water was hot, and he managed to soak everything in the bathroom. He was in a hurry, though, and couldn't wait to mop it all up. He thought, I'll leave the door ajar, it'll dry by morning. He went back into the bedroom, wearing only a towel round his waist. Jo was standing by the window in a striped nightshirt, combing her hair. He went up behind her and put his arms round her. She leaned against him.

'Hello,' she said softly.

'Hi.'

He turned her gently round, and studied her face. 'You've lost your squint,' he remarked. 'Pity, I was beginning to like it.'

'Perhaps you should rush out and buy me another bottle of retzina.'

He bent to kiss her. 'I ain't rushing anywhere,' he said in her ear. Then he kissed her again. She pressed her body against him, and he felt himself stir. The towel seemed in danger of falling off.

There was the sound of voices in the alleyway. The volume increased until it couldn't be ignored. Heavy feet sounded on the steps, and at least three doors opened and banged shut. Then they opened again, and there was a lot of conversation in Greek.

He could feel Jo shaking. 'What's up, kid?' He thought she was crying, but realised it was laughter.

She shook her head. 'We seem to have company.'

He thought of the ill-fitting doors, and the flimsy walls. Privacy, the build-up of passion, had been violently disrupted. Then somebody broke wind loudly just outside their door, and he felt Jo quiver all over with suppressed laughter. 'They don't realise we're here!' she whispered when she could speak.

'No, I'm sure they don't.' He was laughing himself at the absurdity of it. 'It's the ferry-boat crew, they stay here overnight when there's an early crossing in the morning.'

'Do you think they'll be farting all night?' He'd forgotten how infectiously she laughed.

'Oh, yes,' he said, determined to egg her on, 'they'll fart, belch, hawk and spit out of the windows, then eventually they'll settle down to sleep and that's when we get our big chance, because they'll give us a fifteen minute respite till the first of them starts snoring.' She sank onto her bed, wiping tears from her eyes. She looked up at him, love and laughter blending endearingly in her face. He went to sit beside her, and took hold of her hand. He smoothed her hair back, its texture a familiar sensation to his skin.

'Come and lie in my bed,' he said. 'You can tell me some more about Theseus and his pals till we fall asleep.'

# 15

It was only just getting light when Jo woke up. She had been disturbed by some anonymous hand knocking loudly on the crew members' doors, and hoarse voices shouting in Greek. A few minutes later — Greek ferry crew clearly didn't bother with such niceties as shaving or showering — they all clumped off down the steps.

She felt heavy-eyed and slightly hung-over. It had been a restless night, what with the comings and goings from down the corridor and her own uncontrollable giggling. Hal had fallen asleep quickly, despite the snoring that could have been in the same room, and after a while she had crept out of his arms and gone to sleep in her own bed.

She got up and had a cool shower, which did quite a lot to dispel her headache. Then she dressed and began to pack the rest of her things.

'Wake up,' she said, going across to give Hal a nudge. He groaned and pulled the pillow over his head. She leaned down and hugged both him and the pillow. 'I've finished in the shower, you can go in now.'

He uncovered one eye and looked up at her. 'I have no sympathy for you,' she said sternly. 'I've made it out of bed, so can you.'

'You're a hard woman,' he grumbled.

'I know.'

There was a polite tap on the door. Jo went to open it; an old man stood outside. He addressed her in Greek.

'Sorry, I don't understand.' she said. 'Hal, what's he saying?'

Hal sat up. 'He's our landlord. He probably wants some money.'

'How did he know we were going this morning?' Jo asked as Hal handed her the notes he'd counted out of his wallet. 'Is that all it is? Goodness, it *is* cheap.' She gave the notes to the old man, who thanked her and disappeared.

'It's a small community,' Hal said. 'Everybody knows everything. Especially about the doings of the only two tourists in town.'

'Oh, God. How awful.'

He grinned at her, stopping to give her a quick kiss as he passed by into the bathroom. 'Means you have to live a blameless life,' he said.

'No good for us, then.'

They went down to the quay. Jo stood looking along the waterfront. Only two days, she thought — less really, because I didn't get here till evening — and already it's become special, and I don't want to leave. Hal had gone on board the ferry ahead of her, to find a place to stow their bags, and for a moment she was alone. Her eyes misted, and the peaceful scene, brilliant in the sharp morning light, went fuzzy. It's a sort of libation, she reflected, to shed tears on leaving. It's a tribute to how happy you've been in a place. And I've been happy here. She turned and headed for the ferry. What next? Will this pleasure in being together prove only transient? We're going back to the mainland, back to the ordinary world, leaving our desert island. She was suffering from a sudden loss of confidence. She tried to jerk herself out of it: it's probably just that I need some breakfast.

'We'll watch Kea disappear,' Hal said as she joined him on deck; he'd been looking out for her, wondering what was taking her so long. 'It looks great in this dawn light.' She went and stood close beside him. He noticed that she seemed solemn. He put his arm round her.

She said, quite cheerfully, 'There's a snack-bar downstairs.'

'Below.'

'All right, below. We could have a cup of tea, in a minute.'

'Sure.' Another way you've changed, kid, he thought. A while back, you'd have been crying. He found himself hoping her spontaneous response to situations that affected her wasn't gone for ever. It was one of the things he'd first loved about her.

The ferry rounded the headland that shut Kea away from the eyes of the world. It's as if it never was, Hal thought. Maybe it wasn't. Maybe it existed as a place for us, to give us the right environment for a crucial time in our lives. Now that we've finished with it, it's gone back into the abyss. Till the next time someone needs it.

'Tea,' Jo said, prosaically shattering his fancies. 'I can't wait another minute.' They went below, and sat at a small bar with cups of tea made with tea bags and evaporated milk. 'Surprising what you can get used to,' Jo remarked. 'I think I'll have another one.'

They watched other customers satisfying different requirements. A member of the crew came and drank a glass of ouzo, and, seeing their eyes on him, gave them a truculent 'sod you!' look and downed another.

'Such panache!' Jo said admiringly. 'You can just see them doing that on Sealink.'

'Right. And he's the purser, too.'

'Is he? Oh, I don't think so, he had a dreadful old pair of trousers on, and anyway . . . ' She caught his eye, and he couldn't help smiling. 'Rotter,' she muttered.

'D'you want any more cups of tea, or shall we go and watch our arrival in Lavrion?'

'I've had enough, thank you. Let's go upstairs.' She glanced at him. 'Aloft.'

They leaned on the starboard rail, watching as the ferry sailed past the ruins of a foundry and a collection of derelict ships rusting and listing gently, trickling corruption into the clear water. Hal wondered how the sea managed to keep its pure beauty under such an onslaught. It should have been despoiled by all those piles of rotting metal, yet there it was, still lovely, despite man's best efforts to violate it. It was the contrast of Greece, he thought, his mind going back to a theme he'd been turning over on and off for days. You despair at the slackness, the 'it'll-do' mentality, yet at the same time it's exactly that easy-going quality which makes life here so appealing. And then you think back to Greece in her time of greatness — when Pericles built the Parthenon, for instance — and you wonder if Phidias had to holler at his workmen to make them use their plumb lines. He wanted to write out his thoughts, but his notebook was down in the hold, tucked away in his bag. When we get to Lavrion, he promised himself. If I can grab a half-hour.

Jo was proving as much a disruption to his writing as Angela had been. He wondered how Angela was. Her image was receding as he made fewer efforts to recall her. He was stricken with guilt at letting her memory fade and guilt at trying to keep it fresh.

The ferry manoeuvred so that it approached the slip backwards, and the seaman they had watched drinking his breakfast came to supervise tying-up. The ship came to rest at a sight angle to the slipway, and he shouted a long string of instructions to the bridge. They moved a few yards away from the quay and made another approach, but it wasn't any better.

'Maybe they've all been on the ouzo,' Hal said.

'Perhaps a five degree angle is good going, for the seven am sailing,' Jo said, starting to laugh. 'We should have score-cards. You know, like judges at skating competitions before it went computerised — they used to shuffle out onto the ice in bulky overcoats and woolly hats and hold up the marks. Five point three from the French judge.'

'Four point five from the American judge,'

Hal said. 'The vehicles will all have to take a run at the ramp.'

'I don't think I want to watch. Let's go.'

They left the quay and went into the centre of Lavrion, where they sat down at a pavement café for breakfast. 'We have to decide where we're going,' Hal said, 'so we may as well eat while we're looking at the map.' Jo thought she'd like a toasted marmalade sandwich, and Hal opted for a cheese and ham one. 'You go order,' Hal said. 'Good practice for your I-can-make-out-in-Greece attitude.'

'Fine.' She got up and walked into the bar, returning with a big smile. 'Dead easy,' she said. 'Can't think why anyone makes a fuss about Greek.'

'Well done,' Hal said. But when the food arrived, both the sandwiches were ham and cheese. He squeezed her hand. 'Never mind. I'm not so sure I can recall the Greek for marmalade either.'

When they'd eaten, she suddenly leaped up and hurried off. Something I said? Hal wondered mildly. He watched as she disappeared into a shop, then, shortly afterwards, returned.

'Postcards,' she said, holding them out. '*And* stamps — I remembered the word.'

'For the kids,' he said.

'Of course. Here, you start Sammie's, I'll start Edmund's. Then we'll swap and do the second half of each other's.' She began to write; he envied her ability to commit words to paper instantly, without any of the preliminary deliberations he had to go through. I can't even write a damn postcard without ten minutes' preparation, he thought, trying to think what to say that could possibly mean anything to his two-year-old son.

'Hurry up,' she said, waving Teddy's postcard at him. 'I've done mine.'

'But you don't — ' he began. Then stopped. Why take offence? he demanded silently. She didn't mean any. 'OK.' Meekly he put on his glasses and wrote, 'Dear Sammie, The sea is as blue as your paddling pool. Your Mom and I went out on a motor bike and we didn't fall off once. We went on a big ferry-boat which had a picture of a seagull on its funnel.'

'Did it?' She was reading as he wrote.

'Did it what?'

'Have a seagull on the funnel.'

'Yep.'

She looked at him admiringly. 'Goodness, aren't you observant? I didn't notice.' Mollified, he reached out for Teddy's card.

Finishing, he glanced up at her. She had a faraway look in her eyes. 'D'you miss them?'

'Yes. Do you?'

He hesitated. The honest answer was, not very much. But would that brand him as heartless? Not a good idea, when they were getting on so well. But he had to admit — to himself, anyway — that the intrusion created by thinking of the kids had altered the mood. Not necessarily for the better.

'Do you?' she repeated.

'In a way,' he hedged. 'But then they're not so central a part of my life as they are of yours.'

She muttered, 'Tell me about it.'

He thought he should change the subject. 'We should take a look at the temple of Poseidon while we're here,' he said, spreading out the map. 'There it is,' he pointed, 'at Sounion.'

'OK.' She didn't sound too keen. 'Is there a bus?'

'Yes. The temple's on a wonderful site, on top of a headland,' he went on, trying to interest her. 'And it's relevant to what I've been doing. The Bull as a religious symbol for the Minoans — your Minotaur again — then the Bull as Poseidon's creature.' He'd thought that would gain her attention, but he was surprised to see her face fall deeper into despondency. He was about to ask what was up when she spoke.

'Fine, we'll arrange it so you get some working time,' she said hurriedly. 'Will there be hotels open, do you think?'

He shrugged. 'Maybe. If not, we'll travel on till we find one that is.'

Buses ran quite frequently along the coast to Sounion; the journey didn't take long. Although it proved to be a small place, there were two hotels. One, down on the beach, looked deserted, but the other, standing above the shore, had a notice saying *Open All Year*. They went into the foyer, and a friendly woman offered them a double room. 'For you, special rate.' She handed them a key, and gave directions. Then she smiled at them indulgently and went back into her office.

The room proved to be right at the back of the hotel, in a separate block that stood apart from the main building. They were on the top floor. 'She must have thought we wanted privacy,' Jo said. 'I wonder why?'

'Must be the way we look at each other.'

'Oh!' He smiled to himself. He always enjoyed the slight pause, when he'd said something she didn't expect, between her hearing it and her reaction.

'What d'you want to do?' he asked

when they'd finished the small amount of unpacking.

'Mm. I don't want to eat, do you?'

'No.'

'Temple, then?'

He went to look out from the balcony. The view was wonderful. In the foreground was an olive grove, beyond it the sweep of the bay. Beyond that was the jutting headland, dense green with spring grass. On top of it, above the navy-blue sea, stood the temple of Poseidon. Tiny with distance, it looked like an ivory carving. He could make out a string of tour buses slowly climbing up the road to the headland.

'It's crowded right now. Come take a look.'

She came out on to the balcony. 'Yes. I see what you mean.'

'We'll go have a beer on the beach, and go up later.'

'OK.'

★ ★ ★

There was a bar down on the beach, beside the path that led to the deserted hotel. They sat down, and after a while a young man came out and asked them what they would like. They had two bottles of beer, and a little later, two more. They were the only customers. It seemed like a sort of heaven, a continuation of their Kea privacy, to be sitting comfortably in the shade in the middle of an Aegean spring day, together, deep in conversation, with cold beer for the asking. With the posting of the boys' cards, Hal realised guiltily, he'd managed to put them right out of his mind again. He wondered if Jo had. I doubt it, he thought. But she seems to have a facility for having them live in one compartment of her head while letting the rest of her get on with whatever she's doing. He watched her; she was telling him about having supper with the Hawkhurst neighbours. Her face was vivid with amusement, and he couldn't help laughing with her.

Why is it different? Hal wondered. This is the same woman I was only too pleased to leave behind me less than a month ago. But here, now, I wouldn't be with anyone else. I'd sooner be on my own than with anyone but her. He watched her face as she spoke. She'd gone on to talk animatedly about the house, what she'd done to it, and about someone called Reggie who had helped. She became aware that he wasn't answering, and paused in mid-sentence, her eyes meeting his questioningly.

'What is it?'

'Nothing. I was just enjoying hearing you talk.'

'Oh!' She seemed surprised, then frowned slightly. 'Was I holding the floor, then?' she asked.

He said, suppressing a smile, 'Yes. I don't talk much.'

Her eyes flew wide open. 'Oh, you *do*! There's a row of donkeys over there missing a back leg, and I haven't been talking to myself all this time! For the past few minutes, perhaps, but that's all.'

'Well, I don't talk as much as you.' He glanced at her mischievously. 'Nobody talks as much as you.'

'In that case I shall stop.' She folded her arms, turning to stare haughtily out to sea.

'Don't stop, sweetheart,' Hal said, leaning over to kiss her ear. She started to smile, then unfolded her arms and shoved him away.

★ ★ ★

'You're out of condition,' she remarked as they trudged up the scrubby hillside to the headland. The afternoon was half over; there were only a couple of coaches left in the carpark below the temple.

'I'm older than you.'

287

'True. You get less exercise, too, sitting at a desk all day. You should try having children.'

'I thought I had.'

'Yes, but like most fathers, you only have them very part-time. I meant, you should try having them to look after constantly.' He had no answer. She was making a totally reasonable point. But he wished she hadn't, not then. It made him feel depressed.

'D'you want a guidebook?' he asked as they bought tickets.

'Yes, please.'

He wanted to recapture the mood of half an hour ago, but had no idea how to. Jo read her guidebook, walking ahead of him up the path. He went after her; there was nothing else he could do. The crowds had thinned and there were only a few people about. Jo and Hal walked around the temple in silence, letting its impression sink into them. Then he felt her take his hand.

'Let's go and sit in the sun,' she said. 'My neck's aching from looking upwards.'

'OK.' He put his arm round her, and they stepped down to a shelf of rock that spread out a few feet down the headland, right over the sea. Jo lay on her back, her head on a hillock of grass, her arm across her face. After a while, he realised she'd gone to sleep.

He stared out to sea. The surface was agitated and restless, and waves broke with some force against the rocks at the cliff's foot. The water seemed to swell in a great current into the bay, and the mood was different from the Aegean tranquility he'd become used to. He thought about Poseidon, and imagined the building of the temple, the selection of this as the site for the god's most important centre of worship. He had come out without his notebook, and, irritated with himself, he concentrated on the tentative outline he was forming for the last chapter of his book. If I fix onto it, he thought, maybe I'll hold it until I can write it down. Frustrated, because whole sentences were flashing into his mind and he ached to write them down, he turned his full concentration inwards. He became aware that Jo was sitting up beside him. She yawned, and said something about going back.

'Yeah,' Hal said absently. She laughed, and he turned to her, frowning.

'That should have been a 'no' answer,' she said. 'I said, we'd better not stop at that bar on the way home or else we'd never get back in time for dinner.'

'Right.' He was mentally writing the last paragraph. It was proving difficult: he had two opposing ideas to summarise together.

Jo stood up, brushing herself down. 'I'll tell you what, Hal, we won't talk again until *you* feel like it. We'll make an appointment, if you like.' Her voice was light, but he sensed an edge of irritation in her. He was about to tell her what was absorbing him, but her face was set and she didn't look too approachable. OK, he thought, OK.

They walked back in silence, and, once in their room, Jo said she was going to have a bath. He heard the running water and the splashing for a long time in his subconscious as he sat on the balcony, writing with a speed and fluency that made him quite sure he was on to something good.

Some time later, he sat back with a sigh of pleasure, raising his arms above his head and stretching his back. He hadn't realised how tensely he'd been crouching over the table, which was too low for someone as tall as himself to write on. He wondered if Jo'd give him a massage. She had strong hands, and he loved to feel her working on him.

'Is the water hot?' he asked, walking into the bedroom. Jo was lying on the bed reading.

'Mm.'

He went and knelt down beside her, trying to look into her face. 'Will you talk to me now?' he asked penitently. 'I'm through writing.' She raised her head from her book and stared coolly at him. Her eyes looked very green against her tanned skin. Hal thought suddenly of icy water, frozen into emerald in the cold heart of a glacier.

'I'm not through with reading,' she said quietly. 'Why don't you go and have a bath?'

He watched her, rejoinders of a greater and lesser friendliness running through his head. Then he got up. 'OK.' He thought ruefully as he turned on the hot tap — which burped, spat, then let out a trickle of cold — I guess the massage is out of the question.

\* \* \*

Jo was sitting on the bed making up her face when Hal emerged from the bathroom. He brought with him a smell of soap and aftershave. Glancing at him in the mirror, she noticed that his body above the bathtowel was still damp. He was brown from his weeks in the sun — he didn't get that tan wandering around museums, she thought — and she wished she didn't find him so fiercely attractive. It's not fair, she cried inside, it gives him such a weapon, that I want him so much. She looked sideways at him again, turning back to her mirror as he looked over and caught her eye. I don't want to be sweet and nice, she thought angrily. I don't want to be someone he can talk and laugh with when he feels like it and ignore when he doesn't. But what do I do? We're here, two of us alone, and there's not much future in a long drawn-out silence.

'Those are nice,' she said conversationally as he put on a pair of cream trousers. 'Are they new?'

He looked up, surprised. Then he replied, in a similarly light tone, 'Yeah. I got them in Heraklion. They all wear them.' He struggled with the top two inches of the zip. 'Guess I must have put on a couple of pounds.' Jo watched him. She could see what he meant. She smiled.

'Yes, they are a bit form-fitting. Nice, though.' She thought for a minute. 'Men do it on purpose, don't they?'

'What?' She felt embarrassed. Silly, she thought, with Hal. But somehow it was significant, this feeling that there were things she was reluctant to say to him.

'Well, wear trousers that — er — show a bulge.'

Hal stared at her. 'No!' he said indignantly. 'No way! OK?'

'Yes, OK.' But a devil had been raised in her. She didn't want to be dismissed when she had more to say. 'Men ogle women, stare at their breasts and their bums,' she said angrily. 'So why is it so wrong if women look at men's bulges, especially if they're deliberately wearing tight trousers to display it all?'

The mood changed in a flash as a grin spread across Hal's face. Jo realised achingly that it was Hal's moods that set the mood between them. Never her own.

'They don't, do they?' He was laughing.

'Don't what?'

'Ogle. Women don't really ogle men's — bulges.'

'Of course they do.'

'God, Jo, I don't want to know that! I'll never wear these again.'

'Oh, I should. Shame to waste a new pair of trousers.' She stood up. 'Shall we go down? I'm ready.'

'OK.'

He moved to stand in front of her, and she knew he was going to kiss her. She stood aside. He looked at her, his face puzzled.

'What is it? What's upsetting you?' She felt desolate. She had so much to say, and yet it was all so nebulous, so hard to pin down, that she had no idea where to start.

'I wish I could feel you really want to know.'

He sighed. 'Obviously I want to know, or I wouldn't have asked.' Oh, Hal, she thought, you're all heart. She tried again.

'It's just that — I get tired of you being so — so — impenetrable. You're happy, and it's fine and dandy, we're all happy. But when you're not, when you don't feel like communicating, when you're preoccupied or tired, or fed-up, you are just that, and you never seem to think that perhaps you could make a bit of an effort for my sake. For all our sakes, when we're at home. But then you'd probably say, why is it getting you down? It's nothing to do with you.'

'Right. It's not.'

'*Yes it is!*' She surprised herself with her vehemence. 'When I'm with you, we're together, we're two, and our individual moods make the big mood that exists between us. And if you've decided to retreat into yourself, then how can I alone make the mood better?'

'You can't. You just have to let me get on with it.'

'You think I don't know that? I don't give up on many things, Hal, but by God I know when I'm beaten!'

She'd had no intention of making a scene. She had a frightening sense that things had raced away out of her control, and she wanted to rein in. But she couldn't. She picked up her bag, tucked it under her arm, then flung the door open and went out. Banging it behind her, hearing Hal's shout of '*Jo!*' ringing in her ears, she ran off along the corridor and down the stairs.

# 16

Hal listened to Jo's running footsteps until he could no longer make them out. No way am I going after her, he thought, his anger rising as surprise at her abrupt departure lessened.

He went out on to the balcony, and saw her emerge from the building. She hurried on down towards the road, and for a while he lost sight of her. Then she reappeared, and he watched as she stood waiting to cross the road. She ran down the slope towards the beach, then along the sand in the direction of the far headland. She's going back to the temple, Hal thought. Let her. Let her sit up there sulking like a kid.

'Goddam it, what the hell are you doing?' he shouted out across the distance between them, although she couldn't possibly have heard. 'If you want to chew me out, *do* it, don't run away!'

He went back into the room. On the dressing table was a bottle of ouzo they'd brought with them from Kea, a quarter full, beside it a tumbler. He poured a large measure, adding a splash of water and watching the liquid go cloudy. 'Crazy woman,' he muttered. 'What do we do now?'

He was still knocked sideways by her action. He'd known her lose her temper before, sure, and he'd heard her hollering at the kids, or at inanimate objects that refused to do what she wanted. But he realised with a chill that this was the first time she'd shouted at him.

He lay down on the bed, thinking over what they had been saying immediately before she stormed out. Impenetrable, am I? he thought. No I'm not. I just work hard. I don't make an effort for her? Yes I do. Don't I?

He shook his head and drank some more ouzo. It wasn't just that last exchange. Something must have been brewing all day. He recalled that he'd been preoccupied with the ideas for the ending of his book that had suddenly clarified in his head. Maybe I stopped talking to her for a while, sure. But she's used to that, she knows that's how I work. She has no reason to start taking it personally, it's not because of anything she's done.

His mind was sending him red-alert signals. He began to get the feeling that he was almost on to something; a reason not only for this most recent outburst of hers but for a lot of the unhappiness in the months leading up to it. He frowned, trying to grasp the thought that was whispering in the corner of his mind. But it wouldn't come into focus. It was too nebulous, too convoluted, to pin down. Swearing in frustration, he finished the bottle — he'd never drunk neat ouzo before, it packed quite a punch — and went out of the room.

★ ★ ★

Jo ran past the taverna where they'd sat and talked earlier — don't stop, don't think about that — and down on to the beach. It was difficult, running in sand, and she slowed to a trot and then to a breathless walk. She looked up at Poseidon's temple high above her. I'll go up there. It'll be calming, sitting quietly up there.

She put herself at the hill like a hunter following the pack. By the time she was at the top she was panting and aching, and her legs were bleeding from numerous gorse scratches. She stopped to get her breath back, then got some drachmas out of her bag and bought an entry ticket for the site. The sun was setting, and most of the trippers had gone home. She wandered about the headland, not in a mood for the temple itself. She knew she wouldn't be able to stand there without hearing Hal's voice, without seeing it through his well-informed eyes. Oh, *God*, she thought, too much of Hal's influence, bending me to his way of thinking even though he would never say that that had been his intention, never be pleased that he'd succeeded. Too detached for that, aren't you, Hal? Let no-one suggest that it *matters* to you whether someone sees it your way or not.

She followed the rocky path that led around the headland, then stopped at last, tired, sweaty and dusty, flinging herself down among the tall grasses and the wild flowers. She sat with her knees drawn up, arms tightly folded around them and her head bent down to rest on top. The flowers were beginning to close their faces, and she wished she could close up too. How nice it would be, to put everything away until the sun came up tomorrow.

She sat for a long time. Children run away and hide, she thought, hoping that someone will come and look for them, then they can reveal self-righteously what grievance made them dash off. Is that what I'm doing? I hope not, I'd be wasting my time. Suddenly she remembered Elowen speaking to her when, an angry seven-year-old, she'd tried to storm off in a huff. 'The trouble with flouncing out,' Elowen'd said, 'is that, sooner or later, you have to flounce back again. And that's not easy'.

Jo smiled at the memory. Then, the smile fading, thought, there isn't the remotest possibility that Hal will come after me. He'll have gone down to dinner, he'll have chosen what he wants, and he'll be sitting there eating quite calmly. When I eventually go back, he'll just say, 'You missed your dinner. Did you have a good walk?'

Do I go back, then?

The moment was crucial. It wasn't just going back to today, to the present. If she went back, it meant she was going back to Hal, tacitly acknowledging that she accepted things as they were. I can't change anything, she thought with a piercing pain. He's the way he is, and I have to take him like that or not take him at all. Suddenly she knew exactly what had upset her so much: even after the happiness and the togetherness of the lovely day on Kea, today he could revert to his usual self, retreat into his thoughts just as he'd always done.

Less than twenty-four hours after yesterday.

Alone in the fast-fading light, she laid her face back down on her arms and wept.

After a while she stopped. What's the use?

she thought wearily. There's no point in railing against it. People are as they are, and we have the option of accepting them or buggering off.

Shall I bugger off? Shall I go back to the room, pack my rucksack — Hal's rucksack — catch the bus to Athens and fly back to San Francisco? I could collect the boys and take them to England, where I have a beautiful house that's waiting for us to live in it. I could leave word for Hal, and inform him calmly that I have decided he and I can never make each other happy because we understand different things by 'happy'.

And how would life be in England without him, in that same beautiful house, that I worked on so hard? Images of the rooms flashed before her. New colours, new furnishings, not feminine and frilly but subtle with splashes of strong colour, the sort of things you'd choose for a man and a woman living together. Was that why I did it? Is it so obvious? Was that why Jenny and Tom said, almost in passing, that it'd be nice to have us back? Both of us?

It's all just more running away, she thought in despair. I was miserable in San Francisco, so I ran away to Cannes with the boys and Mum and Dad. Then I got a bit braver — perhaps also a bit more desperate — and

I ran away to England on my own. I can't go on shedding people, and I don't think I can go on running away. She saw with sharp clarity that she couldn't go to live in England on her own. Not yet, anyway. Not until she had first talked it all out with Hal, and then only if running away to England emerged as the only thing she could do.

She stood up. It was quite dark now, and she realised the site must be locked up for the night. She wondered how she was going to find her way over the rocky, uneven ground, how she was going to get out with the gates locked. Sod it, I'll manage, she thought, cross with herself for being sidetracked onto unimportant issues when so much lay ahead requiring her total concentration. She smiled slightly, amused despite herself. We are ridiculous, we humans.

She set off back towards the hotel. What will Hal say? How will he react to . . . To what? She hadn't a clue where she was going to start. But it doesn't matter, she thought. It matters that I begin. The rest will come. I hope.

★ ★ ★

Hal wasn't in their room. She hadn't expected him to be, but she wanted the morale boost of washing her face and hands, wiping the dried blood off her legs, combing her hair. She'd decided she'd take a heartening slug of the ouzo, too, but found the bottle empty on the floor. She took a deep breath to try to steady her erratic heartbeat, then went downstairs.

He wasn't in the restaurant, either. She went into the bar, but it was empty except for a grey-haired couple in the corner who looked up and wished her good evening. She went out on to the terrace. The lights were dim out there, covered with red shades that cast a slightly diabolic glow. There were quite a few people, talking and laughing. Then, in the far corner, she caught sight of Hal.

She walked over to him. He looked different, in the strange light. His features looked — disordered, she thought. He stared up at her, his face unmoving. She realised with a slight shock that for the first time ever, she was seeing him really drunk. They'd been drinking a lot since she'd arrived, yes, but this was something else. She glanced again at the row of empty glasses that he had lined up neatly in front of him.

'Well, hi,' he said. 'Why don't you sit down?' He kicked out a chair for her, violently so that the noise it made turned heads.

She lifted her chin. 'No thanks,' she said

frostily. 'There's not a lot of point in staying if you're drunk.' She turned to go. His hand shot out and, with a grip on her wrist like handcuffs, he stopped her.

'Oh, no you don't,' he said smoothly. 'You're not leaving.'

She glared down furiously at him. 'Let me go!' she hissed. He went on staring at her impassively, and his grip tightened.

'What are you going to do?' he asked. 'Plenty of folks about; someone'll come running if you cry for help.'

She said fiercely, 'I fight my own battles!' and saw the grin spread across his face. You *knew*, you bastard! she thought wildly. You knew how I'd react if you challenged me. She sat down, and Hal released her arm.

'What'll you have?' he asked.

'Coffee.' He caught the waiter's eye, and ordered coffee and two brandies. 'I don't want brandy,' she said.

'You'll have it. It'll help.' Help what? she wondered.

The drinks arrived. The waiter, after eyeing them curiously, left them alone.

'I have to talk to you,' Hal said. She didn't answer. 'We have to put some things straight. Then we have to see if we go on with this.' She felt a shiver inside. It was one thing to have doubts herself, to think calmly, do I want to stay with Hal or don't I? But it was another thing entirely to have him expressing the same misgivings.

'Yes, I agree,' she heard herself say.

'Have some brandy.' Hal pushed the glass at her. 'I find you easier to communicate with when you're tight.'

'It's simpler for you than for me, then,' she said angrily. 'I have to wait till you're not only sober — which hasn't been easy, recently — but also have your mind free of all your other concerns that come before me before *you're* easy to communicate with!' She drank the brandy down in a gulp and banged the glass down on the table.

Hal watched her in silence. The drink and the dimly-shaded lights combined to make his eyes reddish. He was quite unfamiliar to her. She wondered if he was still functioning sensibly. With no experience of him after so much alcohol, she had no idea if this all meant anything, if he would even remember. But somehow she thought so; she had never known him when he wasn't absorbing and assessing, and she guessed it would probably take more than spirits to make his extraordinary brain fail to operate at something close to a hundred percent. He said quietly, 'You're wrong. You are my first concern.'

Her head shot up. She felt a great surge of relief, but then it popped like a bubble and was gone. 'I don't believe you. It's easy to say that. You've never given me grounds for thinking it's true.'

'Well, it is.' He leaned back in his chair, his eyes gazing out towards the dark sea. 'I love you, kid. I've probably loved you since the moment I set eyes on you, although God knows why. I've certainly loved you since you flung yourself into my arms and cried your heart out over Ben. It made no sense then, it makes no sense now. You're the most irritating, elusive goddamned woman on earth, but you're a part of me. You're not a habit I know how to break.'

She sat silent, numbed. I've just heard a declaration of love, she thought. I have, I didn't imagine it. It was only the third time he'd laid it on the line for her. She knew that for a certainty; because he'd said it so infrequently, she could recall with total accuracy both places, both occasions. It came to her, in the next instant, just how much she'd wanted to hear it.

I have to make a move towards him, too, she realised. But she wanted to keep her own feelings hidden; to let him into the secret of how much she loved him gave him a power over her which she wasn't sure she wanted him to have. And why am I so sure I do love him so much, when only a while ago I was contemplating life without him? No. That had been a way of coping with what might lie ahead *then*, when he hadn't just told me he loves me.

She watched as he turned from his contemplation of the sea and stared straight into her eyes. This, she thought, was no time for pride. She reached out and took hold of his hand. 'I love you, too.' He didn't respond, not even with a flicker of expression. But she was undeterred. She knew what she wanted to say; his mention of Ben, of their own beginning as a couple, brought to the top of her mind something she had long wanted to tell him. She'd been afraid to, till now. But again, on the many previous occasions she might have confessed it, she hadn't just been told he loved her.

She said softly, 'If I hadn't met you, I don't know if I'd ever have come properly alive again.' She had his full attention, she could tell by the way he was glaring at her. But there was something more. She paused to gather her courage. If this wasn't the best time to tell him, it must come pretty close. 'I realised something about you,' she plunged on, 'that time when I thought you'd gone and I wasn't going to see you again.'

He said nothing, but now that she'd made up her mind she needed no encouragement, 'Thinking I'd lost you hurt worse than losing Ben. So, it came to me that I must love you more than I loved Ben.'

Hal swore suddenly and snatched his hand away. 'I don't want to hear that! I don't want comparisons, I've never asked you that question and I don't want to hear the answer!'

'Oh, yes you do!' she flashed back. 'Don't you realise what I'm saying, Hal? I loved Ben with a perfect love, but he went. He died. Then I came to love you, and you're not perfect, nor is our love perfect, but you're the one I want, till the end of my days. Ben was youth, he was my young love. You're my maturity. And I'm better at loving, now.'

Hal was totally silent, sitting like stone, his face immobile. She watched him for a long time. Then at last she said, 'Just as well, isn't it?' His face twitched slightly. Then he began to smile.

'Crazy dame,' he said, half to himself. He put his hand on her thigh, clasping her leg just above her knee. She looked down. He had big hands, square-shaped and well-formed, the fingers straight and blunt-ended. The signet ring she'd bought him when they were married shone dully in the faint light. With her own hand she traced around his fingers. She thought of his hands when he made love to her, of the joys and the incredible sensations he drew from her. Shivers of excitement ran through her, and a very slight hope rose in her mind. She slid her hand beneath his on her leg, moving her fingers in his palm.

He put his other hand up to her chin, turning her face to make her look at him. His eyes gleamed red, and his expression was slightly questioning. She didn't want to let herself believe; the memory of his rejection, all those months ago, raced back full-blown into her head. Not again, she cried silently, I won't let it happen again. She tried to withdraw her hand, but he wouldn't let her.

'Kid, I want you,' he said.

He pulled her towards him, clasping both her wrists in one hand and still holding her chin with the other. He paused, staring down into her eyes. Then he kissed her.

She was experiencing sensations she'd forgotten she was capable of. There, in the dark corner of the terrace, he was stirring her to such a pitch that she didn't care who saw them. His arms went around her, and she clung to him, her whole self involved in the fierce arousal of his kiss. Her body trembled with the strength of her desire for him. Nothing else mattered; if he'd lain her down she'd have made love to him there and then.

He broke off, moving so he could speak into her ear. His warm breath made her nuzzle against him.

'We have a bed, upstairs,' he whispered.

'Yes.' She looked at him. There was nothing else to say.

They stood up, and began to thread their way through the tables to the door into the bar. He put his hand under her elbow to steady her as she stumbled slightly. She was vaguely surprised that she could walk at all, on legs that shook as if in the aftermath of extreme physical effort.

They left the bar behind, got away from the public areas of the hotel. At the foot of the spiral staircase which led up to their block, amid the scent of freshly-watered flowers — as if he couldn't wait any longer — he stopped to kiss her again. She could feel his body tense against hers, feel him pressing against her with an urgency that swept her with him.

They reached their room, and Hal locked the door behind them. He switched on the bedside lights, and then put his arms round her and lifted her off her feet. For a moment she was held at his height, kissing him face to face. Then he fell with her onto the bed.

He gave her no quarter, pinning her down with the greater strength of his heavy body. And she revelled in him, in the force of his desire which brought her own to screaming pitch. With a roughness born of impatience he pulled her clothes off, ripping off his shirt so violently that the fabric tore, flinging his jeans against the dressing-table and breaking a glass. He entered her immediately, and she was ready for him, pushing herself up to him, wanting all of him, wanting him to be where for so long she'd despaired of him ever being again. They moved together in perfect sympathy, and she felt an unstoppable acceleration. She could sense it boiling up in him, a great tensing and bunching of his muscles, an exertion that brought him out in a sweat that wet her, mingled with her own. His breath came fast, his fingers clenched into the flesh of her hips, moving her to his increasing rhythm. She heard him gasp out something — 'It's been so long,' she thought he said. Then with a last convulsive stiffening of his whole body, he climaxed into her.

★ ★ ★

311

'Sorry, kid,' he said, after a while. He was lying heavily, unmoved from his final collapse on top of her. His heart was pounding so violently that she could feel his chest pushing into hers. Her eyes were full of tears. He misread them. 'Hey, it's OK! There'll be other times. I gotta recover, though, huh?'

She wasn't crying for that. She was going to keep silent, but then she thought, no. There's been too much of that, too much of us not saying what we're feeling, not explaining. That's been our trouble. Now we have to try it another way.

'It's not that,' she began. 'I'm crying because . . . ' But it wasn't so easy, putting things this deep, this personal, into words. 'Because it was so wonderful. You wanted me that much, and it felt like magic. I'm full of you again. And I've missed you so very much.' His arms closed around her as she cried out all the sorrow, all the disappointments and misunderstandings. It was a purification; her tears washed out the accumulated wrongs that had been allowed to come between them and hold them apart.

He rolled off her and lay down beside her, one arm round her and the other hand resting companionably low down on her stomach. She laid her head on his chest, breathing in the particular smell of

312

him, the scent they made together in this ultimate closeness. She lay still; she imagined he'd gone to sleep, and didn't want to wake him.

He wasn't asleep. He could feel a taut excitement in her, and he knew that his own incredible fulfilment had left her unsatisfied. He moved his hand slowly over her body, exploring her in places where his touch brought a reaction like a flower opening to the sun. His hands slid smoothly on her damp skin; she was cool, beautiful. He leaned across her to kiss her breasts, her belly, his lips and tongue absorbing her softness, tasting her slight saltiness.

He had thought only to bring her pleasure, to release her just as he had released himself in her. But her fierce response made his body forget what had just happened, and he found himself ready for her again. He heard her moan as he went back inside her, and her legs wrapped around him in a convulsive grip. He wanted to stay there like that, to preserve that moment of exquisite delight, but he could feel her moving under him. Her hips arched up towards him, her body strengthened by her need of him. Caressing her, at one with her so that he found it hard to tell where he stopped and she began, he felt her body go tense. For a moment she stopped breathing, then a long, deep cry burst from her and he heard her cry out his name. He felt her tighten around him, and, his arms wrapped round her, he clutched her to him as if he would never let her go.

★ ★ ★

He awoke in the depths of the night, his arm sending out pain signals; it was still beneath Jo, who lay curled up against him. He didn't want to wake her up, and he managed to extract his arm without disturbing her. The beside lights were still on, and he shifted round carefully so that he could look at her.

He remembered all that they had said. She'd been quite right to accuse him of being drunk, but he hadn't been so drunk that he was right out of control. Maybe it was meant, that I got as cut as I did, he thought. Maybe I wouldn't have told her I loved her if I'd been sober. He wondered why that should be. Too revealing, to tell someone you loved them? When you tell people you loved them, sometimes they die. Don't they?

His mother had died, despite Sam's love, despite his own. Magdalena had died. Ben had died. He heard in his head an echo

314

of his conversation with Angela, heard his own voice saying, *a shell means nobody knows your feelings. It doesn't mean you don't have any.* That was right, for sure. So what difference did it make to tell people you loved them? The fact of the love existing was surely what mattered. If loving someone made you a hostage to fortune, then whatever malevolent force was responsible for the permanent removal of loved ones probably knew you loved them without you saying so.

His eyes were closing again. There was something I was chasing after, he thought, something about tomorrow. Then he knew what it was; he had slewed away from it because it was so vast. Now that he had it clearly in his mind again he almost wished he hadn't. Tomorrow, he and Jo had to talk it all out. Tonight they had proved pretty conclusively that they had reasons to stay together. That had been easy. Tomorrow, he thought, turning on his side, tomorrow comes the difficult part. We have to figure out how we make it work.

# 17

Jo opened her eyes to see Hal standing barefoot in the middle of the room, pulling a t-shirt over his head. He already had his jeans on. She felt a depressing regret, as if she'd been dreaming it was Saturday and woken up to find it was Monday.

'Are you getting up?' she asked, watching him, crying silently and illogically for him to say no, I'm coming back to bed and I'm going to make love to you.

He emerged from his t-shirt and grinned at her. She was quite sure he knew what she was thinking. He came over and sat on the bed, stroking her hair back from her forehead. 'I am,' he said. 'So are you.'

'Oh.' He kissed her briefly, dodging away from her arms as she reached up for him.

'Kid, we have to talk. And if we stay in bed, we won't. Or, we won't talk about the things we ought to.' She still felt crushingly disappointed. He said, very gently, 'We sorted that out, already. Ain't nothing in the world wrong with how we make love together. It's everything else we have to work on. You know?'

She sighed. 'Yes. I know. I don't find the prospect as nice as staying in bed.'

'Me neither. But we have to do it some time, and here's as good a place as any.'

She pushed him away and yanked at the sheet until it came free from the bed. She sat up and wound it round her, over her head and under her chin. Then she stood up with dignity and headed for the bathroom. She said over her shoulder, 'I'm keeping myself to myself. I'll see you in a minute.' Then, feeling more like her normal self, 'You'd better not have taken all the hot water.'

As she closed the door, she heard him laugh quietly, and the alarming prospect of 'it's everything else we have to work on' didn't seem quite so bad.

They had breakfast by open french windows, the sun forcing a dazzling path into the dining-room. Jo found it hard to think of anything to say. There were so many big matters looming that it seemed irrelevant to comment on the scenery, or gossip about the other people having breakfast. Hal seemed similarly afflicted; all he managed was 'D'you want more coffee?' and, 'You can have the honey'. But when he'd finished eating he took hold of her hand under the table.

The waiter cleared the plates, and they sat looking at each other across the empty table.

317

'Where shall we go?' Jo asked. 'Somewhere dramatic?'

'Right. We'll go sit on the headland, and we'll invoke Poseidon's aid.'

'Funny god to advise on our particular situation. We'd better ask him to send Aphrodite.' Hal grinned at her as they got up to go.

'You're forgetting last night. Reckon he already did.'

★ ★ ★

The temple site was busy with visitors, despite the early hour. Jo and Hal went back to the shelf of rock they'd found the previous day, and sat down with their backs to the cliff. Facing south, out across the Aegean, the temple and all its traffic were out of sight behind them.

'Where do we begin?' Jo said.

Hal knew he had the advantage over her, since he'd been thinking about that very question for the two hours beween when he'd woken and when he'd got up. He fixed his eyes on a coaster that was slowly passing the headland some way out to sea. He didn't want to look at her; it was less difficult to talk when he wasn't watching her.

'We start with the basics.' His voice

sounded more forceful than he'd intended. He tried to make it less harsh. 'You and I have both found out we can live on our own — I'm merely going back to the way I used to live, you apparently have found a new strength that allows you to make your own decisions, and I reckon you'd manage life on your own with the kids OK.'

'It isn't a *new* strength,' she interrupted. Her voice was chilly. 'I acquired it when I lost Ben. I managed on my own then. Remember?'

'Right,' he said. 'I'm sorry, I — '

'What *is* it with men?' she said angrily. 'Why do they hate strong women?' She rounded on him, making him look at her. 'You don't want us depending on you, because that threatens your precious freedom. Yet when we show we can manage without you, that isn't right either.' She leaned closer. 'You can't have it both ways.'

He waited while his irritation faded. Then: 'I can't speak for all men. Me, I like strong women.' Before she could interrupt, he added, 'I like *you*. OK?'

After a moment she said grudgingly, 'OK.'

'When I spoke of your new strength, I didn't mean to diminish what you are. And I hear what you're saying, about Ben. But I didn't want to bring Ben into it yet.' He heard her take in her breath in preparation for another salvo, and he hastily said, 'Unless you want to? It's not only for me to say how we do this.' His uncharacteristic humility seemed to take her aback.

'It's all right,' she said. 'Go on.'

'So, point one: we both can live on our own. Point two is, do we want to?'

'Do you?'

'No.'

'Nor do I.'

He grinned, turning to look at her. 'Great start, huh? Neither of us said 'yes'.'

She nodded. 'Great start. But that's the easy bit. Because we can't go back to how we were, or else the whole thing will blow up again. I've discovered, this past year, that the beneficial effects of a break are purely temporary. In fact, overall they're destructive, because it's much worse when you get back to what you were trying to escape from. The contrast, you know.' The pain in her voice surprised him. He had a moment's urge to stop this now, before he uncovered things he didn't want to hear. But he knew they had to go on; buried resentments would decompose into worse problems. The mood was as right as it'd ever be for sticking them through with a stake and dispatching them.

'What did you have to escape from?'

She moved restlessly beside him. 'I . . . oh, so much!' She paused, and he sensed she was ordering her thoughts. 'Above all, I wanted to escape from a role that I didn't fit,' she said quietly. 'I've never been a housewife, only for the briefest time with Ben. Then I was on my own with Teddy, and I was in charge of our lives. Then there was you, and Sammie came, perhaps too soon, and before I knew it I was no longer boss. I had to fit into a pre-ordained mould, my days were filled — *crammed* — with such a whirl of things I just *had* to do that I lost myself.'

'I didn't put you in a pre-ordained role. Did I?'

'No. You didn't. I don't think it was anything to do with you. It seemed like your fault, then, but it wasn't. It just happened. Things had to be done, and there was only me to do them.'

'That's the same for everyone who marries, has a family.'

'I know. The fault lies in me. But I've come to the conclusion that it's a fault I can't rectify. I'm no good at being a housewife. I can go on in the role; it won't break me or drive me to a nervous breakdown or anything, but I'll always hate it.' She hesitated. 'Alternatively, we can work out some other way.'

Hal let her words sink in. She'd surprised him with the brevity and accuracy of her summing-up; she'd obviously been doing some figuring, too. 'I don't want you to be unhappy,' he said. 'What would you like to add to your life — or take out of it — to improve things?'

'I'd like more time,' she said instantly. 'I want to have some hours that are mine, when I don't have to put everyone else's needs before my own.'

'What would you do with them?'

'Write.'

He smiled. Her answer had been predictable. There wasn't a thing she could have come up with more guaranteed to win his instant sympathy. But he knew it was the truth; she was straight, Jo.

'Surprise, surprise,' he remarked.

'You did ask.'

'Yeah.' They sat in silence for some time. Then Hal said, 'How would we get on if we both wrote?'

She digested the question. Then she asked, 'In what way? Practically, like who fetched the kids and who cooked the meals? Or in the abstract, like would we drive each other nutty by both being absent-minded together?'

'Both.'

'It'd be you that would lose out, because

you write already. If I did too, with your full compliance, you'd have to take over a lot of what I do. Otherwise I couldn't.'

'We couldn't do it unless something went.'

'What do you mean, something went? What?' Her voice was full of impatience. He understood; it must be like a glimmer of light appearing.

'I'm thinking of chucking in the lecturing.'

'Good God!'

He turned at her exclamation. She met his eyes briefly, her own full of surprise. Then she went back to staring out to sea; maybe she too was finding the goddamned coaster an aid to concentration. He wanted to reach for her, but he held back. They were doing well.

'I never expected to hear you say that,' she said. 'You love your work. You do it so well, too.' There was regret in her voice, but he got the feeling she was already accepting his suggestion. Like an offering to save what they had together. A fitting sacrifice. Only it wasn't, and he couldn't let her think it was.

'I do. I did,' he corrected himself. 'What I love about it is getting across to others what I've gotten out of a subject. And that I can do as well by writing it in books as by talking about it in a lecture theatre. And I'm tired of the smell of students.'

'But writing won't necessarily bring in an adequate income,' Jo said. She sounded dismal, as if she'd judged the reality behind the bright dream and found it unworkable.

'Why shouldn't it? We haven't done so bad, so far.'

'Perhaps. But it wouldn't be like a regular salary.'

'We don't know until we try.'

She sat thoughtfully, picking minute flowers from the grass and forming them into a little bouquet. Then she said, 'I've got my own income, anyway. You know — from Ben's life insurance.'

'That's yours. Yours and Teddy's.'

'Don't be silly,' she said impatiently. 'I can just see me, when we hit hard times, going out to spend it on food for Teddy and me and leaving you and Sammie hungry.'

'I don't want to profit from Ben's death any more than I do already.' He hadn't meant to say it. They had enough to sort out already. But the words had leapt out before he was aware of thinking them. She was regarding him with a strange expression.

'Very revealing,' she said quietly. 'I really did say the wrong thing yesterday, didn't I? About loving you better than I loved Ben.'

It was slightly worse to hear her say it now,

in the harsh and clear-headed daylight, than it had been in the haze of last night. She was, although he didn't think she realised it, hacking at a nerve that had never really healed.

'Ben was better for you than I am.' He was saying out loud words that had tormented him for some time. 'I know you say you love me better, but I can't love you like he could. I don't have the ability to love people in the wholehearted way he did.'

'You loved Magdalena pretty whole-heartedly. You must have done, for the echo of it still to be so strong.'

He couldn't believe she'd said it. She had never mentioned Magdalena to him. How did she know what he felt, now or then, about his long-dead, desperate first love? 'It was the way she loved me.' He felt defensive, wanting to hit out at Jo for her trespass into his deep heart. 'She threw her whole self at me, she gave me everything, with no calculation, no holding back. She left herself so vulnerable, so in need of me, that I couldn't help but give her all I had, too.'

He was plunged right back into his own past, feeling vividly again his helpless love for Magdalena, remembering how she looked, how she spoke . . .

'She didn't give you everything.' Jo's voice

cracked across the pretty pictures. 'She didn't marry you.'

There was a moment of utter stillness. The sounds of distant people were a babble in the background, and the restless sea went on throwing itself on the rocks below, but it seemed to Jo that she and Hal were suspended from their surroundings. She felt a sudden sharp pain in her hand; looking down, she saw that she'd been holding the flowers so tightly that she'd stuck a fingernail into the skin of her palm. Her hand was bleeding, a fine red stream trickling down on to the grass.

Magdalena. I said, *you loved Magdalena.* She felt sick. What have I *done?* she cried silently. She didn't dare look at Hal; he was radiating a jumble of emotions, so fiercely that she felt he was attacking her. But I *had* to say it. The ghost of lily-white Magdalena cannot be allowed to assume such idealised proportions.

She heard Hal cough quietly. She shot him a glance out of the corner of her eye. He had his hands up to his face. He said in a whisper, 'She couldn't marry me.'

*Yes she could*, Jo ached to say, anyone can marry anyone, it depends on whether you love them enough to put up with the uproar you may have to face. And she can't have loved you enough, or else she'd have run off with you, hopped on a plane to the States, married you, and you'd have had her for a wife instead of me.

But the words remained unsaid. Why should I say them? she asked herself, unbearably moved by Hal beside her, struggling with something she could scarcely understand. She had no desire to hurt him. Let him keep his memories. She tied a strand of grass around her tiny flowers and threw them over the edge of the cliff. Probably they won't reach the sea, but you never know. Magdalena, rest in peace.

'No,' she said. 'I know she couldn't.'

They sat in silence, the violent emotions stirred up by their words — their thoughts — gradually fading. It's still today, Jo thought, we're still sitting here, although it feels so strange. How odd, how very ironic, that Hal should say he'd felt all that he did for Magdalena because she'd loved him so desperately that he'd had no choice. I could have done that, couldn't I? she cried to herself, I could have given him all the love I had. But I didn't think he wanted it. There was no point, however, in saying so. What either of them *might* have done was quite irrelevant. What they were going to do was what mattered.

Hal found that his mind had wandered away from Magdalena. He was thinking about his father. Sam had said on Hal's wedding day that there was much to his new daughter-in-law that he hadn't begun to touch on yet. Hal had replied, 'She's a surprising woman'. He'd also said it didn't do to be complacent.

Obviously, he had been. He'd gotten too used to his image of her as she'd become. In the domestic role, the one she hated. He'd been blind to think she'd stay there, crazy to forget all that there was to her. She had guts and courage, she'd overcome heartbreak of a magnitude that would have sent a lot of people into permanent hiding. But not her. She'd taken herself off to America, right into the emotional lion's den of Ben's parental home, and she'd kept her head high and outstared the spectres of anguish that would have had her break down. Why the hell had he thought she'd lost her will to fight now? Women like her didn't crawl away and give up when life pressed down on them, they gathered their strength and they punched back.

She wasn't the floundering, fraught mother desperately trying to do a job that was outside her talents. She was a cool, self-assured woman who was forceful and direct, who seemed to know just what she wanted and who was prepared to go straight for it. Her housewifely role was the disguise; that hadn't been Jo at all. Perhaps that was why he'd found it so hard to love her all the time she was struggling to act it.

Magdalena's pale image came briefly back into his mind. But he didn't try to keep it there, and after a moment it broke up and drifted away like smoke in the wind. I held on too long, he thought. Maybe we all do, to our first love. No reason why they have to bear the burden of our resentment, when we try to make them perfect in our memories and we inevitably fail. Goodbye, Magdalena. You *were* perfect, as far as you could be.

He felt he was on a high path, that he had to choose whether to go back into the familiar but unsatisfactory valley that he knew, or onwards to explore what was ahead. 'We can't go back to how we were', Jo had said. She was right. He looked at her. She had rolled on to her stomach, and was watching the waves ceaselessly washing the rocks far below. She'd be for exploring ahead, he thought. She's done it before. Maybe she needs to uproot and settle some place new every now and again. He grinned, amused at the idea of revolutionary changes of venue occurring endlessly down the years.

But then, why not? It was the company that mattered, not the place.

Jo had watched the waves until she had hypnotised herself into a state of numbness. She felt neither happy nor sad. I haven't felt like this since I finished my finals, she thought. It's as if I've been trying very hard to achieve something, and I've done my best, but I'm so exhausted by it all that I've forgotten what the effort was for. Bits of conversation echoed in her head. Did we really say all that? Good grief, we really have had a heart-to-heart. All the old skeletons have been dragged clattering and rattling out of the cupboard. I wonder if we've booted them far enough out to sea? I don't care any more. I don't think I can ever care again. She rested her head on her arms. The earth smelt lovely, so rich, so fertile. She breathed in the smell. It's like breathing in life. It makes Hal and me and our worries seem so trivial.

'How long will it take you to evict those tenants of yours?' Hal's voice jolted her back to the real world.

'There aren't any tenants in at the moment,' she said drowsily. Then the meaning of his words hit her. She felt herself go very still. 'Why?' she asked. Her mouth had gone dry.

He didn't answer for some time. Then

he said, 'Reckon we were happiest, in that house. Maybe we should pick it up from there.'

He was right. He was absolutely right. She buried her face in her arms, happiness welling up in her like the glow of warmth from a fire. She hadn't allowed herself to admit that this was what she wanted; all along she'd justified her hard work on the house with plausible reasons that had nothing to do with Hal. Also, foreseeing his refusal if ever she did suggest returning there, she'd fortified herself with rock-hard reasons why he couldn't go and live in England. To have him propose it all by himself was to have a wish granted for which she hadn't even dared ask.

She became aware that he was waiting for her to speak; she seemed to remember him saying 'Jo?' a couple of times. She couldn't help smiling.

'Yes,' she said.

He waited for her to go on. When she didn't, he nudged her in the ribs. 'Is that it? Just 'yes'?'

She rolled over away from him. Her ribs were very sensitive, and she didn't think now was the moment to start laughing like a ticklish child. But she wasn't sure she was going to be able to help it, with or without the nudging.

'That's it,' she said. God, I love you. 'That's my answer.' I love you more than I realise.

He looked down at her as she lay in the grass. He could see laughter in her eyes, but there was something else in her expression. He leaned over her, and very gently kissed her lips. The laughter receded. She put out her arms to him, clasping them round his neck.

'It's just us, isn't it? When you come down to it.'

'It is.' He kissed her again.

'We're very selfish,' she said quietly. 'We've been considering only what we want. Neither of us mentioned the children.'

'Doesn't mean we weren't thinking of them. Only . . . ' He stopped. He had no wish to criticise her.

'Only what? Go on, it's OK.'

He bent down to lay his face against hers. It was a tender position, for what he was going to say. 'With things like they were — with you like you were — reckon the kids would have been better off with you on your own. The friction would have got to them, any minute.'

She sighed. 'Was I that bad?'

Her softness against him was making him lose the thread of what they were saying. He felt guiltily that it was his paternal duty to put in a plea for his sons, but he didn't feel dutiful. What the hell, they had a mother in a thousand. And ain't nobody perfect.

'You were the bogeyman, the Wicked Witch of the West and Snow White's stepmother, and some,' he said, punctuating the words with kisses down her neck that arrested her laughter before it took a hold on her. He felt her body move closer to his.

'Hal, I don't think we're as out of sight as you think,' she whispered in his ear. 'I think . . . ' He stopped her with a more serious sort of kiss that kept her full attention for some minutes.

'Can't help it, kid,' he remarked when they broke apart. 'It's all these pillars, they give me ideas.'

She started to laugh. 'That's very apparent! Well, from where I'm lying, anyway. Wouldn't that be a libation to good old Poseidon, if we — er, if we did it, here?'

'Sure would.' He raised himself up on an elbow. 'We'll dedicate the next time to him, anyway.' He rolled away from her and, after a while, sat up. He turned to her. 'Now we have a choice,' he said. 'Either we can go into Lavrion and order the best celebratory lunch we can find, or we can do something else.'

She watched him, slowly shaking her head.

'I'm not hungry,' she said. 'What's this something else?'

He stood up, reaching for her hand to pull her to her feet.

'Guess.'

★ ★ ★

In the evening, Jo suddenly needed to talk to her mother. She left Hal in the bath, singing something jubilant from *The Marriage of Figaro*. She felt quite pleased with herself for knowing that much — if I hang around with him long enough, she thought with a smile, I'll eventually know the characters and the names of the arias, too. All in good time.

She went gingerly down the spiral staircase, her knees still weak and her thigh muscles slightly tender. Poor old legs, she thought, first a motor bike and now Hal in his King Kong mood. She had to stop for a moment to allow a high-voltage shock of reminiscent excitement to dissipate. I wonder if it made me blush? She put her hand to her cheek, but since it had felt hot all day, either from the sun or from her own fiercely-pounding blood, she was none the wiser. I don't care, anyway. I've been in bed all afternoon with my Hal, and I'm *proud* of it, proud that I've been loved as much as any woman could want, to the limits of desire and down the other side.

She had reached the bar. She found a quiet corner, and ordered a beer. She tried to compose herself, to steer her thoughts away from making love with Hal; it wasn't really the right frame of mind for talking to Elowen. But if I don't make the call soon, Hal will have come to the end of *The Marriage of Figaro* and be out of the bath. And I want to sit here holding his hand. She jumped up and went to use the telephone in reception.

Hal heard her voice as he approached reception.

'We'll be living in Kent again,' she was saying. 'No, he won't be lecturing, he'll be writing. We both will. So we may as well be there as anywhere. And we want to be there.' Elowen must have made some remark about Sam and the MacAllisters, because Jo said that flying to and from the West Coast was no distance nowadays, and they'd all be able to make frequent visits. Then she went on to talk about how she'd redecorated the house, and he stopped listening.

He left her to it. Her voice was full of happiness, and he didn't need to hear any more. When she's through, he thought, we'll phone home. Talk to Dad and maybe

Sammie. Then call Teddy at Bernard and Mary's. We'll tell them we're coming home. He walked on into the bar. Soon she'd come and join him. She was in his blood just then, and he wanted her close. He went to lean on the balcony wall, watching the moon over the sea. I'll know when she's near. I'll feel her.

It wouldn't last, this extreme intoxication with her. We're just two ordinary people, he thought; we're not gods, and we haven't been lifted permanently on to a higher plane. Aphrodite's influence is likely limited. But we've been given a bonus. Whatever may come, neither of us will forget this. We'll go home, make our plans for moving back to England, pick up our life together — us and the boys — and maybe this'll all seem like a dream.

But we can come again.

He turned away from the dark sea. He'd heard a footstep, and he knew it was Jo. He watched her approach. She looked happy, a tender smile on her face. You mean so much to me, kid. She was wearing a shirt which was open at the neck, and he could see the tanned skin of her throat. She walked with a light step, her very movements sending a singing thrill through him.

Yes. We can always come back again.

And there's still tonight.

# Coda

## Late Summer, 1987

# 18

Jo walked slowly up the garden, snipping the thorns from a bunch of roses she'd just picked. She came to a stop at the foot of the terrace, and stood looking up at the house. Its bricks were russet in the glow of the setting sun, and through the open windows she could hear sounds of her family. The boys were shouting at each other up in Sammie's bedroom, and from downstairs came the sound of the television. They've gone away and left it blaring out to an empty room again, she thought calmly. Silly little things. No doubt they're busy making a rook's nest out of Sammie's room. They'll just have to clear it all away, won't they? Or else I shan't give them any tea.

Looking through a window to her left she could see Hal, working at his desk. If she listened very intently, she could just hear him talking to himself as he wrote, although she couldn't make out the words. Soon after their return to Copse Hill House, he had built himself a study, extending the ground floor out at right angles to the back of the house so that the terrace was now bordered by two walls instead of one. It had made an excellent sun-trap; Jo now had a very healthy-looking young fig tree growing in the corner.

She stared intently at the new building work. They'd sweated blood waiting for planning permission to come through, and the job had cost a fortune. But she knew it was worth it; you couldn't monkey around with a beautiful old house unless you hired the best craftsmen you could find. The end wall of Hal's study was almost all glass, which gave the extension the look of a conservatory. It was only when you got inside, and saw the word processor and the shelves full of books, files and papers, that you realised it was actually an office.

Initially Jo had used the smaller spare room as her study. But Hal's was so nice, so full of him and his work, and, above all, so *private*, that she concluded she'd like a purpose-built room too, and preferably one that wasn't as readily accessible as the bedroom next door to Teddy's room. So they spent another small fortune on adding an upstairs to the new extension, which, although it would mean an embargo on foreign travel for a year or so, resulted in a much better looking end product. The two-storey extension now had an elegantly pitched, tiled roof; Jo's upstairs study had a ceiling which sloped down to small child's height at the end facing the garden, where there was a little window. The boys said it was like Alice in the White Rabbit's house, when she had grown enormous and had to fold herself up. Until the novelty wore off, they kept pretending to be Alice trying to get out, and they would clamour to be kicked up the chimney like Bill the Lizard. 'There isn't a chimney,' Jo'd said firmly when she finally lost patience and shooed them out. 'Go and annoy your father.'

There was a door from her study into the house, but she kept it locked and she had hidden the key. Entry was up a wooden staircase from Hal's room below. To reach her, you had to leave the house, walk across the terrace, knock on Hal's door — at the risk of being either shouted at or ignored, depending on what he was doing — and then clamber up the narrow staircase. Jo found that she was safe from all but the most determined visitors.

She'd bought a word processor, having given up on trying to share Hal's. She and Hal had taught themselves from the manual, with quite a lot of comparing notes and solving each other's problems. Jo mastered the technique more quickly, which annoyed Hal. 'You haven't gone into it as thoroughly as I have,' he complained as she edited and printed out a short story without a single hitch.

'No, I don't suppose I have,' she agreed, quite unperturbed.

It was part of his greater irritation at the ease with which she wrote. 'You don't even stop to think about it!' he grumbled, standing behind her one day when he'd wandered upstairs to borrow an atlas. She smiled. She did write fast, although it wasn't true to say she didn't think about it. But she did all her thinking while she was making the beds, or driving back from taking the boys to school. When at long last she was able to sit down and write, the accumulation of several hours would pour out. Her mind seemed to have a facility for recording whole pages of narrative or dialogue, and, as long as she wrote it down fairly soon after thinking it up, she could turn out half a chapter with scarcely a pause. The frustration came when something or someone prevented her from getting to work; Hal still had a tendency to expect her to answer the telephone, or attend to callers at the door, or see to suddenly-remembered credit card bills that just had to be posted off there and then. But he was improving. Slowly.

He jeered at her sometimes. He said once, 'Anyone could write your stuff fast. It has no depth.' OK, it had been on a day when he had finally given up on a chapter he'd been struggling with for a week. It had come right, later, and he'd apologised for taking it out on her. She hadn't been ready to be forgiving, yet, and had reminded him acidly that her stuff brought in nearly as much money, in terms of pounds per man-hour, as did his own long, deeply-thought-out works. He hadn't answered.

Jo had found a niche writing short stories for a new magazine eager to publish something slightly different from the usual formula of boy-meets-girl, boy and girl have problems, problems are solved and boy and girl get married. Jo wrote stories with a frisson of the supernatural, and, having proved her ability to write a story of a specified length to a specified deadline, had earned a regular commission. The stories brought in a small but steady sum; the majority of her income came from her novels.

She had resurrected the convoluted plot she'd worked out years ago in Rhodes. With a new enthusiasm at her own cleverness and delight at the explosive impact of the twist in the end of the story, she'd raced through the transposition of the book on to her word processor. Then she handed it over to the agent who had sold her earlier children's

343

books and found her a market for her stories. Eleven months later, the book was lined up for publication.

She was writing another one, and had plans for two more after that. She knew it would be a short-lived fad, this demand for her strange supernatural plots in their historic backgrounds. People would get bored with her, and the unexpected touches that were now so exciting would, after four books, be predictable. When that happens, she thought with a new but rock-sure confidence, I'll do something else.

Hal's 'Minoan thing' had been in the bestseller charts for months, on both sides of the Atlantic. It had been his breakthrough work, the book that had widened his appeal to a new, non-academic audience. Jo, who had always loved the way he wrote, had been surprised. It was, she thought after she'd read all three hundred pages in the best part of two days, as though he'd come down from some intellectual pedestal to join the rest of the human race. She returned several times to the chapter on Phaestos, the most hauntingly beautiful part of the book. It was the section that had surprised the critics, too, many of whom said dismissively that it was 'unworthy' of Dr Dillon, and that near-fantasy had no place in a work of scholarship.

One reviewer had suggested caustically that Hal ought to make up his mind what he was trying to write. But clearly the book-buying public were not deterred by such comments; the letters that continued to pour in indicated that most people considered the book money well spent.

Jo went on thinking about the Phaestos chapters. The site, in all its majestic beauty, was painted through the eyes of a supposedly imaginary woman, alone and sad, being shown around by an older and better-informed man. Woven into the descriptions was an overpowering sense that real people had built this palace, and that, although they had been dust for four thousand years, the echo of their emotions, their loves, hates and motivations, still lingered in the very atoms of the place where they had lived. The imaginary modern-day couple came over as real people, too; linked by their common humanity, they were able to reach not only their distant forebears but also — although this was only hinted at — each other.

The photographs that illustrated the chapters showed a deserted site, the raw stones and the ruined masonry pale gold against the intense green of pine trees and the azure of the sky. The shadows said it was early in the day. It looked as though Hal had been entirely alone.

Jo wondered. She wondered very much. Especially after she had accompanied Hal to London for a signing session and, just as important, to share with him the pleasure of seeing his book in the displays of so many book shops and book departments. She had noticed, not without apprehension, that he seemed to be looking for someone.

He was quiet and withdrawn on the way home. Didn't she turn up? Jo thought. But she had learned, over the years. She said nothing.

* * *

The evening was growing cool, and Jo went on inside the house and began to arrange her roses. Damn, she thought suddenly, I forgot to post Sam's letter. She went into the hall and picked up the air-mail envelope. She had left it open, because Hal had said he would add a few pages. She looked inside, and saw that he had done so. I wonder if the boys would like to come with me? No, I think I'd like to walk on my own.

She let herself quietly out of the house and set off up the lane. Sam was on her mind a lot, as she knew he was on Hal's.

They had visited him once since the move back to Kent, and he had come to stay for six weeks in the spring. He's getting old, Jo thought sadly. Perhaps it had only shown up because they didn't see him so often now, but she had been dismayed at his appearance when she'd met him at Gatwick. He looked . . . grey, she thought. Grey and tired. Mind you, that was shortly after Thomas had died. Sam's brother had meant a great deal to him, and Jo knew without being told that, despite Sam's smiling, cheerful exterior, he was grieving deeply.

'Sure, he was getting old,' Sam said to her quietly one evening when they were washing up together, 'and his death wasn't any great surprise, and he died painlessly in his sleep. Fine way to go. But he was my brother, and I'll miss him.' Then he had put down the tea towel and left the room.

He'll come here and live, soon, Jo thought as she strode out up the lane. She knew that Hal was pressing for Sam to come to England; there were nights when Hal didn't come to bed until the small hours, and Jo had gone downstairs once to find him sitting motionless at the kitchen table with a bottle of bourbon, staring at a photograph. Sam smiled up at the camera in happy summer sunshine, Sammie on one knee, Teddy on the other. She'd put her hands on Hal's shoulders, laying her cheek against the top of his head. 'I'd welcome him, too,' she whispered.

Hal didn't reply, but some time later he came up to bed and took her in his arms. He said quietly, 'I love you, kid.'

Sam would be a good addition to the household. Life had an extra dimension when he was with them; he had a quiet patience that was a balmy antidote to Jo's hot-tempered, quick irritation. But he never makes me feel bad, she thought, picturing him lovingly. He's a bit like Christ, in a way, suffering us in our imperfections but not condemning us for them. In fact, he's not exactly like Christ, because he offers a more realistic sort of help. Sam doesn't suggest that I give away my clothes, or that I sacrifice everything to follow him. Instead he sees when the children are about to make me explode, or when one of them needs a bit of extra love, or when Hal could do with a man-to-man chat over half a bottle of scotch, and he's right there, giving us all just what we want.

She thought perhaps she was being unfair to Christ; just because the Bible didn't go into that sort of detail didn't mean to say it hadn't happened. She smiled briefly at the thought of Hal sharing a bottle with Christ. I wonder what they'd talk about?

Sam had had a mild stroke in the summer. Hal and Jo had wanted to go out to him, but he had been adamant. 'I'm OK, son,' he'd said repeatedly over the phone. 'It's a waste of your company if you come now, because I have to rest. Anyway, if you and Jo were here I wouldn't rest — I sure wouldn't sleep away a visit from you! Come when I'm better.'

Now he was better, or so he reported. The letter Jo was posting included an invitation for him to come to stay, for the autumn, for Christmas, perhaps for ever. He's too independent, Jo thought. He won't come without a lot of persuasion. And are we quite sure that we have the right to persuade him? He's entitled to live where he wants, after all. She was aware of a niggle in her mind, though, a worrying suspicion that Sam was holding off from moving in with them because he thought they didn't really want him. We shall just have to show him, shan't we? He's so like Hal, she reflected, loving him dearly. They're both loners, really. Neither of them makes many attachments, but the ones they do make go as deep as the roots of mountains.

Reaching the letterbox, she kissed Sam's name on the envelope, then posted it. She closed her eyes for a moment, her thoughts concentrating on him. He would be seventy-six in October. Although his tall, spare frame seemed still to be reasonably fit, the stroke in the summer must surely be taken as a warning.

Don't go, Sam, she thought. By the most optimistic reckoning in the world, you won't have all that many more years. Not enough. It won't be the same, without you, so come and be with us, while you can.

She turned and walked quickly away.

★ ★ ★

Hal heard the front door slam, and the sound brought him back to the present and reminded him that he was thirsty. He stood up and stretched, then wandered out of his study, across the terrace and into the kitchen. Jo was standing at the sink arranging roses.

'Been out?' he asked, reaching across her to fill the kettle and kissing her cheek as he did so.

'Yes.' She looked subdued.

'What's up?'

'Nothing. I was just hoping Sam will come — I went to post the letter.'

Hal set out cups and the teapot. Then he said, 'He'll come, when he's ready.' She nodded. She still looked unhappy. Hal put his arms round her, holding her tightly. 'Ain't nothing we can do, kid,' he said gently. 'It's the way of things.' He felt her sigh. Then she laughed softly. 'What're you laughing about?'

'I'm trying to hug you back, but my hands are full of roses.'

The kettle began to boil, and he released her to make the tea. 'I have two more pages to write, then I'm through,' he said.

'Good. Tom and Jenny are coming to dinner. But then you hadn't forgotten that, had you?'

'No,' Hal said. He had.

He took his tea back to his desk, sat down and wrote a couple of paragraphs. But his mind wasn't concentrating any more on Mycenae, and he decided to call it a day. He'd get back to it in the morning with more enthusiasm, he knew that without a doubt; he had no guilty feelings about stopping now. He leaned back and stirred his tea, thinking about Jo.

She'd become very good at . . . managing him wasn't exactly what he meant. It was more that she steered him tactfully in the right direction. Like just now, reminding him about Jenny and Tom. Hal was glad they were coming; he enjoyed their company.

He'd had some discussions with Jenny that tipped over the edge and become arguments, but that was enjoyable, too. Jenny held forthright opinions and wasn't afraid to speak her mind, and Hal found her a challenge. People didn't often argue with him, and he reckoned Jenny was good for him. In fact both she and Tom did him good, because Tom seemed to have some private avenue of humour with Jo which nobody else shared, and Hal noticed that there was a slight edge of sexual attraction between them. He didn't think it went beyond that; Jo and Tom were far too relaxed with each other for them to be indulging in a secret affair. In any case, Jo was very fond of Jenny, and Hal didn't think she was capable of spending afternoons of affectionate companionship with the wife before slipping off to share evenings of passion with the husband. I don't reckon old Tom's any great shakes as a Casanova, Hal thought. But you never can tell with the British.

He smiled, beginning to laugh. He had gone down to the pub with Tom the previous Sunday lunchtime, a habit they had fallen into after one memorable morning when Hal had helped Tom reassemble his lawnmower. Tom had dismantled the air filter, then hadn't been able to remember how to put it back together again. Not that Hal knew any more about lawnmowers than Tom, but he had a more logical mind. This last Sunday, Hal had absent-mindedly gone out in his gardening jeans, the ones with a rip in the crotch. He hadn't noticed until he and Tom were seated in the pub, when Tom had suddenly shouted with laughter. When they got back, Tom remarked to Jenny that Hal was a sort of Penis in Blue Jeans. Hal went home and asked Jo to sew him up. When he related what Tom had said, Jo thought it was funny, too.

It was nice, having convivial neighbours. Nice for the boys, too, to have a girl playmate. Any ideas they might have had about Laura being a civilising influence on Teddy and Sammie had, however, long gone out of the window. The reverse was true; Tom said proudly that Laura was the only girl who the gang of small bullies in her class went in fear of. She had hit one little tormentor so hard that she had blacked his eye and given him a nosebleed, and since then her male classmates had left her alone. 'It's all this tree-climbing and football,' Tom said. 'And Teddy can only just beat her at arm-wrestling — it's making a man of her!'

But Hal had been dubious when it came to Christmas. Casual friendliness, the occasional meal together and Sunday pints in the pub were just fine, but he wasn't at all sure he welcomed the big Christmas celebrations that were planned to include all of them. He had been happily surprised, the first year back in Kent, to find he enjoyed it as much as everyone else.

Jo's parents had come to stay, and on Christmas Day eleven of them sat down to lunch in the big dining-room in Copse Hill House. Jenny's mother was down for the week, and Jo invited a retired doctor from up the road to even up the adult numbers. The doctor was a widower, and his courteous attentions to Jenny's mother took most of the sting out of her.

Hal had a great time. He and Jo had still been laughing intermittently when they went to bed, at the memory of Jo's father loudly telling Jenny's mother — apparently impervious to her Glaswegian accent — just how much he loathed Glasgow. If that's a traditional English Christmas, Hal thought, then count me in.

Hal reflected that he must have been in a particularly observant mood that Christmas, because it was then he'd first been struck by how close Elowen and Edmund were. Maybe it's what you'd expect, he thought, seeing again Elowen and Edmund quietly seeking each other out, exchanging glances across other people's heads, exchanging thoughts across other people's laughter. Edmund was ten now, and his physical resemblance to his father increased as he matured. But mentally he was quite different; his facility for deep concentration and his interest in reasoning out the answers to questions that puzzled him weren't traits that he could possibly have inherited from Ben. He's more like Jo, Hal decided. Because he looked so like Ben, Hal found he tended to forget Teddy was Jo's child too.

Teddy talks to Elowen, Hal realised, more than to any of us. Her first grandson, he's bound to be special to her. But it's more than that. Hal was well aware that Elowen had been very fond of Ben. She'd once told Hal, very sympathetically, that Ben would be a hard act to follow. At the time Hal had thought her comment related to Jo, and to the difficulty Hal would have in replacing Ben in her affections. Now he wasn't so sure that she hadn't been talking about herself. He felt no resentment; he was inclined to agree with Elowen, Ben was altogether a worthier character than he was.

Whatever the cause, he concluded, Elowen and Teddy have something good between them. He thought he might suggest to Jo that maybe Teddy could go stay with his grandparents, on his own, some time soon. He reckoned it'd do them good. All three of them.

He had finished his tea. He considered going to pour another cup, but realised it was nearly an hour since he'd had the first one. He went out on to the terrace, and walked slowly down the garden. He stopped by the hedge at the bottom and looked out across the gentle hills, where patches of full-leafed summer woodland stood out dark against the gold of ripe corn. A combine harvester clattered in the distance, and from somewhere closer a lark sang in the evening air.

Hal leaned his arms on the stile that led into the fields. This place was home now to him as much as it was to Jo. It had been right, that almost desperate, last-shot decision to move back to Kent. Although it had been taken under the strain of his adrenalin-charged reunion with Jo in Greece, the instinctive urge to come home to this house had been the best thing they could have done. Don't reckon any place felt so much like home as this, he thought.

It wasn't just the house. Hal liked living in England. Well, I like this piece of it, he reflected, thinking that he mightn't be so enthusiastic had Jo bought her house in some grey Midland suburb, or in some totally inaccessible, lonely spot where the post didn't get through in winter and frozen pipes closed off the water supply. But this, now, this was pretty near perfect.

And I reckon I like the English, too. He was in an expansive mood, and the philanthropic vein continued. I like them for their reserve, and for the way it goes on surprising me to find there's kindness and humour underneath it. In some people, anyway. I like ancient tracts of land like the acres round here, where the people match their environment. They and their ancestors have lived here so long that they're an extension of it.

Images of people came into his mind, the cheerful echoes of characters he'd met and hadn't wanted to let go. He thought of Helen Arnold, and her swallow like a navvy. She'd been one of that particular breed, the travelling English gentlewoman. She was — good grief, Hal thought, she's ninety-one now. Gutsy old dame. He smiled. Helen was still travelling, fit as a flea and — sometimes to his discomfiture — about the only person who ever really told him exactly what she thought of him. She came to stay, when she didn't have anywhere more exotic to visit.

He heard her laugh in his memory, and laughed with her, thinking of how he'd kissed her peachy cheek in a hotel lounge in La Paz. She'd said no man had done that since VE Day. We ought to go see her soon, he resolved. Just Jo and me. We'll take her somewhere smart for lunch.

Angela. It was a direct line of thought to go from Helen to Angela, since she was a modern-day version of Helen. Was that why I took such a shine to her? Hal mused. Helen had provided a moment's kindness and affection at an all-time low in his life, so it was obvious he'd keep a place for her. Then along had come Angela, and maybe she'd just slipped into that place beside her predecessor, and for much the same reason.

Hal thought frequently about Angela; today was no one-off. But there had never been any question of him looking her up, even if he'd known where to look. It was just as well he didn't; he wasn't sure he'd be able to walk away from her again, so he kept his communication with her to a sort of attempted telepathy. It was wish-fulfillment, he was sure, to think that there were times when she was simultaneously thinking about him. I loved her, in a way, he thought. If there was ever to be another woman, if I was ever to be in a situation when I no longer had Jo, I'd go find Angela.

He knew with utter certainty that he and Angela would go straight back to where they'd left off. God, he thought, it was another example of something being wrenched away while it was red-hot. She was another Magdalena — I didn't have the chance to get used to her. To get bored with her. To live with her. Not even, in Angela's case, to make love to her. Magdalena was gone. Angela was, too; all that he had left of her was her gallant spirit, captured for ever in a chapter of a book.

The thought made him sad. He'd wanted to dedicate the whole 'Minoan thing' to Angela, and he very nearly had done. But it hadn't seemed fair to Jo. It didn't seem right either to dedicate it to Jo — it would have made her seem like second-best, and that wasn't how he thought of her, ever. In the end he'd dedicated it to his father. Appropriate, since Sam had after all been the person who'd set off Hal's fascination for the past in the first place. But I hope you got to read it, Angela, Hal thought. I hope you recognised yourself, and that it told you all the things I couldn't say.

As he stood there in the gathering gloom, the apparent irreconcilables in his life seemed to grate less violently than before. It's distance, he thought. It's all a long time ago. I don't reckon it'd have mattered to Jo if I'd told her about Angela. It made no difference; she was never any real threat. The main effect she had was to make me realise how much I love Jo.

His thoughts had come round to Jo. They always do, he realised. Guess she means more to me than I'm prepared to accept. You're like a tune that my mind likes singing, kid. It's easy, having you around in my head. He thought again about telepathy. He had it, with Jo. He was becoming used to it now, but at first when she'd started coming out with the exact thing he was thinking about, it had knocked him sideways. Once or twice, sure. But after so many occurrences, it had to be something other than coincidence. He smiled. He wasn't about to lose any sleep worrying about it. And it sure as hell made for a great relationship, in every way.

Jeez, he thought suddenly, looking hastily at his watch, it must be time I was somewhere else. Dinner. Someone's coming to dinner. Yes. Jenny and Tom.

He walked quickly up the garden. Then, coming on to the terrace, he slowed and stopped. He could hear voices: Jenny and Tom were there already. He must have been down the garden longer than he'd thought.

He realised they couldn't see him out there in the evening light, and he was just about to go in and announce that he wasn't going to change, they'd have to put up with him as he was, when he became aware of what Jo was saying.

Tom and Jenny were laughing, and there was amusement in Jo's voice. But there was something else, too. Tom, or Jenny, must have been making a joke at Hal's expense; probably, he thought guiltily, about the courteous way he'd been waiting for them in the hall with a welcoming tray of drinks.

'I know, and it's just like living with a zombie half the time, you're quite right,' Jo was saying. 'It's his way, though, being absent-minded and far away. But,' and abruptly her voice changed, 'the time he's entirely here actually beats most people's all the time.' There was some more laughter, and Tom's voice started to say something about jammy buggers who didn't know when they were well off.

I know, pal, Hal thought, running round to the kitchen door. I do know when I'm well off. He didn't mind being referred to as a jammy bugger, he didn't mind about anything. He had one thought in his head, and intended to act on it. He went into the kitchen, quietly closing the door. He hoped he wouldn't have to wait long.

After about ten minutes, he heard the living-room door open. 'I'll get you another tonic, Jen, hang on,' Jo's voice said. 'I'll give Hal a call, too — I can't think what the hell he's — '

She had come into the kitchen looking back over her shoulder, and Hal had taken her in his arms before she'd seen he was there. He turned her face up to his, and stopped what she was saying with his mouth on hers. He didn't have any other way to express what he wanted to get over to her, but the way she began to respond, once she was over the surprise, suggested that this was achieving the desired result.

He'd always loved kissing her. He remembered telling her once that he'd never enjoyed kissing any woman as much as her. Still applies, he thought distantly. Still reckon you're the best, kid. She was wrapped tightly in his arms, her body pressed against his, and he realised in a flash that he'd never known her unresponsive. I know when I'm well-off, he thought again, oh, boy, do I.

After some time they broke apart. Not far apart, but enough to speak to each other.

'We have guests in there,' he said.

'I know. I wasn't so sure you did, though.'

'Right. I'm sorry, kid.' He looked down

into her eyes. She can still make me shiver, he thought. He bent to kiss her again, lightly, and she put her hands up behind his head to pull him closer.

'What's this for?' she whispered, after another lengthy time of non-verbal communication.

'Ain't for nothing,' he began. Then he changed his mind. 'Yes it is. It's for, thank you. And, I'm glad you're here.'

She looked at him for a long assessing moment, pulling slightly away from him. Hope the telepathy's not working now, he thought, remembering all that had recently been running through his head. He went on staring straight into her eyes, and her expression softened. What the hell, he thought. It doesn't matter.

She smiled at him. He knew what she was going to say. For devilment, he said it first.

'Let's hope they won't stay too long.'

She shook her head, beginning to laugh. He put his arm round her shoulders, and together they left the room.

## McLEAN AT THE GOLDEN OWL
### George Goodchild

Inspector McLean has resigned from Scotland Yard's CID and has opened an office in Wimpole Street. With the help of his able assistant, Tiny, he solves many crimes, including those of kidnapping, murder and poisoning.

## KATE WEATHERBY
### Anne Goring

Derbyshire, 1849: The Hunter family are the arrogant, powerful masters of Clough Grange. Their feuds are sparked by a generation of guilt, despair and ill-fortune. But their passions are awakened by the arrival of nineteen-year-old Kate Weatherby.

## A VENETIAN RECKONING
### Donna Leon

When the body of a prominent international lawyer is found in the carriage of an intercity train, Commissario Guido Brunetti begins to dig deeper into the secret lives of the once great and good.

# A TASTE FOR DEATH
## Peter O'Donnell

Modesty Blaise and Willie Garvin take on impossible odds in the shape of Simon Delicata, the man with a taste for death, and Swordmaster, Wenczel, in a terrifying duel. Finally, in the Sahara desert, the intrepid pair must summon every killing skill to survive.

# SEVEN DAYS FROM MIDNIGHT
## Rona Randall

In the Comet Theatre, London, seven people have good reason for wanting beautiful Maxine Culver out of the way. Each one has reason to fear her blackmail. But whose shadow is it that lurks in the wings, waiting to silence her once and for all?

# QUEEN OF THE ELEPHANTS
## Mark Shand

Mark Shand knows about the ways of elephants, but he is no match for the tiny Parbati Barua, the daughter of India's greatest expert on the Asian elephant, the late Prince of Gauripur, who taught her everything. Shand sought out Parbati to take part in a film about the plight of the wild herds today in north-east India.

## THE DARKENING LEAF
### Caroline Stickland

On storm-tossed Chesil Bank in 1847, the young lovers, Philobeth and Frederick, prevent wreckers mutilating the apparent corpse of a young woman. Discovering she is still alive, Frederick takes her to his grandmother's home. But the rescue is to have violent and far-reaching effects . . .

## A WOMAN'S TOUCH
### Emma Stirling

When Fenn went to stay on her uncle's farm in Africa, the lovely Helena Starr seemed to resent her — especially when Dr Jason Kemp agreed to Fenn helping in his bush hospital. Though it seemed Jason saw Fenn as little more than a child, her feelings for him were those of a woman.

## A DEAD GIVEAWAY
### Various Authors

This book offers the perfect opportunity to sample the skills of five of the finest writers of crime fiction — Clare Curzon, Gillian Linscott, Peter Lovesey, Dorothy Simpson and Margaret Yorke.

## DOUBLE INDEMNITY
## — MURDER FOR INSURANCE
### Jad Adams

This is a collection of true cases of murderers who insured their victims then killed them — or attempted to. Each tense, compelling account tells a story of cold-blooded plotting and elaborate deception.

## THE PEARLS OF COROMANDEL
### By Keron Bhattacharya

John Sugden, an ambitious young Oxford graduate, joins the Indian Civil Service in the early 1920s and goes to uphold the British Raj. But he falls in love with a young Hindu girl and finds his loyalties tragically divided.

## WHITE HARVEST
### Louis Charbonneau

Kathy McNeely, a marine biologist, sets out for Alaska to carry out important research. But when she stumbles upon an illegal ivory poaching operation that is threatening the world's walrus population, she soon realises that she will have to survive more than the harsh elements . . .